MW00910477

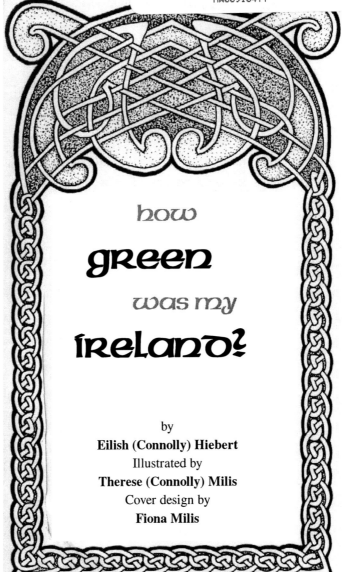

how

green

was my

ireland?

by
Eilish (Connolly) Hiebert
Illustrated by
Therese (Connolly) Milis
Cover design by
Fiona Milis

© 2001 by Recursion Press. All rights reserved.
No part of this publication may be reproduced, stored in a retrieval system,
or transmitted, in any form or by any means, electronic, mechanical,
photocopying, recording, or otherwise, without the written prior permission
from Recursion Press, contact through Trafford Publishing..

'Altnamore' is a fictitious village, reconstructed from elements in many
rural communities in Northern Ireland, where the author lived, worked,
visited, sang, and had crack in. These elements are woven into composite
fictitious characters. Resemblance of these fictitious characters to real
people, living or dead, is purely coincidental.

Celtic designs from Celtic Art Sourcebook, by Courtney Davis, Blandford
Press, 1988, are used with permission from publishers Cassell & Company,
125 Strand, London, England.

Thanks to Celtic Clipart for some designs

National Library of Canada Cataloguing in Publication Data

Hiebert, Éilish
    How green was my Ireland?

ISBN 1-55212-967-5

    I. Title.

PS8565.I379H68 2001   C813'.6   C2001-903116-5
PR9199.4.H53H68 2001

TRAFFORD

This book was published *on-demand* in cooperation with Trafford Publishing.
On-demand publishing is a unique process and service of making a book available for retail
sale to the public taking advantage of on-demand manufacturing and Internet marketing.
On-demand publishing includes promotions, retail sales, manufacturing, order fulfilment,
accounting and collecting royalties on behalf of the author.

Suite 6E, 2333 Government St., Victoria, B.C. V8T 4P4, CANADA
Phone   250-383-6864   Toll-free   1-888-232-4444 (Canada & US)
Fax   250-383-6804   E-mail   sales@trafford.com
Web site   www.trafford.com   TRAFFORD PUBLISHING IS A DIVISION OF TRAFFORD HOLDINGS LTD.
Trafford Catalogue #01-0369   www.trafford.com/robots/01-0369.html

10   9   8   7   6   5   4   3

Dedicated to

Murray, Paul & Quinn Hiebert

Therese, Hans, Fiona & Lisa Milis

Kate (Quinlivan) Connolly

May (Quinlivan) Sheeran

&

to Murty

(impetus for publishing this):

"It took a whole village......"

heartfelt thanks to:

- ❖ Doreen Masran, who showed me that you *can* express complex ideas in simple terms.

- ❖ Bernice Mattinson. This world just ain't the same without you, Bernie!

- ❖ Mary Blakeslee & Jacqueline Guest, Canadian literary greats, for their editing, encouragement & friendship.

- ❖ Anne (Barry) McElroy, for her friendship, support, insight, discussions, and 'emigrant-sharing'; and Anne Connon.

- ❖ Mary Jane Novokowsky, Judy Paterson, Susan Scott, Mary Robertson, Therese Milis, Sally McCloskey and the 7Cs: Su, Sharan, Doreen, Susan, Janet & Liz; Irene Punt.

- ❖ My children Paul and Quinn — I'm willing to bet that I learnt more from you guys than you ever did from me!

- ❖ Murray, my husband, for your love and encouragement to publish this, long before I was ready to. I *couldn't* have done this without you — on many levels. *You* know what I mean.

- ❖ Lou & June Torok, and Vinay Dattani.

- ❖ The people of Northern Ireland, personified in fictitious characters of the fictitious village 'Altnamore.'

- ❖ Murty, Mary Pat … & Roberta.

how green was my ireland?
table of contents

illustrations:

1

in celtic knots

*t*he woman sat painstakingly carving Celtic knotting designs into the surface of a freshly made clay pot:
over-under,
inside-outside,
turn left-turn right,
up-over,
down-under …

She usually found contentment and peace working with clay, carving into the not-yet-firm elliptical surfaces, transforming them from smooth to decorative, imagining how they'd look fired and glazed. But she felt the old, familiar frustration beginning to mount inside her as her eyes, hands, even her very soul, began to be drawn into this design she was carving. As a moth to a flame, she was drawn to these ancient designs, exquisite from a distance, looking so incredibly beautiful and straightforward, illustrated in the various books scattered around her studio.

"But just try getting inside them," she said aloud drily. "No wonder it was a bunch of celibate monks working in silent monasteries who had time to design these," she thought "working in the middle of nowhere in the Middle Ages, with no telephones nor computers, no kids roaring in and out, no getting ready for work."

Ails had lovingly shaped on the wheel the sturdy, squat, three-legged pot, drying it under plastic to optimum carving condition. But she hadn't planned out the design and measured it, the way she'd learned to do it on paper in a design class. This was a curved surface. This was clay. This should work, shouldn't it? Copying the design from the paper beside the pot, Ails carved carefully. It worked for a little while. But she could feel it going wrong before she could even see it. If she concentrated on the overall proportions, she inevitably lost the interior of the design; conversely, if she concentrated on the interior details, the overall design got lost. She jabbed the carving tool into the clay in frustration as she watched the proportions of her planned design go hopelessly haywire — yet again.

"What's the matter with me?" she thought. "If drawing these designs drives me crazy, how come I keep doing them?"

Deep down somewhere, though, she knew.

Looking out of her studio window at the huge expanse of blue Canadian prairie sky, Ails breathed deeply, content to be where she was, able to do what she was doing with such freedom, yet inexplicably drawn like a magnet to these infuriating designs, indelibly carved in her mind's eye, flowing and meandering in and out, over and under. She had begun to think of these designs as a metaphor for her emigrant relationship with her former birth country, Ireland — a country so beautiful as a whole, at a distance — so ancient and complex. When she had been there in its mantle of safety, humour, music and ancient beliefs, it had indeed been such a wondrous place that she wondered how anyone could ever leave it. Yet, once she left, it was like stepping out from a postage-stamp view to a bird's eye view of a larger world, of which this little island was only a part. Like these frustrating designs, once she tried to re-enter its beauty and charm, she ran into a maze of almost geometrically controlled, complex, contained systems, requiring acute attention to detail, precision and cultural cues. At one time, Ails instinctively knew how it all worked, knotted together perfectly, where each behaviour was contingent upon the next one, or the last one. Just like growing up in her skin from babyhood, she had absorbed how to read cues and behave correspondingly. But that was while she was still enfolded. That was a long time ago.

"Am I screwed up, or what?" she asked herself, throwing the three-legged pot aside, nearly damaging it in her frustration. How many times had she done this on different pots, different shapes, with different clay?

But she'd go back to it. She knew she would.

As she got up and walked over to her studio window, her eyes were drawn again to the sky she loved outside, almost frighteningly huge, free, and untrammeled. As her eye muscles relaxed, unfocused and gazed deeper into that sky, she saw another sky, in another place, what seemed like eons ago.

2

monument parade day

Ails awoke to a heavy sky, laden with thick, dark, clouds, where it felt like the sky was coming down on top of her. "Perfect," she said to herself in awesome anticipation. "Couldn't be better!" She replaced the curtain. Slowly and carefully, so as not to wake her sleeping sister, Ails lay back down under the blankets, stretching her toes into the corner of the bed near the window. She had awoken as usual to the sound of the cock crowing, after what seemed like only a few minutes since the 'ting, ting' of the blacksmith's hammer down the yard had lulled her to sleep. It had taken her a few seconds to figure out the strange feeling of apprehensive excitement coursing through her waking body. Then it hit her — the Annual Altnamore Monument Parade was today.

"Perfect day for it," thought Ails. The mood was just right. The Monument Parade Day wasn't like the monthly village Fair Day, where senses were high with the activity and hustle and bustle of buying and selling and bargaining. No, the Monument was different. When she had looked out through the lace curtains, it was a Monument Day sky — grey and heavy and foreboding, like the monument itself, like the faces, and the menacing clack-clack-clack of the boots that marched there.

She manoeuvered herself gingerly so she could stretch over to look further up the hill, but her sleeping sister lifted her tousled head and said "Will you stop pullin' all the blankets off me!" Darn, she hated that! Now she'd have to get up, for she was no longer alone. She knew her sister would start yapping and wake up the whole house.

Ails got up quietly and slipped on her blouse, plaid skirt and cardigan and her woollen knee socks and crept along the landing and down the steep, dark brown wooden stairs carrying

10

her shoes. She was getting pretty good at stepping between the creaking boards. Even in the semi-darkness she could measure from one creak to the other and avoid each one gingerly. She got halfway down and sat down in the cubicle of velvet darkness, framed by the light which formed a thin line around the wooden door at the bottom of the stairs. This was the time when she could travel alone in her imagination to her secret place and dream, before the house started to stir. As soon as she opened the door into the hall at the bottom of the stairs, Ails knew that Lizzie would wake and come clucking down the stairs, pretending she'd been awake for hours. It seemed such a threat to Lizzie for anyone to be up before she was, judging from the trouble she took to prove she had been awake earlier:

"Ach, that damn rooster of McCann's had me up before the 'screach' of dawn, but then I never was one for sleepin' in anyway. Lyin' in me bed half the day would be a terrible waste."

Ails knew perfectly well that Lizzie was usually peeved if Ails was up out of bed before she was. She could just see Lizzie's beady brown nuts of eyes glancing at her with annoyance, in between clearing out the ashes, as if to say "You're a right nuisance of a chile, always up snooping around before it's time for you to be up."

Sitting on the dark stairs, Ails was jolted from her quiet reverie by the splash of Lizzie's pee in the chamber pot across the landing. Sure enough, Lizzie was up. Ails quietly opened the door, wincing as it creaked and yawned. She slipped on her shoes before stepping on the cold cement floor of the hall leading to Lizzie's kitchen. Oh, good, there were still a few dying embers on the hearth. She loved to poke them down and watch the white ash float around the delicate sculptures that were once crumpled cigarette packets, bits of scrunched up paper, and chocolate bar wrappers. Lizzie's ceilidhers were up late the night before, singing, storytelling and cardplaying, She knew, from the amount of embers in the grate, and only three turf left in the creel. Ails knew exactly how to light the fire and put the kettle of water on the crook, but, of course, the one time that she had done that, Lizzie was furious. Somehow she had infringed on Lizzie's territory, so Ails sat quietly making a magic kingdom with the poker in the ashes beside the sturdy, squat, three-legged sooty black pot that hung on the crook. She stirred when she heard the thump, thump of shoes on the stairs. Lizzie thumped in, bringing her cloud of resentment with her.

"Oh, I heard you getting up. There's no need for you to be up out of your bed this early in the Easter holidays, you know," said Lizzie; then quickly, her eyes registering that she suddenly remembered about the Monument,

"Excitement about the Monument, I suppose?" She pushed Ails aside, dumped the kingdom of ashes in a newspaper and sent Ails outside to empty them in the ash pile out the back, telling her to refill the creel with turf.

The fresh, cold, damp air enveloped Ails. She filled the creel with brown, dry, brittle turf from the stack in the shed, savouring the damp smells and sights of the morning, the raindrops hanging from the nettles and glistening on the moss of the wall. Ails felt at peace, at home, and safe there. Her eyes travelled contentedly around the higgledy-piggledy stone wall enclosing the yard behind the house, where Ails's family rented rooms from Lizzie. Lizzie had been left the big rambling house in her Aunt Nelly's will. Nelly, 'with neither chick nor chile of her own' according to Lizzie, had 'sent for' Lizzie to come in from the country and live there when Nelly's husband died, leaving Nelly widowed and alone. Ails's eyes moved on down to stop at the stone forge at the bottom of the sloping yard, where the horses lined up outside the stone wall, waiting to be shod by Fergie, the blacksmith, who also rented the building from Lizzie. The seeping, damp air snapped Ails's reverie. She shivered in the mist and hurried in with the creel of turf.

No doubt about it, Lizzie was a wizard with a fire. Three turf, matches and a bit of paper and she had a cheery fire dancing in the kitchen. She was cutting the bread in thick slices.

"Ya want the Protestant end or the Catholic end?"

"Dunno why she even asks," thought Ails, knowing that Lizzie always wanted the crescent shaped 'Catholic' crust to curl into the top of her cup and dip in her tea, so Ails selected the 'Protestant' end, the square, close-grained bottom half of the slice of plain loaf bread.

"We'll need to be gettin' ready soon for the Monument," said Lizzie, running out to the window to watch the first marchers gathering outside Callaghans' flour storage shed. Ails joined Lizzie, who was leaning on the windowsill with her mug of steaming tea and the bread and butter in her hand, with her bum stuck out. They peered through the curtains. Everybody knew Lizzie watched the entire goings-on of the street from her house. Usually she was well hidden, but today was different. Faces were blatantly peering out of windows everywhere.

"I s'pose yer father'll not be goin' again this year?" asked Lizzie, with a rasp of disapproval.

"I dunno. I asked him. He didn't say." Ails knew he wasn't going, but she didn't want to listen to Lizzie's tirade about her father reading English newspapers "an' him an Irishman, for God's sake. . ." and how he thought Churchill was a great man, and "what in God's name had Churchill ever done for Ireland? Just-answer-me-that," and so on and so on. It was easier for Ails to say "I dunno."

Ails was wondering how to get to the Monument. Her father didn't like her to go. When she asked him why they didn't learn anything about the Monument and related events in school, he had just answered cynically. "Irish history is complete turmoil, child, and you don't want to be growing up bigoted." Ails wondered vaguely what 'bigoted' meant, but she was too busy planning her getaway to pursue it, and anyway, her father was quietly intent on reading the newspaper, with the bowl of his big curved pipe resting on his chest.

As long as she kept out of everybody's way and didn't get expressly forbidden to go, she could always say she had to run after her sister who had wanted to follow the band.

Now if she could just sneak out quietly and join the excitement ...she heard the stairs creaking. It was her mother with the baby, waving her tiny arms, all dewy eyed and gurgly. Good, she wouldn't have to take the baby out to settle her down or anything. Her mother was singing softly. She'd be sitting in the rocking chair playing with the baby and her father would be

13

reading quietly. Things were pretty lax during the Easter holidays.

"You goin' out to play, love?" asked her mother. "Can you take Fiona with you and mind her in the crowds?"

"Ach, mammy, do I have to?"

"Now, she's younger than you. Remember, you're a big girl now."

"Awright then," sighed Ails, conveniently remembering that Fiona was her excuse for the Monument. "I'll be outside."

Ails slipped out the front door and into the street. There were bicycles leaning on every wall. Serious-faced men and women proudly displayed paper Easter lilies with the green, white and orange colours of the Irish flag. They were on lapels of Sunday suits and coats, and stuck into the seams of caps. Red, work-worn hands grasped tall tricolour flags and beat drums and played tin whistles and fiddles — which kept slipping out of tune. Seamus Callaghan was pompously shouting orders and getting everyone in line.

"That big galoot," said Lizzie, "thinks his own farts don't smell." But today, everyone was uncharacteristically attentive to Seamus's orders. Today in Altnamore the atmosphere was different — deadly serious. The band struck up. The marchers defiantly eyed the two village policemen standing apprehensively at the corner. The policemen were ostracized because they were Protestants, and seen to be enforcing British authority in Northern Ireland. Today, they were particularly conspicuous, casting nervous glances at the marchers, and shifting awkwardly from one foot to the other in their shiny, black policeman boots.

"Wait for meeeeee!" Ails was mortified as her sister came running across the cobblestones and stared in wonder at the gathering parade.

"Pest, nuisance, pest! Have to bring you everywhere," muttered Ails. She spotted Jinny and Maura and Brigid, free as birds, wearing their lilies. Ails had no Easter lily, and she was stuck with her yappy sister, Fiona.

The drum roll sounded. The procession started to move lugubriously forward. The drum beat a slow, menacing rhythm as the marchers began to move in orderly, stony silence. Were these the same people who laughed and sang and told stories in Lizzie's kitchen, who bartered and shouted and gossiped and got drunk on the Fair Day? It was hard to believe, thought Ails, as she moved along, dumbstruck, pulled by a force which she didn't understand, which hung like lead in the air.

They marched in a slow cumbersome parade down past the big stone Celtic cross at the corner, then further down, past the Rocks, which didn't even look like the Rocks where Ails and her friends usually played. A few very old people were standing erect on top of the Rocks, wrinkled faces in a stony trance, hands held over black aprons, bony frames held proudly, leaning on whittled walking sticks. Even the chickens and ducks knew to move out of the way. The band was now playing the rousing rebel marches you never learnt in school. Even her father had to admit liking those rousing songs, but had told Ails and Fiona that the government didn't allow them to be sung in schools.

Suddenly the Monument was in view — a random load of grey granite blocks, piled shapelessly and precariously on top on one another, waiting endlessly to be arranged into a real monument. Ails looked up at the unlikely silhouette, sticking shapelessly up into the grey sky, ominous grey clouds hanging over it. The whole parade filed stonily into the Monument field and stood on the stubble — freshly cut with a scythe by Mickey James the day before. Usually when Ails and Maura and Brigid and Pat and Shamie and Jinny and the rest played 'Monument' throughout the year, they had to trample down the overgrown grass first. Today the grass looked like Mickey James's short, sprickly haircut. Everyone looked dogged and serious.

There was a speech in Gaelic by an important man from the 'Free State' — the name given to the 26 independent counties of Ireland. He reminded the sombre crowd — as if they didn't already know — that Altnamore village was part of one of the six counties under British rule since 1921. Then there was a two-minute silence while all eyes were focused on the Monument. The scene was compelling. Ails could feel something beyond everyday Altnamore life. "The Dan" Coyle held himself upright and had a strange, dogged, grim look in his eyes. Jinny said The Dan was "all for his country." He had been held on a dreaded 'prison ship' bound for 'Botany Bay,' Sydney

15

Australia, where Britain sent her prisoners — forever. Somehow, though, The Dan had ended up in a jail in England. His mother died while he was in jail. When he was released, he came home and spat in a Protestant policeman's face, saying "Yiz killed me mother!" Jinny said The Dan was a 'real nationalist — no doubt about it.' All the old men had the same look as The Dan, and even the younger ones looked proudly and defiantly up at the Monument while the drum beat slowly. Even Old Bella Coyle stood erect and silent alongside The Dan, her brother. Her grey straggly hair was tied up with a huge green, white and yellow ribbon, the colour of the flag of the free 26 counties part of Ireland. Bella's strange amber eyes were fixed on the shapeless Monument.

The coarse grass growing up through the bumps in the gravel hurt Ails's feet, but she didn't dare move. Nobody said anything. The tension in the air was so thick you could cut it with a knife. The required two minutes of silence seemed like an eternity. Then The Dan Coyle starting speaking loudly and menacingly about St. Columba prophesying a war of many years. He rhymed off a list of names of men killed in the rebellion against English rule of all of Ireland, after which Ireland was divided, six counties only remaining under British rule. The list of dead men started with Daniel O'Connell and Padraig Pearse, and ending with "while Ireland holds these graves, Ireland, unfree, can never be at peace." Ails knew this piece off by heart because when they were playing 'Monument,' she had to beat the drum while Pat Doran said that speech. 'The Soldiers' Song' started up. It was the national anthem of the free part of Ireland, a symbol of rebellion, and they sang it in Gaelic. Ails knew all the words like a parrot, they way she knew her prayers in Gaelic. She had no idea what the Gaelic words said. But all she had to do was look at the faces of the singers to know this was a deadly serious, burning issue. 'God Save the King' was supposed to be the national anthem of that part of Ireland under British rule, but you'd never know that in Altnamore. It was never heard there. The last words of the rebel, nationalist, free state anthem were belted out "Shaw live connie oran a laoch!"

16

Ails was relieved. It was over. The air rang with the fervour of the singing and the dogged resolve reiterated in the final crescendo.

As if on cue, just at that moment a downpour started. The tension burst. Umbrellas went up and everyone started up the road into the town straggling in groups of twos and threes, talking and exchanging greetings for the first time today, it seemed. The old Altnamore atmosphere was back, if somewhat subdued.

Wasn't that just great?" said Jinny, as she and Maura and Brigid joined Ails.

"Powerful indeed," added Maura. Ails looked at their wilting paper green, white and orange Easter lilies and vowed that next year she would have a lily. They all traipsed up the town, where everyone had scattered into various pubs. They went in through the door of Heaney's pub, unnoticed in the commotion, and settled in their usual hiding place under the stairs, surrounded by hundreds of corks and the pungent smell of stout. They listened in fascination to old stories, retold yearly, about the time when the I.R.A. was in full operation. They heard how, years ago, the Black and Tans, a particularly savage corps of British soldiers, raided houses and shot people; how P.J. McFarlane ran down out of the town, hiding behind ditches and in bogs and in 'safe people's' houses and barns, eventually escaping to England, and living in permanent exile. Ails instinctively knew that these IRA men could be 'lifted' (arrested) at any time. She felt the tension of the serious work of rebellion against the lilting, bantering songs being sung in all the pubs and houses.

The two lone policemen stood beside the big stone Celtic cross, glancing nervously in the direction of any sudden sounds. Silhouetted against the heavy sky, they were like silent sentinels watching over the village. It didn't make them feel very secure to know that village life moved forward furtively, cannily, with an infuriating air of normality around them, through them, past them, in the rhythm it had kept for centuries, no matter how many policemen came and went from Altnamore village.

Later, when Ails sneaked out quietly to shoo her pest of a sister out to pee, the sounds of music, raucous singing and laughter drifted out of the pubs and houses into the early evening air. She wandered slowly homeward, up around the corner of Altnamore's long street, where she knew every house, and cobblestone, and the smoothest surfaces to play hopscotch and skipping.

Ails was suddenly very, very tired — almost weary — and confused, feeling an undercurrent of fear, mixed with merry, raucous songs, pent-up tension, and heroic, glorious stories.

Altnamore Celtic Cross

3

oh, to be a monk!

*t*he adult Ails was leafing through celtic designs in the books she had taken from the Calgary Public Library. If she looked closely at any overall design, a heroic, glorious picture became obvious, with heads emerging from tails, lines turning into roads, which then turned back on themselves, somehow creating a pent-up tension. Each time she tried to draw a design, she looked forward to capturing its ancient, exquisite precision and wonder.

"Curve up-curve down;
show surface-hide;
ravel-unravel,"

went Ails's mind as she tried to carve the surface of the sturdy, squat, determined-looking, three-legged pot. She had moved away from painstakingly copying the design. She began instead drawing freehand, keeping the overall geometric proportions. It began to take shape, meandering and flowing in and out, over and under. Carving into the clay was sensuous and satisfying. As the tool changed the clay surface, the thin rinds of clay curled up under her fingers "like bacon rinds on a pan," thought Ails. The snaking, crossing lines began to shape into a complex design.

'Twist-turn';
'now-you-see-it-now-you-don't'

was the rhythm accompanying the growing design.

'Push-pull;
love-hate;

20

bad-good;
laugh-cry;
open-close;
grasp-let go;
stay-go,'
continued the rhythm as Ails looked at the emerging design and thought, "Hey! Not bad!"

She was rudely awakened from her reverie by the noise of her children bursting downstairs from school, with their friends and appetites, clothes and boots strewn everywhere.

"Hi, guys," she greeted them, as they all crowded in the door of the tiny laundry room-cum pottery studio.

"Hey, cool!" said one kid. "What's that your mom's doing?" asked another straggler friend.

"Oh, my mom does pottery," said Ails's son proudly. "She cooks it in a kill."

"Kiln," corrected Ails.

"Oh, yea, that's right. What's for supper?"

"Can we have those buns on the table upstairs?"

"Did you hear what Madame Miquelon SAID to him?"

"Yeh, she spazzed."

Ails got up to face the supper hour and said to herself,

"Oh, to be a monk in the Middle Ages, working in a monastery in the middle of nowhere."

"No school tomorrow — professional day!" she heard, as a foam football went flying across the room."

"Hey, no football inside," admonished Ails.

"Oh, yeh, sorry mom, I forgot, can we make a boxing ring? We're going to have a boxing tournament tomorrow, us an' Mike an' Jason an' all" asked her older son, already spreading the quilts on the floor.

"It'll be great. No school tomorrow!" added another kid gleefully.

"Schools smell the same everywhere," sniffed Ails as she waded through canvas knapsacks, crumpled paper worksheets and shoes carrying the smell.

"A chalky, paper, learning institution smell," she thought, musing that schools also educated their children to fit into the society where they lived.

21

"Try as they might to educate objectively," thought Ails to herself, as she mechanically began to get supper ready, "it filters through to students all over the world how they should behave for that society. What's perceived to be 'good,' for that society, is reinforced; what's perceived to be 'bad' is discouraged, she thought. Sometimes it's not even spoken; kids just absorb it."

Looking at her home, which looked like a bomb had just hit it, the familiar feeling of inadequacy nagged Ails, the feeling that she didn't know how to raise children in this, her adopted community and country. Here, children were strangely individuals from birth, with their own beds, desks, toys, even their own rooms, and their own individual rights. The childraising familiar to Ails from her upbringing in Ireland, was that the good of the village came first. She knew that from babyhood, without anyone having to tell her. It was reinforced in school, society and home. There, children were not individuals. They were 'one of the Jimmy Joe twins', or the 'Barney Ann boys' or 'the wee cuttie that moved in from the country with Sarah Ann when her man died.' They were born to fit into a space in the family, village and community; or if there was no space, everybody just pushed over and made a space. The child squirled around until she fit, just like a dog twisting around until the spot was just right to lie down or sleep. If fitting into the space meant picking the smallest spuds from the ground, going over to sleep with your granny, or just staying out of adults' way, then so be it.

Here, in this strange land of Canada, Ails often felt lost in her ideas of childraising. She somehow knew that her children needed to be raised appropriately to live in this society, yet in so many small ways, she reacted at a gut level from patterns playing in her brain. God, it was so lonely sometimes, just Ails and her husband raising children, so many miles from any family.

Later that evening, back to carving her pot, the feel of its solid shape and squatness was comforting, even as her mind contradicted itself with the pattern of the design.

"Up-down,
in-out,
'Do your homework'—'Can we play outside?'

not their fault-they must take responsibility,
right-wrong."
Ails's mind drifted back, back, back in time, to her own
schooldays, far away — tonight it felt like on another planet.

4

school drones on
– till hannah!

Get up, girl, it's time for school!" said Lizzie, shaking
Ails's shoulder.

"Yuk!" thought Ails. It was Monday. It was warm and
cosy under the blankets, and the more she thought of
school and Mrs. Digby's watery blue eyes targeting her, the
more she wanted to curl up under the blankets and go away to
her secret place. She wiggled her toes, thinking how they felt in
the summer when she could to go school barefoot, with the tar
bubbling up through the gravel on the street, squelching up in
thick streaks through her toes, warm and sticky. But it was
centuries till summer, almost three months, in fact, and not even
a Fair Day for three whole weeks to break the monotony.

Lizzie was banging the bannister with a spoon.

"Ails, you'll be late!"

The bed was so comfortable with her sister already up.
Fiona was Lizzie's pet. Lizzie called her "Fiona Miona" and
called her 'an old soul' and thought she could see into the souls
of people. Lizzie heeded Fiona when she hid behind her skirts,
because, she said, "that chile has another sight; she senses things
about people." Lizzie always saved the curly, chewy bacon rinds
on the pan from their parents' breakfast for Fiona, who bartered
the few remaining ones to Ails for being allowed to play at the
Septic Tank.

24

Ails trailed down to the kitchen.

"It's about time, me girl," snapped Lizzie, slapping down a plate of bacon, egg, and black pudding in front of her. The egg was sliding around in clear bacon grease, and the circles of black pudding looking at her like two bloodshot eyes. Worst of all, when she cut her bacon rinds off, they curled up like worms, not nice and crispy like Fiona's, which were cooked longer. Fiona was sitting scrunching on the crisp ones. It was O.K. for *her* to sit there drawing pictures and munching. She didn't have to face Mrs. Digby, who looked exactly like a pig, with balding white hair, a round pink face, and white bristles sticking out of a mole on her chin. She even talked squeakily, like a pig. That's why she was known as 'The Pigby,' or 'The Pig' for short. Ails pushed back her bacon. She nibbled on a piece of toast.

"You eat up your fry," said Lizzie, "there's starving children in India."

"Ach, why don't you parcel this up and send it to them?" thought Ails miserably. "I bet you they wouldn't want it either."

"Youse have the quare days of it, with nothin' to do but go off t' school, and only havin' to walk up the hill. Now when I was young...." Here she goes, thought Ails, about milking the cows before leaving home; walking barefoot over unpaved roads and over fields and stiles and hedges and ditches. She'd be pointing out her scars from chilblains, itchy bumps that came from cold, damp feet, in the hoar frost and damp numbing cold. Ails knew all of this off by heart. She thought of it when she looked down at the surrounding countryside from the school on the top of the hill, where the children came from miles around, climbing up from all sides of the village, in all weathers. They came with fried egg sandwiches for lunch and tins of raspberries and blackberries, and wild flowers with the dew still on them, to soften Mrs. Digby.

Ails's thoughts were riveted back again to the Pigby.

Ails didn't feel at all privileged to be going to school. It was more like torture, she thought, while Lizzie was still ranting. This time it was about somebody putting a mouse under the outhouse door when Mrs. Digby was in the toilet, and cackling

25

with laughter about the squealing coming out of there. Fiona was entranced. Ails was not.

Her sister was lucky. Miss McCartney taught Fiona, and the other Infants. Miss McCartney even liked the children that had green snot on their noses and no rag to wipe it; also the ones who got their numbers all wrong and stuttered when they were reading. She even gave the girls with straight black greasy hair princesses' parts in plays. She kept telling Ails and the other chattery ones to keep quiet and let the shy ones talk. She had skinny ankles and wore bronze sandals. Her grey hair was dyed red — you could see the grey when it grew out. She talked to herself and chewed tapioca. Of course she had bad days, too, but she didn't yell much — just hit you hard and fast on those days. She was easy to bribe, and didn't stay mad for long. Her square, kind face and big brown eyes would soften, and she'd let all the children sit round the fire while she told a good story. She'd always know who had babies, or whose mother was sick. When Dan McGarvey got crushed to death by the new tractor, she went to the funeral and cried. She gave out holy pictures to every single child for First Communion. She got mad at bullies, who were strangely frightened of her. She was uncharacteristically shy when Ails met her in the village.

"It's such a pity she's only smart enough to teach Infants," thought Ails sadly, wishing Miss McCartney was still her teacher instead of the dreaded Mrs. Digby.

Ails didn't eat her fry. She couldn't. She dragged herself up the hill to school, trailing her school bag, dawdling along the ditch, looking down at the countryside, which reminded her of her secret place, except hers had more sunshine and there was always a rainbow.

All of a sudden panic struck. Lizzie was right. She was late! She started running. She tumbled through the door, with Pat Doran right on her heels.

"Here they come, the teachers' children, late again!" It was the dreaded voice of Mrs. Digby, The Pigby herself. Ails and Pat got a stinging slap with the cane. Her eyes smarting, Ails saw Dingo Devine looking at her, and was determined to hold her head high. Dingo was ugly and not too smart, and when he kicked Ails savagely in the stomach for confronting him, (she

26

had insisted that girls were as smart as boys) she longed to be The Pigby, or The Master so she could massacre him. Pat rolled his eyes and grinned. This scene was a constant occurrence every Monday, and sometimes other mornings.

'Little Red Hen' was this morning's story. Ails began writing answers to the questions, from time to time looking over at Philomena Gorman's jotter. Viewed sideways, Philomena's left-handed writing had a strangely artistic patterned look. If Ails half-closed her eyes it looked like Miss McCartney's tweed skirt.

Ails jumped with the pain of a cuff to her left shoulder:

"Get on with your work, young lady!" Then The Pigby spied Philomena's writing and quickly whipped up Philomena's jotter from her desk. She took a closer look at the chequered handwriting and caned Philomena twice on each hand for 'backhand writing.' Philomena was crying, and Ails was almost ready to cry with her. It was less than an hour since school had begun, and Ails felt hopeless, trapped, jailed. Suddenly the door opened with a small girl carrying a note for The Pigby.

"Ails, go to the Infants' Room!"

Phew! Escape! Whatever the reason, Ails didn't care.

Miss McCartney was holding Peggy McGinty's head. Peggy was 'delicate' and smelled of Vicks and red flannel. She had adenoids and a hare lip and was exhaling a loud rasp with each breath. Lizzie's, where Ails lived, was near the dispensary, and the Wee Doctor occasionally ate at Lizzie's. Miss McCartney wanted to know if the Wee Doctor was back from Loughmacnilly where he had been sitting up all night with a young lassie who had the scarlet fever. Ails told her 'yes,' eagerly offering to accompany Peggy to be examined at the dispensary and bring her back to school. Ails longed to get away from The Pigby. Alas! Peggy's brother Rory, the one who always carried in the coal and stoked the fires, was sent for in the Master's room to go with Peggy in case he had to bring her straight home. Lizzie always said it was terrible to keep a big strappin' lad like that in school till 15 years old when he could be helping his father.

"But them's the laws" said Lizzie, "an' if ye keep them home that damn truant officer'll be snoopin' round the fields lookin' to take them back."

Ails did get a short break, though. The Master had to come and see the delicate, ailing Peggy. In the commotion, Miss McCartney forgot about Ails. Great! Ails sat down with the smaller Infants and started to shine a blackboard square, in the way she'd perfected when she was in Junior Infants. The little ones sat engrossed watching Ails, then started imitating her as she quietly spat a row of spits across the middle and wiped her blackboard square whitish-dry with her spitting duster. Then she found a thick part of her cardigan sleeve, placed it carefully over the bone in her elbow, scrunching the cuff and gathering the rest of the sleeve part in her fist. Then she carefully rubbed her elbow up and down in geometric lines, turning the board sideways to repeat the same thing. It took quite a while to get the squares shiny clean, during which time the Master came in.

He arrived in a cloud of smoke, coughing, with a pen behind his ear, and one eye closed to avoid the smoke curling up his face from the omnipresent cigarette dangling from his mouth. It was always a surprise that he knew anyone's name, he was so vague most of the time. Miss McCartney talked sideways at him behind her hand so the children couldn't hear. He grunted back, squinting at Peggy's gormless face.

"Whatever you think, Miss McCartney," he rasped.

Ails stared at the Master, noting the deep lines on his face, his bloodshot eyes, nicotine-stained fingers and crumpled tweedy trousers. She only ever saw The Master at close range when he taught The Pigby's room singing every week. The Master couldn't sing a note with his rasping, coughing voice, but the Lilter McMenamin's nephew, Whistler, could whistle or sing any tune on the face of the earth, and everyone followed him. Occasionally the Master would step in and make everybody go higher than anybody could. Of course it was always Whistler who could sing the highest, after he nearly busted his tonsils. Children always felt anonymous until the Master hit on something they couldn't do — like speak loud, or say multiplication tables. Somehow, the Master could detect every child's weak spot. Then he'd magnify it. He would make those who whispered stand in the big tall windows and yell their tables. Ails had visions of herself, all grown-up, yet the master, with that menacing, sleepy grin on his face, making her stand in the window and memorize that hated song "Ver-me-oooo, oo-ro-van-oh,".

"O.K. I think your boards are clean enough, children." It was Miss McCartney again. "Ails, go back to your class." Noticing the black elbow of Ails's cardigan, she added "Tch, tch, what'll your mother say about you wearing your elbows out of your cardigan?"

Back to The Pigby.

Ails's class was just finishing the play of "The Little Red Hen" with the smart ones getting the dramatic parts, as usual. Then it was the dreaded "Round the room for sums," where you propped your jotter up on the wall, and did five calculations that Mrs. Digby called out. The more you got wrong, the more slaps you got with the cane.

It wasn't the sums Ails dreaded. She was good at them. It was watching the same children every week who got one or none right. They'd cry hopelessly and bitterly every week after The Pigby had whacked them almost senseless.

"Even the snotty-nosed ones shouldn't get it every week," thought Ails as the humiliating process was repeated. You couldn't win with The Pig. Even the smart ones got sarcasm, because they shouldn't look smug for getting things right. Sometimes while still wielding the cane she'd hit Ails for picking her nose, or someone else for biting their nails. She couldn't be bribed, either, with apples or flowers. She didn't trust anybody.

Jinny had told Ails that ages ago Mrs. Digby had had a terrible tragedy, when she was young. "Hundreds of years ago," thought Ails.

"The whole country knows about it," insisted Jinny, appalled at Ails's ignorance. Mrs. Digby was in love with this soldier called Michael Digby. They were going to get a baby, and her father forced Michael Digby to marry her. Michael married her. Right at the chapel gate, he got into a car and drove away, and nobody ever saw him again. She had twin baby boys and they both died. Ails felt deathly sorry for Mrs. Digby for a few hours after Jinny told her.

It didn't last. Mrs. Digby was bitter at the world.

"No need to take it out on us," muttered Ails. Mrs. Digby didn't like anybody much. She didn't like the world much either, it seemed, nor school.

"Neither do I" sighed Ails sadly. School droned on, and on, and on.

Mrs. Digby in School

Then the word spread like wildfire. Hannah McAfee was back! Brilliant, reckless Hannah, hated and feared by everyone, was back! They had tried to get her out, but she was back! The last time she was expelled she'd stuck wads of softened chewed gum on The Master's chair and owned up shamelessly when he sat down on it half-blindly, and got it stuck all over the ass of his trousers. Then she had run out the door and down Gortnabwee, a rough, stony, rutted narrow road by-passing the village. When The Master realized she was gone he stumbled out the door, started his old rattletrap of a car, sounded its "a-googah" horn, and clattered down Gortnabwee, after Hannah. Everybody in the Master's room stood on top of the desks and in the big tall windows so they could see all the way down Gortnabwee. From time to time they could spy Hannah darting through the bushes, probably sticking her tongue out at the Master, and making faces with her eyes turned in. In his cumbersome car, he'd lose Hannah hopelessly, only to find her darting out again like quicksilver, just out of his reach. While everyone was jostling and pushing and fighting over the binoculars from The Master's desk, the Pig walked in, wielding the cane. All stood firm and deadly silent. It was like a mutiny. The Pig looked scared — cornered. She backed slowly out of the room.

But The Master did catch Hannah. He brought her back, kicking and screaming unutterable oaths at him. All were seated working diligently and silently. The silence only emphasized Hannah's defiant back talk and The Master's discomfort while he tried to ignore her.

"She has him beat," thought Ails with quiet glee, "and he knows it, and we all know it!"

Yes, Hannah was back.

This time she had it in for The Pig. The Pig had confronted Hannah's brother Pete, in Ails' class. Pete was real smart. Pete could figure out multiplication before Ails and the rest all knew what it was all about. He could remember whole pages of books, use big words in compositions, say the whole catechism off by heart, and tell you what day Easter was for the next 20 years. Pete got terrible headaches and black, black moods. Ails liked Pete, but he scared her. He got everything right, so The Pig didn't harrass him, and tended to leave him

31

alone. But one Friday when she was caning the same kids as she did every single week, Pete told The Pig: "Leave them ones alone, Miss. They just can't do them stupid sums." The Pig asked him who did he think he was anyway, the teacher or something? She said that indeed she'd wipe that look off Pete's face.

That was her mistake. Pete told Hannah. Now Hannah was back. And Hannah had mice in a jam jar.

If there was one thing The Pig was terrified of, it was mice. She had mousetraps set all over the room, and wouldn't let the country children eat their lunch in the room "in case of crumbs." Packie Gorman from the Master's Room had to inspect the mousetraps daily.

They all got out for break. Hannah was outside the door with her jam jar in a paper bag. She let the mice into The Pigby's room, where The Pig was having her flask of tea all by herself.

The whole school waited for the squeals.

They climbed up to the windows and watched The Pig standing on the table squealing and wildly stepping down over the tops of the desks till she came tearing through the door, her bosoms jiggling, amidst peals of laughter. Hannah was yelling "You no-good bitch" and "don't you ever tackle my brother again, or I'll malevogue you!"

The Master came stumbling out in the commotion. He walked The Pig back in and tried to look superior, but Hannah knew, and Ails knew, and they all knew that both the Master and the Pigby longed to tear Hannah limb from limb, but they wouldn't dare.

Miss McCartney walked calmly up to Hannah and said quietly:

"Don't you think that was cruel, Hannah?" Ails felt a twinge as she watched Hannah about to answer.

"No crueller than them ones is to us, Miss" she said, "but I'd never do nothin' to you, Miss."

Miss McCartney walked inside.

There were no repercussions.

School went on, and on, and on.

Hannah feared no-one, and all feared Hannah.

And Hannah was back, as unpredictable and rebellious as ever.

Ails admired and marvelled at Hannah, free-spirited and unafraid.

What on earth would Hannah do next?

5

flying free!

Seeing the sunset over the Canadian Rocky Mountains for the first time, 24-year-old Ails was filled with a sense of beauty and awe. This was magical. Ails felt her spirit soar, free, unfettered, winging like a bird out into the deep purple sunset. Stars were winking in the indigo and dark blue sunset afterglow. Pinlights of luminous bright blue shone along the airport runway. Hills, dotted with houselights, rose against the sky's afterglow in the gathering dusk. She had seen that strange velvet sky in American movies. There was probably a scientific explanation for this heart-stopping colour and light scene. Ails's heart was captivated, and she felt some kind of invisible shackles fall from her spirit.

This Canada was such a vast, unending land, so vast, in fact, that when she saw others getting organized to disembark, she had gathered her stuff to get off the airplane halfway across the country, before the plane flew off the end of the continent, in her mind.

"You U.K. people!" said the flight attendant impatiently, "always thinking that you've arrived when you're only halfway across the country. Sit down. We've a ways to go yet!"

But Ails had arrived. This magical place was branded into her soul within the first moments of arriving. No matter what happened, she knew she'd come to the right place.

"How could this be?" she thought. Raised on a tiny verdant island, she was, nevertheless, immediately at home, instantly rooted in this huge expanse of continent, under the

34

interminable dome of sky. Ails was puzzled. Even though the exquisite scene of mountains, city, sky and light was not familiar to her, Ails had a strange feeling that she'd been waiting for this. It was a feeling akin to 'deja vue,' but without the actual recognition. She thought of the nurse on the delivery ward, who could look at a newborn and say, with conviction, "Yes. This one's been here before. I just know it." She thought of Lizzie many years before, talking about her psychic sister Fiona, "She's an old soul, that one!"

But mostly, Ails thought of Bella.

6

Bella

Back in Altnamore village in Ireland, a long time ago, Ails was sitting on the pillar by the gable, swinging her legs as she watched the lengthening shadows and the glistening wet black slate roofs and the wet black street. She was in her secret place where the flowers were brilliant colours and the trees were the same as those silhouetted on the hill of the plantin behind the village houses. At times like this she was in harmony with herself and the world.

Bella was suddenly standing there silently. Didn't she hear the old woman, Bella Coyle, sneak up on her? Or was it that Bella respected her solitude, and had perhaps been waiting for a while? Ails didn't know. Bella seemed as ancient as Altnamore. Bella's usually grey stringy hair had turned orange. She asked shyly:

"Like me hair, Ails?"

"It's nice" said Ails.

"It's a new bottle I got at the Chemist's." Bella turned her wrinkled face with its vacant amber eyes towards the glow of the setting sun.

"The cows — only if ye wanna, ye mind."

Ails climbed down and yelled in the front door:

"I'm away with Bella for the cows!"

"Shamie comin'?"

Ails nodded. Shamie, Ails's cousin would be there with his dirty fingernails and knees, pocketfuls of marbles and a stick cut like Bella's to 'cap' the cows. Ails liked Bella's button boots

36

— not so much her orange ankle socks, but the button boots were perfect — the people in her secret place often wore ones like that. Bella saw her looking at the boots, and said:

"Found them in The Dan's trunk in the attic. Musta been ma's." It was hard for Ails to imagine that Bella and The Dan Coyle, her brother, had ever had a mother. They seemed to have always just been there. The Dan had been one of many Altnamore men imprisoned in England — 'jailed for fightin' for Ireland, they were," Lizzie had told Ails. "An' them tryin' to get them British gentry outa this country, people with no right to be here, taking our farmers' land," Lizzie went on, almost spitting with rage. "Wasn't God good to send The Dan back to look after Bella. Just missed getting sent to Botany Bay in Australia with the rest, he did. May God look down on them brave men, wherever they are," she added, making the sign of the cross, and looking heavenward.

Ails and Bella climbed the hill, and waved to Shamie, coming into view, waiting for them at the plantin stile.

They ambled silently on up the hill, with the birds heading nest-wards. Bella took a handful of sticky boiled sweets out of a rag in her flowered apron pocket. Today the sweets were orange like her socks and her hair.

They took a shortcut through the graveyard on the way to the fields on the other side of the hill from the village.

"That would be a nice place to lie if you were dead," thought Ails, "nice cool clay over you, with the birds in the trees around you and God above keeping watch over the countryside. Peaceful."

Bella nipped into the chapel. She always lit a cigarette off the 'Candles for Good Intentions' in the big glowing candle frame in front of the Virgin Mary statue. Shamie and Ails waited at the back, smelling the musty, holy chapel smell, dabbling their fingers in the holy water font. The church was empty except for Biddy McGinn.

"Kneelin' there mutterin' at the altar rails like a goat chewin' a hedge," Lizzie always said about Biddy. Bella tiptoed down the aisle again and scattered a handful of holy water on the floor as they went to leave, wiping her hand on her apron, puffing away on her cigarette.

Suddenly the silence of the evening air was shattered, as the deep resounding voice of the huge parish priest echoed throughout the chapel. He was towering above them in the dark shadows of the tiny entrance, blocking their exit through the heavy wooden doors.

"Have you no respect for the house of God, woman?" boomed the voice of Father McStay. His jowls were shaking formidably, his huge finger pointing at Bella. Even the look of him made Ails and Shamie quake.

"Don't you ever let me catch you lighting cigarettes in my church again! D'you hear?"

Bella drew herself up taller, her amber eyes flashing fire:

"Your church!" she retorted "an' who do you think you are, God Almighty Himself?" and she shook her cow-stick at him. Ails and Shamie watched his big face get more and more furious, his stubbly white hair bristling. Bella fixed her eyes on him, speaking in a low, dangerous tone of voice, devoid of its usual childlike lilt. Father McStay was glaring at her in a purple rage.

"Youse McStays are nothin' but a bundle of gatherups from Macnatassy," Bella said evenly to the glowering Father McStay. "Just because you have a collar that's turned backwards and you call yourself a priest — that's no reason for you to go tellin' off people around here," Bella continued relentlessly. "So don't you tell me what to do! *God* knows what I do, and *GOD doesn't* mind." By now Father McStay had backed them into the church, moving away from the doors. Bella deftly maneuvered in behind the huge man, quickly pushed open one big door, skilfully holding it open for the frightened Ails and Shamie, who skittered nimbly out ahead of Bella. Then she let the door swing slowly back on the astonished figure of the massive Father McStay. Bella marched off, brandishing her cow-stick, her button boot heels clicking determinedly on the tarmac. Ails's mind was boggled at the way Bella was able to talk to the huge Father McStay, when everyone in the whole parish was terrified of him, and wouldn't dare say a word in protest — even though Ails had heard them all criticize and talk in the pubs about Father McStay's interactions with many villagers. Sitting in Lizzie's chimney-corner hiding place, pretending to be reading a book, as people were eating, Ails had heard about Father McStay visiting Mrs. Tague when her second child started school, inquiring why there were no more babies coming. She hadn't been denying her husband her wifely duties, had she? He also called in on the 13-member McHerrity family, to ask whether there was a vocation for the priesthood among the older boys? Or maybe some of the girls to the convent life of a nun? He'd even called into Lizzie's one day. "God, I near had heart failure when I saw His Reverence coming to the door — he had to stoop down to get through the door," said Lizzie. "He asked me about my 'parish dues' money envelope — but sure, hadn't I stuck it in between the plates on the dresser and forgot all about it, so I left it in the collection plate the very next Sunday."

Nobody challenged the huge Father McStay, except Bella, "but she's crazy anyway. The whole village knows that. Sure, there's a mental streak in that family," said Lizzie, "the whole, seed, breed, and generation of them has got it." Then Lizzie made the sign of the cross pensively, probably remembering with genuine sadness the periodic spells her Aunt Nelly's husband had spent in the Mental Hospital in Unragh. Lizzie had often seen the mother of Bella and The Dan, rocking, rocking, rocking, and muttering about going home.

Ails's daydreaming and dawdling meant that she now had to run to catch up with Bella, who was walking quickly now, with a kind of satisfied confidence that she had done what was right. She didn't say a word, even though her eyes glowed orange like her hair in the sunset. When they reached the field where the cows were, Bella slowed down to her usual pace, talking to each cow softly, calling them 'A store' and 'A roon' and 'A leanbh.' "The trouble with cows," thought Ails "is that you never know if they hear what you say or not. They just chew and stare and moo at nothing." But Bella cooed on. Ails loved watching the cows' big soft brown eyes, twitching midges off their ears, with their huge tits almost bursting; chewing and staring, chewing and staring.

They couldn't cut through the graveyard on the way back, in case the cows would trample on the graves, so they went around by the road, staying in a triangle around the back of the cows to guide them home for milking.

39

Biddy McGinn, who'd been praying in the chapel, was on her way home down the country. She got off her bicycle and said to Bella:

"You can't talk to the Holy Father like that, Bella. He was chosen by God!"

Bella's mouth curled up thin:

"There's them that thinks they're chose by God and can hide behind one of them white round collars. God made us all, she added, and pointing her stick at the cows said pointedly, "them cows, too." Ails had never heard Bella talk so much and with such conviction. In fact, she rarely said anything. Bella quickened her walk again, briskly swinging her arms, until she got out of Biddy's sight. As they walked in silence, a calm settled over them again, with Bella crooning to the cows, Shamie kicking stones and Ails ambling along quietly. By that time, they'd reached the plantin stile again, and Bella signalled wordlessly to Ails and Shamie to herd the cows into the triangular patch of grass beside the stile. She took out some more orange boiled sweets from the hanky, and they sat sucking on them, just looking around, all of them drinking in silently the gold-orange sunset and feeling warm, secure and content.

Looking out to Cranny Glen on one side and back towards the bogs of Tuggan on the other. Ails looked around at the glory of it all, and back at Bella who smiled a shy smile like a child, and Shamie, who had a look of quiet contentment on his face. The village was spread out in the valley, with the road winding up the hill and out over the bog. All was still, except for the creaking of a bicycle with someone leaning on it, pushing it up the hill. The rattle and clop of a horse and cart would occasionally break the stillness, but usually it was silent except for the birds winging homeward.

It was different from a sketching lesson of Cranny Glen by the Master, or an observation of 'Nature' for an English composition, or even the poetry in school that talked of the ancientness of the land:

The greybeards rave of highwaymen
And of a cave in Cranny glen
Of ghosts that walk before the dawn,
But that's a tale of years long gone. "

40

The feeling welled up inside Ails that the three of them were an extension of the timeless landscape of Altnamore. There they belonged, this strange trio. Their ancestors formed part of the soil and the spirit of Altnamore. Ails could never imagine not belonging. This countryside was as much a part of her as were her hair, her eyes and her soul.

  That night they helped Bella milk the cows in the sweet dungy smell of the barn. Bella always let Shamie squirt the milk into the kitten's mouth. Ails often tried but usually missed. Maybe Shamie could aim straighter because he was the best in the village at shooting marbles and spent hours doing it, thought Ails idly. Ails wouldn't have minded playing marbles, but the boys wouldn't dream of letting her or any of the other girls join them. Bella talked away to the cows, and Ails watched the straws float down the gutters while the cows peed green streams of water.
  The easy silence was broken by the chattering voices of Maura, Brigid and Jinny. They ran towards the barn, then stood a respectful distance from Bella.
  "Ails, you get home this minute!" scolded Jinny gleefully. She always seemed to know everything, thought Ails, but she didn't come in over the byre gutters. Jinny knew Bella didn't like her, so she stayed carefully outside the door, looking almost gloatingly at Ails.
  "Yer father sent us out lookin' for you." added Maura threateningly.
  "He said you were to go straight home this minute," said Brigid with authority.
  "Go on Ails," said Bella, who didn't like Ails's father much. "See you tomorra."
  Ails's father was not happy that she had been away so long, even though Lizzie had told him she had shouted in through the door to say where she was going. Ails felt sullen. Nobody ever came looking for Shamie, she thought enviously, just because he was a boy.

41

Later that night, before bedtime, Ails was sitting in Lizzie's kitchen listening to the crickets chirping in the chimney, and poking the shapes of turf around the hearth. Lizzie was talking to Mary Margit in the doorway. They were talking about Bella and the parish priest. Probably that busybody Biddy McGinn had come straight down into the village and told everybody she met about Father McStay and Bella while Ails, Bella and Shamie were out getting the cows, thought Ails. When eavesdropping, Ails had discovered, as soon as Lizzie's usually shrill voice got hushed, it usually disclosed secrets.

"Talk of the town, they were, her cheekin' aff His Reverence in front of them innocent children. Sure she's not right in the head at all, y'know." Then Mary Margit's voice:

"I just came from the Post Office, Lizzie, an' I declare to God if she didn't write letters on 'Government Property' toilet paper from the Mental and sent them to Americay — with no stamps. The postmistress was terrible annoyed." Then Lizzie again:

"Ach, sure The Dan's a livin' saint to put up with her." Ails's father's footsteps sounded, approaching the front door. He didn't turn into Ails's family's tiny sitting room, but came instead up the cement hall to Lizzie's kitchen. Lizzie and Mary Margit scattered, not wanting him to see them 'gossiping,' as he always called it.

"Evenin' Master! Soft evenin' it is. I'm just leavin'" said Mary Margit.

Lizzie had begun whistling in the kitchen, very business-like, a little taken aback to see Ails sitting in the chimney corner in the shadows.

"Time you were gettin' ready for yer bed, me girl!" said Lizzie briskly, as if she knew all along Ails was there, as if she hadn't been engaged in deep conversation with Mary Margit. It always amazed Ails how Lizzie could shift gears so quickly.

Ails went to bed with a dull nagging feeling. It wasn't to do with the telling-off she got from her father about wandering away after dark with 'that woman' (Bella). It was something else. Lizzie's conversation with Mary Margit, about Bella, kept playing, replaying and echoing through Ails's head while her guts seemed to churn around. She stared out at the dark blue heavy sky for a long time before she went to sleep, troubled. Somewhere inside her she knew it was something to do with Bella, but what?

The troubled feeling didn't go away. She woke up with a sense of foreboding.

Lizzie wasn't as sharp-tongued as usual. This unfamiliar calmness of Lizzie's produced more uncertainty in Ails's already troubled mind.

Lizzie was speaking softly to Sarah Callaghan. It was about Bella.

"They carted her aff t' the Mental again in the middle of the night. Up on the roof fixin' slates roun' the chimney with glue an' a penknife, she was."

Ails's heart stopped. It *was* Bella. "She's gone again," thought Ails in a panic. She just knew that Bella had gone away, yet again, on one of her regular disappearances into the Mental Hospital in Unragh.

Sarah: "Just kills The Dan, you know, to let her go, cracked and all as she is. Ach, he'll not let her stay long in that terrible place."

It sank into Ails's being with a thud. Bella Coyle was gone again. Ails's churning guts turned into an ache of loneliness .

Ails pushed back her wooden chair with a grating rasp on the cement floor, and fumbled with the door latch, hardly hearing Lizzie saying to Sarah:

"Ach, let her go on. She's a funny chile that. Just doesn't understand."

Ails ran blindly down the yard, through the back gate, past the forge, down the lane. She stopped and looked out over the fields.

Bella Coyle was gone. No more orange hair, sticky sweets, button boots, going for the cows …Ails felt heartsick, lonely, apprehensive, worried. Would Bella ever come back? What would the Dan do without her? What would Ails and

Shamie do without her? What would happen to Bella in 'the Mental'? Most of all, there would be a huge hole in Altnamore, with Bella gone.

Ails's silent, aching cry was wafted away by the wreaths of mist that hung over the fields, as far as she could see.

Bella, Shamie & Ails Going for the Cows

7

colmcille

Working away in her Calgary studio in Canada, Ails had decided that a flat clay surface made it easier to manage the proportions of these Celtic designs. She was decorating a large plate, now painting with a brush instead of carving — that made it easier to correct mistakes. She'd made lots of them, and corrected them — this was progress, she thought, the large Celtic design taking shape under her hand. She followed the plant-like lines as they turned into tails, interweaving into heads, legs and feet. Nothing was complete — bits and pieces everywhere, but the overall design was exquisite. She imagined those Celtic monks, inventing more and more of these intricate designs, those faceless, nameless monks with cowls and beads and sandals — a bit like Jesus with a tonsure. But surely those monks must have once been individual people, living in families, in villages and farms like those in and around Altnamore? They must have missed the laughter, singing, dancing, fiddle-playing, arguing, and storytelling they came from, mustn't they? Imagining their lives, Ails continued painting. "Up-down,

> in-out,
> point-counterpoint,
> melody-harmony,"

sang the design. When those ordinary men became monks, they sang in dank, dark, stone monasteries instead of cheery kitchens with fires and ceilighing faces. Did the monks bring to these designs the lives they missed, or did they weave elaborate designs to *avoid* the lives they missed? No smiles or happiness were evident on the fierce bird and snake heads. The curving, winding lines were contained and geometric, suggesting a strict, serious life. Those monks had to keep the rules. As she painted,

in-out,
up-down,
home-exile,
resident-emigrant,

Ails remembered from long in the past, a monk with a difference. His name was Columba, the name for dove, or peace. He didn't seem to Ails to be very aptly named, given reports of subsequent events in his life. In Altnamore village he was known as St. Colmcille. The name came from:

Columba + Cill (church) = Columcille

She continued painting, thinking of St. Colmcille, the monk who was different. He liked drawing these designs. He was fascinated by them, just as she was. He too copied designs and calligraphy — a whole book of them, in secret, at night, by candlelight. She imagined him listening for the creaking of a footstep or a door, and pinning blankets over the windows so nobody would see the light. He dared to do this. He was caught, and was exiled for it, to the island of Iona in Scotland. The book must have meant a lot to him, thought Ails, to have taken this kind of risk, in such a censored environment. Did he love the symbols, or the colours, or the content? Or did his heart wind and twist and curve along with the complex patterns, while he wished he had done the original himself? The author of the original book was furious at Colmcille for copying it, reporting this travesty to the Ard-Ri — the High King. Ails couldn't remember the details from school, but she knew that Columba, called after a peaceful dove, got pretty riled up, got exiled to Scotland, and made a vow never again to set foot on Irish soil. To be exiled was one of the worst punishments anywhere, she knew from legends, and songs, and stories of Irish emigrants.

Instinctively, Ails looked around furtively from her clay work, as if someone might hear or read her forbidden thoughts. She would never dream of saying in Ireland how she dearly loved Canada, her adopted country, and how she felt the inner peace and optimism she had decreasingly felt in Ireland, as she grew beyond her teens. She instinctively knew it would be considered high treason to even breathe that, so, when she visited Ireland, she quietly agreed with how terrible it was to have to leave Ireland. Did Colmcille feel terrible, she wondered? Or was he perhaps fed-up with rules? Was he maybe even secretly relieved to go?

Although exiled for many years, St. Columcille had to come back to Ireland before he died. In order that he keep his vow of never again setting foot on Irish soil, St. Colmcille filled his boots with soil from Iona, Scotland. Ails pondered gleefully on how inventive this was, especially for a monk who lived such a restricted, ordered life.

Ails thought Colmcille would have done well in North America, in a new world, a frontier, where inventiveness was survival, where many of the norms and rules of the former culture were turned topsy-turvy; where climate extremes tended to blow away the cobwebs of tradition and class. Often, to cope with unfamiliar agricultural land and strange peoples, immigrants had to bend and twist and massage their own behaviours, attitudes and values — formerly held sacred. The very act of daring to draw, and possibly invent his own designs was so 'new world' of Columcille, thought Ails, even if he did live centuries ago.

"Like living in Canada these days," she thought. No mystique, no preparation, no research, training or apprenticeship; just reading a book on a bitterly cold night and saying "Hey, that looks interesting. I think I'll try that!" Nobody saying, directly or indirectly, "No, you can't. You're not qualified. How dare you think you can do that! There are rules, you know!" On this side of the Atlantic, whether it was art, plumbing, making garments, or tents, or bridges, or electrical wiring, or bridges, or pottery, or painting, you just figured it out and did it!

Ails looked up from her clay work, her reverie interrupted by her sudden consciousness of the tension in her neck, wrist and elbow, holding them in one position for too long "Whew! Am I getting carried away!" said Ails to herself. "I bet that was what happened to Columcille when he got caught. He probably stayed at it too long, too late and got discovered." She felt her eyes straining, and decided to leave her unfinished plate painting until the next time she had some time free. She thought of the lunches to make for the morning, clean clothes, notes for school, and getting her work stuff together. As she began wrapping up the half-decorated plate in multi-layers of drycleaning plastic to keep it at the right consistency to paint, Ails admired her fairly well-constructed design, and her mind wandered, unbidden, back to Colmcille.

He'd been gone a long time when he went back to Ireland. Did he perhaps go back to Altnamore? Did what was once familiar and second nature to him now seem strange, forced, contrived? Had he forgotten what to say, how to say it, who to say it to? Had he become so used to a different way of living, adapting to new ways and relationships and language and thinking and food and customs, that maybe he couldn't go back? Had exile perhaps made him a different person, now that he'd been banished? Had he now become a great leader, instigator, agent for change, or scribe? Someone who invented, took risks, and soared with the glory of accomplishment?

If so, could he ever go back again? Ails wondered.

She didn't think so.

Uir
iner
Uir
pro

49

8

a hospital love story

ypical Irish November weather, it was a crisp, cold, damp day, with the odd shower of light rain. Seven-year-old Ails and her friends were all playing up on St. Colmcille's Rocks high above the town. They had run up the hill, and Ails had a terrible stitch in her side. But in Jinny's empty milk room, on the cement floor, while Brigid banged the churn in time, they had worked out a whole dance routine. They were going to use the usual 'stage' — the huge slab of rock that was known as St. Colmcille's bed, so Ails stumbled on with her side aching, up, up, up the hill, to get there.

Ails and Maura and Jinny and Fiona and Brigid tapped their shoes on the smooth, damp, flat, flint-hard granite of St. Colmcille's bed. Of course, Jinny and Maura and Brigid had steel taps and shiny silver buckles on their dance shoes. Ails and Fiona were banging as hard as their leather-soled, sensible, laced shoes would allow. Their father insisted they wear practical footwear where their feet could grow healthily. "None of those dancing patent leather shoes," he'd said.

"A-h'aon, do, tri, cahir, cuig, shay, sheacht," (1, 2, 3, 4, 5, 6, 7) they chanted in Gaelic, keeping time to the 'seven steps' of the reel, as they'd been taught in Irish dancing class, continuing "A-h'aon, do tri, agus a h-aon, do, tri," (and a 1, 2, 3; and a 1, 2, 3) for the two triplet steps at end of each seven. As she felt the hard rock through her shoes, Ails thought "They called this St. Colmcille's BED? Some bed! You'd need a heap of straw covered with moss or grass or something to sleep here, never mind the cold!" Ails shivered. "He must have been a big man to sleep here, that St. Colmcille, judging from the fact that there's room for all five of us to dance here," she thought. They danced for a while, then started arguing about who was supposed to be where, and who was not keeping together. Then Jinny decided it was time for all of them to put the steps to music, lilting the deedly-diedly music for the steps. But Ails had to stop. The pain in her side was still there.

"Where you goin'?" accused Jinny bossily.

"I got a stitch in my side running up the hill and it won't go away," said Ails defensively.

"Namby-pamby," said Jinny.

Ails put out her tongue at Jinny.

"Miss Bossy-Boots," she mimicked in Jinny's voice. Ails went over a short way from St. Colmcille's bed, then sat down heavily on the two slabs of damp, cold rock that looked remarkably like a big chair — St. Colmcille's chair, it was called. The pain eased a little, but that chair needed cushions, thought Ails. She would have gathered some soft grass, but she didn't feel like moving.

She woke up from an uncomfortable half-sleep, feeling kind of groggy when she heard voices coming up the hill. It was four older people, strangers to Altnamore, probably coming up to put money in St. Colmcille's well to pray for somebody to get better from being sick, thought Ails. People often came to Altnamore to pray at St. Colmcille's famous well. Everybody knew when strangers came to Altnamore, especially the boys. She noticed Jinny and the others cleaning grass stains off their dancing shoes on the other side of St. Colmcille's stone bed, and wondered, since they'd finished dancing, how long she'd been dozing. She felt cold and stiff and sore and miserable.

"Hello," said Jinny to the people heading towards the well, in her inimitable way that could charm adults. "They just can't see through her," thought Ails jealously. The others sidled along. Ails knew Jinny would wheedle money for sweets. Her huge eyes could do that, somehow. Even Jinny didn't have the nerve, as some of the boys like Dingo Devine did, to lift the money out of the well after the donors had gone and brazenly go and buy sweets. The ancient, awesome nature of the well, with its myths, legendary cures for skin rashes, pains, aches, and

51

seemingly magic qualities, had seeped into the girls, and most of the boys, but a few boys didn't care. Ails knew these boys had probably seen these strangers coming up to the famous well. Later the boys would follow and take the money out and wash it and spend it, but they'd leave enough so nobody'd notice. Jinny always said they'd get warts if they did that, but so far, no sign of warts. Ails wouldn't have minded hanging around to talk to these people, then spying on the boys later, but she was strangely tired, and the pain in her side wouldn't go away. It got worse again that night, and Fiona told their mother that Ails had fallen asleep on St. Colmcille's stone chair.

"You shouldn't be sitting on damp rock," said Ails's mother.

"Probably a chill in her kidneys," said her father, and he gave her a spoonful of whisky, which she hated. It burned its way right down through to her stomach.

There it came again, that pain in her side — off and on all day yesterday and today. It was Christmas Eve.

"Why couldn't it have happened before the holidays?" thought Ails. On Christmas Day each year she went to her Auntie Cora's. All of the kids were allowed into the sitting room. It was one of the few days the children got to use the sitting room, with its cream coloured sofa covers, the doll hanging on the wall, and a big dancing fire. You could sink down into the stuffing of the sofa, just like you were on a cloud. It was even better if you rolled over the back of the sofa, and tumbled into the cushions, landing on their softness. Auntie Cora had great things to eat, with pretty paper doilies and Christmas crackers that you pulled to crack them loudly, releasing a beautiful miniature toy or ring. Ails and Shamie were the youngest ones that went there. Ails didn't have to bring her sister. She could dress up and it would be wonderful.

"Ooowwwh!" She caught her breath sharply. There it was again. That nagging pain kept coming back like a hot ember getting hotter each time. She went into McAleavey's shop, hardly able to remember what Lizzie had sent her for. A pound of tea, that was it. She lifted her arm up to put the money on McAleavey's counter for the tea, but the pain was so severe, she crumpled down onto the floor. The pain took over.

"Are you alright, Ails?" asked Maureen McAleavey, leaning over the high counter to look down at Ails on the floor.

"Just turned over on me ankle," muttered Ails, struggling up. The pain had passed but she felt really strange. Her body didn't feel like her own. Her head was confused and woozy, and the crippling pain could come back any time, she felt.

"Not on Christmas Eve," she thought, as she moved automatically homeward, clutching the package of tea. "I can't be sick on Christmas Eve!" But she had to stop and lean on the pump and pretend to be getting a drink.

When she got home, her mother had her egg-in-a-cup and bread ready. She felt a wave of nausea, but she *couldn't* be sick, not today. She thought of the big soft cushions, the way her aunt loved to spoil Shamie, her youngest, and Ails herself who was Shamie's age. She thought of the doll with the braids hanging on the wall. She was going there tomorrow, she thought, determined. Ails swallowed a spoonful of boiled egg. It felt like rubber. The bread tasted like gravel.

The pain was duller now. Her daddy said she had to go to bed early for Santa Claus. On the way up the stairs the pain came again, like hot lava pouring over her inside. Ails hung onto the bannisters. She could see the doll with the flaxen braids smiling at her from the wall of the Auntie Cora's sitting room, but the pain was searing through her, and she couldn't hold onto the bannister any longer. She fell back against the brown door which crashed open at the bottom of the stairs. She landed in a crumpled heap on the mat, protected somewhat from the cement floor .

"My God, what is it, darlin'?" It was her mother.

"I'm not sick, mammy. The pain went away before in McAleavey's. I *can't* be sick. It's Christmas! I'm going to Auntie Cora's tomorrow, and wearing my red velvet dress. I'm not going to be ..." Ails felt herself floating and heard everything through a haze.

"My God, run quick for the doctor, Paddy. Something's terribly wrong! Lizzie, take the baby and Fiona. Oh, God, make her be alright, my Ails, my girl, oh please God.... " Ails felt herself being rocked against her mother's body. It felt soothing, but the pain, the awful pain, and the wooziness..."

She came to, and felt the blue satin ribbon on the edge of the good blue blanket, and her father's strong arms tightly around her. The bumping and clanking of the car was deafening. They seemed to be moving awfully fast.

"God protect us, he's drunk," said Ails's mother's voice. Then louder, "Take it easy, Doctor, or we'll all be killed."

"Jay-sus, woman, don't tell me to take it easy. That chile has to be got to the hospital quick."

Ails woke up briefly on a flat bed that seemed to be flying down a strange white corridor. She felt hot tears on her face. She was sick and it was Christmas Eve...

When she woke up in her hospital bed, Ails knew it was Christmas Day. She was sore, but it was a different sore. It wasn't her whole insides. It was outside, but she couldn't move, not even her legs. Her mother was crying softly beside her, looking white and exhausted.

"You're alright, love, thank God you're alright." But Ails just said "I missed Santa Claus and Auntie Cora's couch and the Christmas crackers and the plum-pudding and the doll with the button boots and the bonnet ..." Tears streamed down her face. Her father leaned over and said "We nearly lost you, Ails, we're just glad you're here."

It was burst appendix, she was later told. Had been burst for a number of hours and the poison had to be drained from her whole body. Did she have a bad pain sometime earlier, they asked her? When she told them about collapsing in McAleavey's shop, they thought her appendix must have burst around that time.

From her hospital bed, Ails looked around groggily at the lights, carol-singers, a man in a Santa Claus suit, Christmas trees and people with presents. It was beautiful. It was all a kind of haze. Suddenly her eyes focused. She blinked in disbelief.

Was it really? ... It couldn't be ... It was.

There was the doll with the flaxen braids, the bonnet and the button boots, and her Auntie Cora smiling tenderly above it.

"The doctor told us you kept talking in your sleep about the doll on the wall. Is this it?" She gave Ails the doll, and hugged her gently.

"And how's my best girl?"

"I missed your house."

"No, you didn't, Ails, we're keeping the day for you till you get better."

Ails looked at the doll with delight, as her mother and father and Auntie Cora talked in hushed tones. As she drifted into wooziness once again, Ails could hear quite clearly the three voices, as if she were listening to a radio drama. First her father, sounding angry, his whispering growing louder:

"I *know* he saved her life, Eileen, but *something* has to be done about that man's drinking. He could've killed all of us. Sooner or later, for every life he's saved, he's going to kill somebody else." Then came her mother's placating tones,

"Ach now, Paddy, sure he's no worse than a whole lot of other men in the village." Then her father's voice again, in controlled anger, hissing in the loudest whisper

"Listen, you two, other men are not responsible for the lives of innocent people. That man's a danger to himself and everyone else!" Then her Auntie Cora,

"Ach, c'mon now Paddy, sure everyone knows he's a great doctor, you have to admit that, don't you?" Ails could hear her father pushing back his chair. He must be standing up now; his voice was now coming from above her.

"That's some way to keep his Hippocratic oath, for Chrissake!" Then her mother,

"Paddy, stop cursing and calm down for God's sake, you'll wake Ails." She could hear her father's strides leaving the room, and the swinging doors swinging hard, sending a kind of breeze whooshing through the room. She expected to hear some kind of violin music, just like listening to the radio. But all she heard was her mother and Auntie Cora's whispers, ebbing and flowing like the sound of the river. Ails thought she heard — naw, it couldn't be — could they *really* have prayed for her at Midnight Mass? Jinny always got to stay up and go to Midnight

Mass. Had Jinny heard Ails's name announced by the priest from the altar? Ails was filled with a mixture of pride and embarrassment. She suddenly thought of home, her sisters, her own bed and Fiona sleeping alone in it, and Lizzie. What were they doing? Were they alright without her?

"Where's Fiona and the baby?" she asked suddenly. Her mother put a hand gently on her arm.

"Ssh, darlin', Lizzie has them. We're goin' home now to let you sleep." They kissed her and left. Ails felt weary, fatigued, and washed-out tired. A nurse came in. She had one of the most serene, tranquil, lovely faces Ails had ever seen. The nurse took her pulse and temperature, saying:

"I believe The Wee Doctor from Altnamore brought you in last night late. That was some Christmas present for you!" Ails had forgotten last night. Now she remembered the Wee Doctor driving like a maniac, smelling of booze and cigarettes, his warbly whistling sounding like the birds in the morning. Suddenly Ails felt herself fading out. She drifted off, her head feeling heavy.

In her sleepy grogginess, she could see the doctor's hand. It was awful. It had a finger missing — the index finger. The next two fingers were stained with nicotine. That's how he held his cigarette. This small ugly hand was pressing on her side and it hurt something awful ... How did he lose his finger anyway? Ails had asked many different people many times about this missing finger. Nobody seemed to know. Everyone loved a chance to tell a story about the Wee Doctor, just as if he were a person in a story book, yet nobody seemed to know how he lost his finger ...Ails's dreamy sleepiness wafted her woozily to her hiding place under the stairs in Heaney's pub, where she could see herself playing with the corks and listening to stories about the Wee Doctor "jist put that wee lassie in the back of the car and him as drunk as Bacchus and careered aff to the awspital. Saved that chile's life, he did. Another coupla hours, and yon wean woulda been dead. She was that bad they prayed for her at Midnight Mass. Her da had to come to this very pub to get the Doc to look her over. I tellya the Doc's a genius, no doubt about it. Through all the drink he knows what's wrong with a body." Ails's father seemed to be the only one who ever questioned the

56

Wee Doctor's drinking, driving, swearing and betting money. As she had heard Lizzie say to Mary Margit about her father, "That Master there, you'd nivir think he was from around these parts. Mind you, he's not, but he's from up Armagh way, and should be as Irish as the pigs of Connemara. But he thinks like an Englishman for God's sake! Should be ashamed of himself, he should."

Ails opened her eyes sleepily, not sure whether she was awake or asleep, or how long she had been this way. She saw the form of the Wee Doctor's ugly face above her, smelling of cigarettes, with his ugly brown hand on her forehead.

"How's me girl?" he asked her. Ails grunted. Her mouth seemed filled with glue and she couldn't get any words to come out. She smiled a watery smile:

"Good. Now you shoulda got sick when school was on, not during the holidays. That wasn't very smart of you. You're in Mrs. Digby's room, aren't you? Mrs. Digby was asking for you — real worried she was." He winked and chuckled.

"Even The Pig knew," thought Ails. The Pig seemed so far away. They all seemed so far away. Altnamore seemed in another land ...

"Yeh, a real celebrity, that's what you are, Ails!" She yawned wearily and dozed off, the word 'celebrity' spinning around in her head.

"Celebrity, that's what he was, the Wee Doctor, around the country," dreamed Ails "not a character in a book, but a celebrity."

"Mind you it's not for his looks that people admire him," Lizzie would say "but he's the best doctor you'll find in the length and breadth of Ireland, and sure looks aren't everythin'. And sure he's great crack!" And he was. He made a joke out of everything. And everyone told his jokes in the pubs and at ceilidhing nights. A favourite story was about the chapel congregation saying ten Hail Marys, while counting the compulsory ten beads of each decade of the Rosary. Instead of using rosary beads, the Wee Doctor counted them on his fingers, but with one finger missing, he only had to say 9 prayers to everyone else's 10.

"He gets finished the rosary before all them holy ones that's wearin' out their Rosary beads!" Ails had heard Mickey Faddy telling over and over again in Heaney's pub. Mickey would laugh and cackle, showing his one brown front tooth.

"But the drink has a terrible hold on the Wee Doctor," Mary Margit would retort to Lizzie.

"Ach, never mind that. He's powerful crack when he's drunk, an' smarter drunk than thon smart new wart of a doctor sober, and that's a fact."

The next time Ails opened her eyes in a kind of haze, the Wee Doctor was still sitting in her hospital room, this time looking out through the window, pensive. She saw it again, that strange look she'd seen before. It was a sad, haunted look, as if someone else was looking out through his eyes behind the thick glasses, someone with a lonely, lost soul, a soul that was reaching out to try and touch someone or something. Ails had seen that look before, but it was fleeting. She had also seen it last longer, and if it did, Ails had even seen the Wee Doctor turn mean and nasty. She almost felt guilty saying that silently to herself. Sure wasn't the wee doctor one of the great characters of Altnamore? Sure, hadn't he saved her life? But unbidden, a memory came back to Ails of the Wee Doctor, when nobody could see him, in between the two doors of the pub, giving money to Dingo Daley to beat up Jinny. Ails didn't even think he would have noticed Jinny. He never looked at children, and seemed to treat them like the dogs and cats walking around — unless they were brought to him sick. Then, it was said, he knew what was wrong with them immediately. He then looked at them as if they were just like big people. Hadn't he done that with her? But the memory of him driving drunk and swearing at the weather and the winding road frightened Ails. She could still feel the sharp breaths her mother drew in as the car rounded a corner, sometimes on the wrong side of the road. Still, he was the only doctor Altnamore had, and wasn't that lucky? Usually someone in the ever-present crowd surrounding the Wee Doctor would call him out of this strange, dangerous-looking mood, drawing him into the limelight, with:

"Isn't that right, Doc?" or

"A penny for yer thoughts, Doc?"

58

When this happened, Ails imagined she could see a look of weariness flash across his face. He'd crack some joke and be off with the crowd. That sad, haunted, sometimes dangerous look would go back into hiding behind his eyes again. Now, however, in Ails's hospital room, he was staring, transfixed, alone, sober. Stripped of all his admirers in the empty setting of the hospital, the wee Doctor looked to Ails to be deformed and ugly, a crooked little figure, alone, and somehow, to her childish mind, suffering.

She watched him in this state from her half-closed eyes for what seemed to Ails a very long time. Yet she knew it wasn't her imagination. The longer she watched him, Ails could see that look of pain — almost torture — and a kind of longing. Then her throat tickled and she tried to suppress a cough.

"Darn it!" thought Ails. At her cough, the Wee Doctor gave a start and put on his bright, cheery, people-surrounded face again. She had broken his reverie. The cough hurt her insides terribly, but she had to cough again.

"Keepin' me up half the night, girl, and now you wake me from me daydreamin'. You're an awful case! Well, I have to go now. See you tomorrow." Suddenly he was gone, whistling his warbly whistle, a comical, crooked, short figure of a man, forever pushing his glasses up his strawberry red nose, and laughing his deep, raucous laugh. Ails felt guilty for thinking bad things about him earlier. Sure wasn't he a saint?

Without the distraction of the Wee Doctor, Ails now realized how rotten she felt. Tubes were sticking out of her ankle and abdomen; big ugly stitches pulling folds of skin together on the side of her stomach. She was tired and sore and homesick. She hugged the doll that smelled like Auntie Cora's sitting room. She tried to visualize the sky behind the plantin, which always made her feel calm on those golden Altanamore summer evenings. She couldn't visualize anything. Another nurse gave her a drink of sickly pink stuff. She drifted off to sleep, a fitful sleep. She kept seeing the Wee Doctor's face, its expression changing from weary to frightening to understanding, to mean. Then Lizzie's voice:

"Definitely was behind the door when the looks were being given out, the Wee Doctor was. Ach, sure I mind him as a lad, the runt of the litter, and then he got polio on top of it. That finished him, but he's a great doctor even if he is no oil paintin'."

Then in Ails's fitful dreamlike state, she saw him outside the pub, handing out pennies to herself, Jinny, Maura, Brigid and Fiona. Fiona! Ails woke up with a start. My God! She'd forgotten Fiona! Fiona would be afraid of the dark without her!

"Fiona will likely sleep with Lizzie," Ails comforted herself, settling down, exhausted, into the hospital pillows to fall asleep once more. This time in her dream, the Wee Doctor's car seemed to be weaving all over the road down to the Monument, hitting the hedges on each side. "He's drunk," thought Ails wildly. She kept trying to run down to the Monument after him, but she couldn't move her legs. Then the Wee Doctor's car bashed into the Monument and he was hurt badly, maybe even dead, she thought in panic. Ails woke up screaming, shivering, drenched in sweat and frightened.

"I wanna go home to Altnamore!" cried Ails weakly. The gentle, tranquil nurse was there again. She comforted Ails and changed her into a fresh nightgown and big long socks and rocked her back to sleep like a baby. Ails slept for a long, long time.

When she awoke, what seemed to her like weeks later, Ails's head was clear. The wooziness was gone, and two nurses were talking in hushed tones in the corner of her room:

"I tell you, Mary Ellen, he fancies you!"

"Ach, go on, Jane …. what makes you say that?"

"I don't know. Every time he brings a patient in when you're around he gets nervous. He hangs around where you are, and …d'you fancy him?"

"Well, there's no point. I'm sure he has a girlfriend."

"They say no. He's always with a bunch of men. Would that wee girl know, d'you think?" This was better than eavesdropping in Heaney's pub, thought Ails, pretending her eyes were closed:

"I'll ask her for you when she wakes up," whispered Jane. "She was awful scared yesterday evening — woke up screaming. I bet you that sleep will do the trick. She's slept for almost two whole days!"

Ails was surprised. She thought she had slept for over a week, but her mind was still on the nurses' conversation.

"They're talking about the Wee Doctor!" thought Ails, "did he have a girlfriend?" Ails honestly didn't know. She thought back to things Lizzie had said. Lizzie and Jinny always knew these things.

"Never bothers with women — ach mebbe on account of the way he looks. Sure where would he find the time anyway?" Ails remembered Lizzie telling someone in the kitchen.

"So he doesn't have a girlfriend?" she surmised. Ails had never seen him talking to a woman except in the dispensary, to patients. But Ails saw him spend long hours in the pub, and playing cards in a haze of smoke, and staggering home when the crowd left. Sometimes he even staggered up to his dispensary to examine people.

The nurses didn't get a chance to talk to Ails again before the Wee Doctor arrived to do his rounds.

"How's Ails today? They tell me you're doin' great sleepin'!"

"Have you got a girlfriend?" blurted out Ails. She didn't mean for it to come out that way. Just for a moment that sad, haunted look flashed across his face. He laughed quickly:

"Just too many to choose from, Ails, can't make up me mind!"

"So he doesn't have a girlfriend," thought Ails. Maybe that was part of the reason for the sad, brooding look, turning to hardness — even bitterness, when he was alone, when there was nobody to cajole him out of himself. When the gentle, calm nurse came into the room, Ails watched. He became fidgety, unusually quiet and confused, and didn't look at the nurse at all. Indeed, he just concentrated on Ails's stitches, and muttered something about 'watching infection, medication, record chart' without looking up. He couldn't seem to meet the nurse's eyes. She went out of the room again.

"It's just that the nurses were wondering — about the girlfriend, I mean," Ails continued from before. He looked distinctly uncomfortable. "They were teasing Nurse Mary Ellen about you." Ails was enjoying herself now. The Wee Doctor gave a start. He almost seemed shocked, but he didn't say a thing. Ails had never known him not to rally from his quietness. He was never stuck for words, always coming up with some kind of banter. But now, no answer; five minutes must have ticked by. Ails was quiet as a mouse. The Wee Doctor continued to stare out through the narrow hospital window, with the same haunted look on his face. This time he even seemed frightened, thought Ails. He seemed to forget Ails was even in the room. The quiet nurse came silently into the room carrying a chart. Ails had heard the other nurses calling her Mary Ellen. The Wee Doctor stayed quiet, reading. The Nurse was looking at him, quiet as a shadow. Watching from her half-closed eyes, Ails somehow knew that Mary Ellen was watching not only Wee Doctor, but also the person behind his eyes, the complex person who appeared when nobody was watching, when he was alone. In Altnamore, nobody seemed to acknowledge this side of the Wee Doctor. Maybe they just didn't want to see it, thought Ails, perplexed. She was so confused about him.

The Wee Doctor, suddenly realizing he was not alone, stood up abruptly, awkwardly. Ails noticed that Nurse Mary Ellen was taller than he was, even without her nurse's hat. Then everything all seemed to happen so quickly. The Wee Doctor simply put his arms around Mary Ellen and kissed her, right on the lips, in broad daylight in Ails's tiny hospital cubicle. Ails was watching in open-mouthed astonishment, her stitches almost melting. Nurse Mary Ellen was flushed and pretty and reeling with surprise. The Wee Doctor was silent with embarrassment. It was Nurse Mary Ellen who broke the silence.

"Now, Doctor, and in front of the chile!" He looked enormously relieved when she spoke. They both stood for a long time, looking tenderly into each other's eyes. Ails felt warm and glowing inside. She pretended to be engrossed in the doll, As

62

other nurses' voices approached, the Wee Doctor and Mary Ellen left the room — separately.

Ails was moved out of the special cubicle into a big long ward. "Out of the woods" they said she was. She grew to love the hospital with all its kids from other villages and towns all over the countryside. Many had been just as sick, many much sicker, than she was. Every time the Wee Doctor came in, the nurses nudged each other and giggled. Mary Ellen blushed and didn't look directly at him when other people were around.

Ails seemed to have forgotten a lot of things about Altnamore, even what Lizzie's kitchen looked like. She read nearly all of the hospital's many library books. She named Auntie Cora's doll Ingrid. She found the name in one of the books. She knew Ingrid would have to go back on the wall in Auntie Cora's sitting room, because Ingrid had been sent from America to Mags, Auntie Cora's grown-up girl. Ingrid had been too good even for Mags to play with. Ails was very careful with Ingrid. She made her part of her own secret place, so she could talk to her even after Ingrid had to go back on the wall. Having come through her operation and discomfort and bad dreams and recovery right along with Ails, Ingrid now knew Ails almost better than anyone.

9

that 'home' feeling

I n a Calgary pottery studio, Ails and her Dutch-Canadian friend Theodora (Dora for short) were taking some glaze lessons. That was one thing Ails loved about living in Canada. You could experiment and fool around and dabble in things. As Bernie, her other friend in experimentation, was prone to say "Hey, Dabble is my middle name!" The neat part was that when she screwed up, or got stuck, or couldn't go any further, Ails didn't have to feel ashamed of her 'failure.' Rather, armed with her own experience of doing it the hard way, as long as she had time and a little money, she could take formal lessons, paying a modest fee to avail herself of the expertise of someone who had already solved all those problems.

For instance, on the advice of the instructor, Ails had given up her carrot peeler when the instructor introduced her to a much more efficient carving tool. Also on the instructor's advice, she had changed her technique, now rolling out medium-thin pieces of clay and painting them with a glaze colour. She then carved through the colour, so the Celtic design was the original clay colour inside the actual glaze. Then she attached this piece to the outside of the curvy pot, by roughing up both surfaces with a toothbrush and water, and they stuck like glue. The pot ended up with a kind of embossed decoration that was easier to keep in proportion, and really quite lovely. Ails' instructor was excited and enthusiastic, looking upon all of her students' experimentations as further experience for herself, as well as for all the other students, in what seemed like a huge adventure. The level of the instructor's education was not important. Here, in Canada, it was how a person performed that was important — 'where the rubber hits the road' was how people here described it. In this part of Canada, out west, it was a feature of the fast-moving, entrepreneurial, vibrant city they lived in. In this way, Ails had tried guitar-playing, stained glass, sewing, and many other things, getting hooked on some, discarding others. She held the opinion that it was because of the diabolical winters that people here got into all these things.

The winter had never become easier for Ails in Calgary. With the end of October — often earlier, came a freezing over of the earth, and gradually, a freezing over of the brain, and emotions, if she was not careful. As the winter worsened and lengthened, ordinary, everyday life became more difficult. Almost inhuman conditions required layers of clothes, heaters inside engines of cars, shovelling snow, chipping ice, and the four walls of a house closing in on her. Worst of all about the winters, though, coming from the warming glow of Irish people-centeredness, was the isolation — in a city full of people, everyone all but disappeared, coming out again like moles out of holes, into the melting, brown-grass rebirth of a Calgary April Spring. That was a whole six months of winter. And above it all, an interminable blue dome of sky, making it seem all the more vast and eternity-like.

She cosied back in to the warmth and cheeriness of the pottery studio, where she and Dora were working with a group of mainly women in the class. As she wove in and out with her carving tool, the design seemed to grow under her hands, its rhythm saying:
"Winter-summer;
Hot-cold;
Crowded-lonely;
Rigid-flowing;
Separate-stick together. "
It was working a lot better, this carving on a flat surface. It removed the element of trying to work on a curved surface, thereby technically changing the length, direction and proportion

65

of lines. It was amazing how, in isolation, it was hard to see this. When other pairs of eyes looked at it, it seemed so obvious.

"Somehow, you know," she confided to Dora, "these Celtic designs keep their own character better if I carve them on a flat surface first. THEN it's easier to introduce them as an element onto the pot, instead of trying to carve a complex, geometric design on a curved surface." Dora, with her scientific, logical mind, looked at her in open amazement, responding in her strong Dutch accent.

"You mean, you didn't figure that out before?" Ails looking sheepish, tried to explain it away, "Well, I mean if it's done separately on a slab, it's much easier to attach it to the pot later," she said lamely.

"That makes perfect sense," responded Dora in her inimitable way of connecting things differently from Ails.

"Take ourselves, you and me, for example, "When we go to a new place, isn't it easier to sort of attach to the outside first, and then become a part of the society as you gradually adapt to it?" Ails hadn't thought of it that way.

As a child, it had seemed so natural and wonderful and easy to blend into where she had belonged — like soaking down into a bath of warm, soothing water. If it was mizzling rain outside, she could always find something to do, somebody to talk to, a way or a place to escape the drizzling soft dampness, or even the biting, slicing Atlantic winds. Everyone lived so close to each other, and to everything they needed — shops, the pump, the pubs, the church, the fields, ceilighing neighbours looking for places to get together. That, to Ails, was what it was like to feel grounded, in tune with her environment, to feel 'at home.'

She looked out through the frost-encrusted panes of the Calgary pottery studio windows, at the merciless, brilliant, blue sky, and felt that familiar sense of isolation and separation from her environment. It didn't seem to affect Dora. She loved the coldness, the vast white isolation, and walked for miles with her dogs in deep snow, near her almost-rural house. She suddenly realized that Dora was still talking to her. Pretending to be concentrating on her carving, she said:

"Sorry, Dora, I wasn't listening. What was that you just said?"

"I was talking about how attaching your personal design to the outside of a pot is just like attaching to the outside of Canada. Then you gradually become part of it as you adapt. Attaching the designs onto your pots are just like that." Not for Ails, it wasn't. She thought of how she, herself, jumped right in at the deep end, and often wished she had moved more slowly, but she didn't know how. Dora always had such a logical, charming way of explaining the kinds of things that Ails got tied up in Celtic knots inside herself.

"Yes, I guess so," said Ails getting up from her workplace stool and pretending to go to her locker to look for something. She was looking for something, but not pottery-related. She had cut a quote out of the newspaper a number of weeks before. She searched through her books and papers, and found it, stuck with a piece of grimy sellotape to the back of a clay-stained glaze book. She re-read it in the shadow of her locker door. It was a strange, cryptic comment about the Irish which puzzled, yet intrigued her:

"we are lazy and feckless by nature, but driven by our own demons that force a reckoning with the complexity of merely being Irish in a world that is always alien to us, no matter how orthodox we pretend to become. All society is upside down to us because of its inherent insistence on simplifying the complex. We rail against the enemies within, because outrage is our escape from reality, because in confusion there is order; in symmetrical precision there is disorder. We suffer from the excesses of our own highly strung strengths."

"Good God, it's no wonder I'm feeling screwed-up," thought Ails, going quietly to the washroom to clean up. She didn't really have the heart to tell Dora about her newspaper clipping, nor did she feel like going back to her clay decorating. She made some excuse about having to leave early. Dora, oblivious, was working away quietly with the other people in the studio, all of them seeming grounded, content, at home there in the warm cocoon in the midst of the cruel Calgary winter.

Ails was feeling alone, alien and desolate inside herself. She didn't know any more what it was like to feel grounded and completely at home. Maybe she never would again. Her mind and heart drifted back to a homecoming many years ago.

10

When you've Been away

Young Ails got more and more excited driving home from the hospital in Unragh, Ireland. It was the first time she'd ever been away from home. It seemed like a year since she'd left, and she couldn't wait to see everything and everyone again.

"Drive slow, daddy, drive slow!" The marked contrast in the houses had never struck her before. She had always heard village people say houses were 'Protestant looking' down the lower end of the village where the Protestant school was. Now she really noticed sparkling windows, whitewashed walls, window boxes with flowers, neat gardens, trimmed hedges. 'Sweet William' and 'Orange Lilies,' were both blooming in the tiny, perfectly-kept gardens of Protestant houses. Catholics never grew these flowers, with their 'partisan' names, mindful of King William of Orange — their sworn enemy from 1690, although nobody seemed to know much about this king. These beautifully kept houses and weed-free gardens contrasted with the squads of grubby-looking children playing around Catholic houses, unruly rose bushes, vines climbing all over the walls, and a welcoming look about them.

"Daddy! can you drive through the estate? Please, daddy, please." Her father was beaming all over, delighted to have her home. An avid gardener with no garden of his own, he loved to look at the golden privet and the hedge sculptures and the rose trellises of the estate.

"Alright, then, Ails, just a quick detour. The scenic route home." She saw him wink at her mother. Since, according to Lizzie, Catholics 'wouldn't be seen dead in the estate,' Ails's mother was glancing furtively out the window to see if anyone they knew happened to be watching from the surrounding roads. She was pretending to rummage in her bag for a safety pin for Ails's skirt, who'd got so thin that her underwear and skirt kept falling down. Even her knee socks wouldn't stay up on her skinny legs. From being in bed so long her hair stuck up in spikes and felt like straw.

They were stopping at the gatehouse of the estate.

"Just driving through," said Ails's father, "my girl just got out of hospital."

"Fine, Sir," said Basil, the gatekeeper who lived in the picturesque 'Protestant-looking' gate lodge, with its burst of colour from a huge bed of orange lilies.

"Slow, daddy, slow," said Ails. She had never seen such glorious profusion of colour. Gardeners were out working between rhodendron bushes, laden with blossoms. Copper beech trees shone like burnished gold and the light shining through the translucent green of the beech trees formed a stunning canopy. Ails felt like a royal princess. They passed an English looking lady in her jodhpurs, going in the direction of the stables, and she said " How do you do?" through the open window of the car. "Wonderful weather we're having, isn't it?" There was the lake with the boat and the boathouse, and grass with no thistles or nettles.

"See, Ingrid," she said, holding the doll up to the window. Then she pulled Ingrid back, remembering she'd better not tell Auntie Cora she was driving through the estate of the "landed gentry," as Auntie Cora called them, "with nobody living there half the time, gallivantin' aroun' the colonies, and them with a whole bevy of servants, and the Catholic farmers not even allowed to fish in the lake that they could throw a stone in from their own homes. Don't talk to me about those people!"

No, Ingrid had better not look.

Ails caught her breath. There was a peacock in full regalia, his tail spread like a fan in the dappled light shining through the beech trees. "Just like a picture in a book," thought

Ails. They reached the other gatehouse, and drove out onto the main road again — much bumpier than the smooth roadway within the estate. Ails's side still hurt a little, not being used to bumping around on roads like this. They passed the bog, with the men out cutting turf and putting it in little stacks to dry, and children jumping over bog holes and sinking into marshy, wet ground. Altnamore was experiencing a freak heat wave. Still, used to hospital heat, Ails shivered from the open window of the car. They started climbing the hill into the village, past the football field, past Auntie Cora's at the foot of the town, past the forbidding barracks, and the austere Protestant church behind its stone wall and neatly groomed hedge. The house of Trevor Tunbridge, the caretaker, looked smart and manicured among the higgledy-piggledy Catholic houses and shops with people out enjoying the heat, waving to Ails in welcome. They drove slowly on up into the village, where every house was like a person welcoming Ails back. The schoolchildren were all around the pump. Ails felt strangely shy waving out at them. She felt like hiding! On up past the Celtic Stone Cross at the corner and finally up to Lizzie's, where her sister came running out to meet them, looking at Ails with naked admiration. Neeve, the baby, 'made strange' with her and started to howl. Lizzie screwed up her face:

"My God, girl, y' got terrible thin, but Altnamore air'll soon put the colour back in yer cheeks." The group of children at the pump came running up the street to see her. They were all looking at her as if she was different and she didn't know what to say.

"They said your name off the altar," said Jinny with reverence, "an' I was there." Pat Doran grinned sheepishly and said

"Mrs. Digby made us pray for you."

"Where'd you get the doll?" asked Jinny.

"I got a rubber stamp printing set for Christmas. I'll let you make your name, Ails," said Maura.

"Can you play hospital with us?" asked Brigid.

"There's a new policeman. He has three weans at the Protestant school, an' they say the Wee Doctor has a girlfriend," related Jinny. Then they all started talking together.

Ails's legs felt wobbly.

"O.K. Ails, you can go out to play tomorrow, but for today you have to take it easy," said her father, leading her the opposite way from Lizzie's kitchen, into their sitting room, which looked so tiny after the hospital ward. Her father let her sit in his chair by the fire, but Ails longed to walk around and see Lizzie's kitchen and the yard and the turf, and feel the air, and look out the window at the happenings on the street. She'd been gone a long, long time. Everybody's attitude to her seemed different. Ails had a warm feeling inside her. It was good to be home.

In the days and weeks that followed, Ails couldn't get enough of playing in the village. She felt like she had been born again with new eyes. She wasn't allowed to go to school till she got her strength back. She was allowed to sleep in, get up late, go out for some fresh air, yet stay close to Lizzie's while her parents were gone to teach school. She read books and more books. When she went alone to play at the rocks, she didn't feel lonely at all as she sat between the big craggy boulders in the grassy dips. She picked up handfuls of pebbles to make squares to form the walls of gravelly rooms. She used Lizzie's balding besom to sweep the gravel out through the space left for a door. She had old broken teapots and dishes and imaginary children called Gloria, or Denise or Jillian from the library books. Lizzie and Kate and Sarah were such ordinary names. The children in books always said 'shan't,' solved mysteries, made models from paper and glue and went shopping. Sometimes Lizzie let Ails take her baby sister out in the pram. The baby was sitting up now and cooing and gurgling, and Ails would pretend to be her mother. She remembered the day she and Fiona had come home from school with the fat midwife there and the new baby already born, and how scared she was by the big pads filled with blood sticking out behind the wardrobe.

"What a disappointing baby!" Ails had thought, "like an eskimo with black ugly stringy hair and a fat yellow-brown, screwed up face. Yuk!" She looked at the baby now, wheeling the pram home and jiggling it to make the baby laugh. Neeve was the baby's name. It was really "Naombh," but inside Ails's head, she thought "Neeve." It looked more like it sounded. She didn't know how to write Irish, or Gaelic; the letters looked funny and mixed-up. She just knew how to say some of it. Neeve fitted her name now. For a long time she wasn't real enough for a name. Ails liked Neeve now.

"All that blood and stuff — no wonder the baby was ugly," thought Ails. She began thinking of the Christmas story of the birth of Jesus. Mary, the mother of Jesus in Bethlehem, had no blood in the stable. She just appeared with the baby. That was the way to have them, thought Ails. No mess.

When the rest of the kids came home from school, they played hospital. Ails showed them how to take pulses and temperatures, and check stitches and change dressings with old torn-up sheets. They used McMenamin's wheelbarrow for a wheelchair.

Ails was soon strong enough to be allowed farther afield, to go swimming in Foggy's Hole down in Tonnegan River. She could fish for minnows, make dams for paddling pools, make St. Brigid's crosses from rushes, then peel rushes to tie the ends of the crosses and extract the white glistening pulp. She could go in wellington boots with tin cans to pick raspberries and blackberries.

Soon Ails was ready to go back to school. She was surprised to realize that she was almost looking forward to school, even with the Master and Mrs. Digby!

That 'Home' Feeling

11

the poweR of Designs

In the Calgary pottery studio, Dora, Ails's Dutch-Canadian friend was painting native North American Indian designs on her red-clay pottery. Unlike Ails, Dora read books and books and talked to Native people to better understand the symbols and figure out what they told about the Native Indian way of life. Ails didn't ever seem to get around to that. Mind you, the Druids were all dead, but there were books she could've read.

One day when Ails was cursing and swearing over the bird's head and what looked like a lion's paw in a Celtic design on a platter, Dora stopped her dead in her tracks by saying, "What you're doing is really reverend, you know, Ails"

"What?" said Ails.

"Well, a lot of those nature-based religions were remarkably similar. Birds and animals and all kinds of creatures were sacred to many of them." Dora was painting a buffalo, mainstay animal of Plains Indian life on the prairies and foothills of the Rockies, the land surrounding where Calgary now stood. Dora's lone buffalo was standing on top of a cliff looking over a high cliff at a whole pile of dead buffalo bodies lying at the bottom. Dora kept painting as she compared, for Ails, how nature-based peoples had reverence for what they killed for food.

"Eat or be eaten," said Dora. "It's the law of the wild."

"Hard to believe in these days of mass-produced food and supermarkets!" remarked Ails, carving slowly, with more care.

"The Native peoples give thanks to the slaughtered animal for giving up their lives to feed humans," said Dora. "In Ireland, they used every single part of the cattle, just as the native Indians used every single part of the buffalo," continued Dora. "The ancient Druids even hunted similarly to our native people, cornering the animals and running them over a cliff. I also read that the Irish burned what was left that couldn't be used from the cattle, their logic being that the smoke from that fire would put the cattle spirit back into the air." Although somewhat surprised, Ails vaguely remembered hearing one time that this was actually the origin of celebration bonfires in Ireland. She just hadn't thought of these designs in terms of sacredness or reverence. She stopped carving to watch what Dora was doing. Dora moved up on her design, up into the sky above the standing buffalo, pointing out an eagle in the design she herself was working on.

"That's awfully like what's on that corner of your pot," she indicated to Ails, tracing each bird in turn with her finger. "You know how sacred the eagle was to Native peoples," she went on. "There are Aboriginal peoples all over the world, and I'm sure some are descended from Druids," said Dora matter-of-factly. Ails got so bogged down in the details of the

    in-out;

    over-under;

    hide-surface

designs, that sometimes that was all she could see. Sometimes she had glimpses of connections as she went through these animal-looking designs: connections with Africa, where people invoked the spirit of an animal, in trance, for spells, for water, for fertility. Some Hindu gods looked like animals. Somewhere she had read that in the process of moving from Druidism to Christianity, the four evangelists were represented as different animals and birds.

"Actually," said Dora, a geologist by profession, "many of these animal patterns first appeared in the Bronze Age, in the British Isles." The way Dora looked at things, although intrinsically interesting, didn't help Ails's confusion at all.

"The trouble is," Ails thought dimly, "no amount of intellectual understanding seems to be able to allow me to become detached from the intensity and tension of these complex patterns." Working on them, it often felt to Ails like she was an ant in the middle of the design, making her way through its complexities. Maybe the spirit of these designs came upon her, as the spirit of the animal came on those other human beings seeking enlightenment, fertility, guidance ...

"I'm definitely losing it," she said to Dora, as they packed up their tools to go home.

"Don't worry, Ails," laughed Dora, as if Ails had been thinking aloud. Maybe she had been?

"My designs get to me sometimes, too," said Dora kindly. "They do have a certain power, you know. And mine don't have half the complexity yours do," she added; then, as an enigmatic afterthought:

"But then, yours are Irish."

As if that explained everything.

12

human, after all?

Seven and a half year old Ails climbed the hill to Altnamore school in anticipation. As it happened, hardly anybody even noticed she was back in school after her hospital stay and long recovery. The whole school was in an uproar. The school inspector was coming!

The big lads from the Master's Room who usually came early to light the fire were cleaning everything in sight. As the other children arrived, they joined in and started cleaning shelves and windows, dusting the globe, sweeping the floors with wet sawdust, cleaning the desks: washing inkwells, hoking out the dirt and then blowing it out of the ancient deeply carved initials, turning the desks upside down and scraping off the wads of chewing gum before scrubbing them. Mrs. Digby was loading the Irish history books and Fenian rebel song sheets into a box to hide them. Even though these books were forbidden to be used in the British-ruled Northern Ireland school curriculum (Ails knew from her father), most teachers had a stash of books full of legends, songs, poems, and stories of ancient Celts and their great deeds, of such events as the 1798 rebellion and the 1916 Easter rising — all of them with an Irish perspective. Into a box went all of these incriminating books — which could "lose a teacher her job, or a school its licence to operate," Auntie Cora had said angrily. "The priests who run these school boards know all about the books — some of them have even written some of them!" Auntie Cora had continued proudly. "The priests turn a

78

blind eye," adding with finality, "The history of survival in Ireland is our ability to outwit the colonizer."

The big boys were scraping cow dung from the yard, pouring bottles of Jeyes fluid (Jay-sus fluid, Dingo Devine called it), down the big hole of the toilets and all around the outhouse walls "in case His Lordship's shit doesn't have no smell," sneered Dingo. Everyone received strict orders to come dressed up and HAD to have shoes, and *anybody* that had two pairs of shoes in the house was to bring them for extras. There were to be no bare feet and NO wellington boots that had been used in the byre, for no matter how much they were scrubbed, the manure smell still lingered.

Even though Ails had missed a long, long time at school, she wasn't too worried. She could read really well, and her father had been doing sums with her at home.

"Always keep your eye on your education, child," he'd say. "It's the thing that separates the civilized man from the savage. Every time there was a 'going away to America' party, Ails's father would go into a heated monologue about 'the youth having to leave their country "for lack of education, skills and opportunity' and go as America's 'hewers of wood and drawers of water.' Whatever that meant, his daughters were certainly not going to do it. He'd see to it that they got an education even though, as Lizzie and everyone in Altnamore knew, it was a waste to send girls to school. Sure, weren't they just going to get married and have babies anyway? Ails's father was a real puzzle sometimes. He took an avid interest in her schoolwork, doing school work with her at night, with Fiona and even Neeve listening. No, Ails wasn't worried about the school inspector coming and asking her questions, not at all.

The day the inspector was due to arrive, everybody was shining. The school was clean as a new pin. Mrs. Digby was wearing a 'Tara' brooch on a tweed suit with a mauve blouse and powder on her face. The Master was very jittery with not smoking.

A big, shiny car drove up. Everybody was at the window watching. The inspector didn't see them waiting. He didn't even look at the windows. He had a real English face — chiselled-looking — and wore a tweed hat and coat. "The crease in his trousers would cut you like a knife," said Jinny. He had really shiny shoes and a waistcoat with a watch and chain. He started picking his steps carefully over the freshly washed cobblestone path. As he approached the school door, everybody dived into desks and started working. His name was Mr. Heatley-Jones. First, he would inspect the school in general, it seemed. When he came in, they all stood up and said:

"Good morning, sur," in unison.

"You may sit, boys and girls," he said, without looking at them. He went through to the Infants room, and back through again to the Master's and they all stood up again and said:

"Good morning, sur," in unison. Mr. Heatley-Jones seemed a bit annoyed.

"Please do not have them bobbing up and down so much, Madam. Very disconcerting."   Mrs. Digby looked crestfallen.

It was nearly an hour before he came back to inspect Mrs. Digby's room. They all stood up again, with Mrs. Digby trying to signal them not to. Pens, nibs and pencils clattered on to the floor in the confusion. Eventually everyone sat down. He was inspecting all of the books, notes and attendance records kept in the drawer of the teacher's desk, while Mrs. Digby asked them questions on their reading book. All of a sudden, Mr. Heatley-Jones called out in his accent like the BBC news announcers, who, everyone agreed, talked with big round stones in their mouths.'

"Who is Ailsa . . eh ...um . . ?"

Ails's heart jumped when she heard him try to pronounce her name.

"Me, sir," she gulped, raising her hand.

"Would you come here, please?" What on earth had she done?

"What's the meaning of this long absence? You haven't been to school since Christmas. That's against the law, you know!"

"I was in the hospital with burst appendix, sir," stammered Ails apologetically.

"Oh, that explains it, then. Does this child have a doctor's certificate, Mrs. er — Rigby, sorry, Digby?" He didn't listen for Mrs. Digby's answer. Then, without looking at Ails, he said perfunctorily "You may return to your seat."

"You know," thought Ails when she sat down, "he never even looked at me once. Just looked through his gold-rimmed half glasses at the attendance register." Again, he addressed Mrs. Digby.

"I trust this child has a doctor's certificate for the Ministry's records, Mrs. er — Rigby, sorry, Digby?"

"It's her first day back, Mr. Heatley-Jones," answered Mrs. Digby, with just a hint of annoyance, both at his persistence, and at his seeming inability to get her name right.

"I'll leave it to you to make sure she gets that certificate."

"I'll take over now, thank you, if you don't mind, Mrs. er — Rigby, eh, Digby."

He asked them a few more reading questions (they had done them all yesterday anyway), and then said:

"Close your books, boys and girls. I have a few questions of my own which require *spontaneous* answers," he said drily, looking sideways accusingly at Mrs. Digby, as if she'd prepared them for his visit, (which she had)..

"Describe what you saw on the way to school this morning, er-eh, you, young man, back there." You could almost hear the silent groans. He was pointing at Barney Og Toner. Mrs. Digby never asked him anything.

"Nice lad," was Lizzie's opinion of Barney Og, "but them Toners is all as thick as champ."

"Well, sur, I come up through the plantin, an'..." Barney Og began.

81

"...Just a moment, young man, you mean you CAME up...?"

"No, sur, I COME up the same road every day."

"Well, awwl — right, then, I suppose. DO carry on."

"Well sur, I come up through the plantin, an'...."

"The WHOT, young man?"

"The plantin, sur."

"What on earth is that?"

"You mean you dunno what a plantin is, sur?" Barney Og showed open amazement.

"No, I'm afraid I haven't the slightest idea. But DO enlighten me; I'm all ears," he said, with Barney Og completely missing the sarcasm that everyone else in the room was able to hear.

"Well, it has a lot of trees, sur, an' a path wore in it where people take a shortcut, an' rabbits live there, an' birds, an' there's a fox this year." Barney Og's face lit up. "The fox has a lair an'll mebbe have a litter this year. Now, some of it's fields, an' some of it's hilly, an'..."

"Oh, you mean a sort of PLANTATION. Well, why don't you call it that, for Heaven's sake? We speak the Queen's English here, young man."

The familiar voice of Mrs. Digby cut in — with unfamiliar composure:

"Thank you, Bernard," she said, using Barney Og's full Christian name. "You did that very well. Yes, we do speak English here, Mr. Heatley-Jones. And Bernard is speaking English. We call it "the Plantin" here. It's a very beautiful piece of countryside. I'm sure Bernard would be glad to show it to you. As you hear, he is quite an expert on the wildlife there. And we ALL call it the plantin here," said Mrs. Digby with quiet dignity.

Everyone in the room was thunderstruck — including Mr. Heatley-Jones. The Pigby! She stuck up for Barney Og, and called him 'Bernard'. Everybody was incredulous! Waves of admiration for Mrs. Digby surged around the room. Barney Og's face was beaming with pride.

Mr. Heatley-Jones looked flustered.

82

"Well, I dare say one doesn't need to argue the point, really, although technically the proper form of the word should actually be used." He fidgeted with his watch and chain. "Well, I'd best be off now. I have a luncheon appointment," raising his hand in a halt sign "No, don't stand up."

But nobody was going to stand up anyway.

He left.

Everyone in the room sat staring at Mrs. Digby, speechless, and a quiet pride settled in. She looked back at all of them for a moment, with pride also. Then she seemed to remember where she was and didn't seem to know what to do with herself — or with them. She spoke with a stammer:

"Well, get on with it, the description of the plantin."

They all worked quietly, contentedly, confidently. A new respect reigned.

It was all over the village about Mrs. Digby and Barney Og Toner. Lizzie questioned Ails up, down and sideways till Ails was sick to death talking about it.

"An' what did he say then?"

"An' what did Barney Og say?"

"An' what did the Inspector say?"

"God, that man's an ignorant wart. Sure everybody knows it's a plantin. Mrs. Digby was right. Well, good on her. Ach, she's not bad, y'know. Just very sharp of the tongue, is all. Well, imagine that, now." Lizzie looked pleased, and just as surprised as everybody else in the village was about Mrs. Digby.

Later Ails, Maura and Brigid were sitting round the Post Office gable when they saw Mrs. Toner running across the street waving. She was Barney Og's mother, and Ails always thought of her as 'The Old Woman who lived in the Shoe', for she was skinny as a rail, had huge feet, and always had a baby under one arm, and another one in her tummy. She was waving at Mrs. Digby, who was coming out of the Post Office.

"It's great what you done for our Barney Og, Mrs. Digby tellin' that English inspector fella how smart our Barney was. He never was that good at the books, y'know, but he's a terrible good lad, is our Barney Og, an' a great help with the weans. God bless y', Mrs. D!"

Miss McCartney told it in the Post Office that "Mr. Hyphenated Heatley called the Infants 'offspring of peasant families.' "

"Sounds so romantic," thought Ails, a picture forming in her mind of people wearing kerchiefs, with ribbons sewed on costumes, the way they were in some folk dances. This contrasted wildly, however, with the feeling in the school when the inspector lorded it over all of them. It was like this strangely dressed man, chiselled out of stone, with his strange radio accent, came from a different human race than did the people of Altnamore. It seemed like there was nothing at all in common between this Englishman and the Irish. How could this be? Puzzled, Ails told her father about all of this, and asked him if he knew whether the school inspector was really a Protestant, or an Englishman, or both, and why was he so different? Her father said an inspector was probably an Irishman educated in England.

"But I don't want you growing up bigoted, child. Mr. Heatley-Jones is just a person doing his job, just like any other person," adding, as an afterthought, 'We don't get those kinds of jobs.'

Ails thought of how the inspector never looked at her when he talked to her, nor did he look at any of the children. He focused his attention on books, charts, maps and school surroundings. It was like they were all non-persons.

"How could he be a person?" thought Ails, "when he doesn't even know WE are persons?"

13

eyes

Quietly working in the Calgary pottery studio, Dora and Ails were around a table with Kanti and Inder, Canadian immigrants from India. These two women had developed an interest in meticulously painting moulded ceramics. It was easy company, the four of them working parallel, quiet most of the time, talking sometimes about not much. The annoying thing was that Ails's complex Celtic design was making her bug-eyed. It seemed like a collection of eyes cropping up in between birds' heads and dogs' feet, all turning from time to time into some other snake-like creatures. She stopped working for a moment to let her own eyes relax from their focus. Rubbing her eyes, she said unthinkingly,

"I need some of that St. Brigid's water."

"What?" said the other three voices in unison. Ails looked around to see three pairs of eyes curiously fixed upon her. She'd forgotten that she was speaking almost a foreign language.

"Sorry," she said, laughing. "It's just that I was thinking of well water in a place in Ireland that everyone went to for a cure for eye diseases." Analytical Dora said, "But what has that to do with Saint somebody you mentioned?"

"You know, I'm embarrassed to realize that I don't even know why it's called St. Brigid's Well, or river, or whatever," said Ails. She always felt woefully inadequate at her own peripheral knowledge of the myths and legends which had pulsated and reverberated, often as undercurrents, all through her growing up. She just knew that anybody with eye problems went to wash their eyes out in St. Brigid's water at Faughart. It wasn't until someone from outside the Irish culture questioned things, that Ails had to think about the who, what, where, when, why and how of what she took totally for granted. This had happened to her a lot in Canada. She was busily delving through her memory, but to no avail.

"That's like Holland," said Dora. "You know, there was an ancient weigh scale near my home town, and I never knew until I left Holland that it was used during witch-burning times to weigh women to find out if they were witches."

"Are you serious?" asked Ails incredulously. "What did weight have to do with being a witch?"

"If you weighed below a certain weight, you were assumed to be a witch," Dora tried to explain, but Ails and Inder, both plump, just burst out laughing.

"Ails, you and me definitely would *not* have been condemned as witches," said Inder.

"But seriously, Dora, wasn't that a little arbitrary?" asked Ails. "Sounds like the stories you hear about people being condemned to death in primitive tribes, by the direction a chicken falls after its neck has been slit."

"Well, I guess they needed some kind of criteria. Seems pretty weak to me," laughed Dora. Looking more serious, she continued. "When I discovered what that weigh station was for, I thought of how many thin women went to their deaths from that place, and I couldn't go back there any more. I even used to dream about it," she added fearfully. "I was haunted by that idea — and I had passed it hundreds of times and never questioned it

86

before, and no-one ever mentioned it." An involuntary shiver seemed to pass through all of them.

"We have many such places and rituals in India," said Kanti "and people ask us about them too."

"It's funny," said Inder, you just don't think about things you've been around all your life, unless you have to explain them to someone else." Dora, who was fascinated by all stories, said to Ails, "I wouldn't mind knowing something about you Saint Birgitt's eye water." In her Dutch accent, Dora pronounced it the German way.

"The Irish form of the name is Brigid," corrected Ails, "and I know she was a very powerful woman in the changeover from Druidism to Christianity in Ireland, but darned if I can figure out the eye stuff." By now all four of them were packing up their stuff to go home.

"O.k. Ails," said Dora, "for next Saturday, we want to hear a story about your eye saint."

"I might have to make it up!" quipped Ails.

"No, we want the real thing!" said Dora.

"O.k. when I phone my mother I'll ask her," said Ails. But when she phoned her mother, she asked Ails in a worried tone:

"Are your eyes alright, dear?"

"Oh, yes, they're fine, mam," answered Ails quickly, "I just wanted to know for a friend." However, at the end of the phone call, Ails was none the wiser.

"Sure everyone goes there for the cure," said her mother, "I don't know why, but it works. Look at this eye of mine. Right as rain again," she said convincingly.

"I can't see it over the phone," responded Ails, "but I remember you telling me about it." Ails then phoned her friend Anya in Vancouver, who sent her research done by her niece, another Anya.

"Well, lo and behold!" exclaimed Ails to herself aloud. St. Brigid, even as a child, was quite the wean ('wee'un, as they'd say in Altnamore), it seemed. She had strange powers and made all kinds of things happen. Once as a tiny girl, she was left alone in a house that caught fire. People saw the fire from afar, but when they went into the house, the child and the interior of the house were fine. To Ails, she sounded a little bit like a Disney fantasy character, with the deeds she did — until the eye business, that was.

The following Saturday, Ails went in all excited to the pottery studio. She was so disappointed that Dora wasn't there — one of Dora's kids was sick. But Inder and Kanti were there, eager to hear her story.

"Well, did you find out about the holy woman and the eyes, in Irish-istan," Kanti greeted Ails. It was their familiar joke that she always called Ireland that, after states in India seeking their freedom.

"Well, she was a holy woman, o.k.," said Ails excitedly, "born holy, it looks like," she continued, relaying Brigid's childhood miracles.

"Then she got to marrying age," said Ails, "and, of course, there was a guy wanting to marry her, but she had promised herself to God as a virgin." Inder giggled.

"Well lots of saints did that," Ails explained, not quite understanding the giggle. "Brigid managed to divert one suitor to another marriageable girl who lived down the road, but her brothers got really mad at her for doing that. They wanted the bride-price, of course ..." Ails stopped when she saw the two women's eyes grow wide with amazement.

"Did I say something?" she asked, puzzled.

"You mean, they would pay a girl's family to get the girl?" asked Kanti.

"I never even thought about it," said Ails, looking up Anya's notes, checking and re-reading the part about the bride-price.

"In India, the girl's family pays to get the man's family to take her off their hands," said Inder. "It's expensive to have daughters in India."

"Actually, come to think of it, it was sort of that way when I left Ireland," said Ails, vaguely remembering her father talking about his daughters' education being their dowry, because education gave them the capacity to make money, but she was too excited to finish the story.

"Hey, you guys want to get to the eye part or not?" Ails cajoled them. She went on to tell them how her brothers were making fun of Brigid and teasing her unmercifully. One brother, Bacene, said:

"The beautiful eye which is in your head will be betrothed to a man, though you like it or not." Ails read in a man's deep voice the old-fashioned way of speaking straight from Anya's notes.

"And you know what?" said Ails, creating suspense.

"What?" asked Inder expectantly.

"Brigid put her hand in and plucked out her eye, held it in her hand, and said 'I deem it unlikely that anyone will ask you for a blind girl!' " The brothers and their friends were grossed out with shock," said Ails, enjoying the women's reaction. She wished Dora were there.

"Wow!" said Inder and Kanti with one voice. "And then what happened?"

"Well, these brothers looked wildly around for water to wash the wound of the hole where her eye came from. There was no water nearby. So Brigid said 'Put my staff about this sod in front of you,' and a stream gushed forth from the earth. *That's* the stream I was talking about," said Ails triumphantly. "Of course, Brigid's father then said, 'Take the veil, then, my daughter, for this is what you desire.' "

"What does 'take the veil' mean?" asked Inder, but Kanti, educated by Irish nuns in India, explained to her that it meant becoming a nun, and Ails explained that becoming a nun meant dedicating your life to God.

"Hey, great story," said Dora, who had arrived late and was standing by the door listening.

"All the same," said Kanti thoughtfully, "It's a pity women have that kind of power *only* in stories."

14

auntie cora's dilemma

As a child in Altnamore, Ails hated Sundays. This Sunday morning as usual the church and chapel bells would start ringing. The ringing was not the problem. In fact she and Fiona had a rhyming game to try and figure out when they would ring in unison.

The Protestant church bell always started really early, and had a very regular, stately ring. Even though it was the Protestant bell, it sounded just like the magnificent grandfather clock in the Catholic priests' house — a huge stately house on its own manicured grounds above the village. This morning, as usual, Fiona got to start the rhyme first, because the Protestant bell-ringer seemed to get up earlier, even though people had to be at both churches at the same time. Fiona started rhyming in time with the Protestant bell:

> "DONG, dong, DONG, dong
> This is how we sing our song.
> DONG, dong, DONG, dong
> Sing it right don't sing it wrong."

Ails was getting impatient waiting for her cue. The Catholic bell always started later.

"If that damn Jimmy Pat Mary (God forgive me for cussin' an' it Sunday!) would get out of his bed of a Sunday mornin' our bell would be as early as them ones," Lizzie always complained about Jimmy Pat Mary, the man who carried the names of himself, his father Pat, and his grandmother Mary. Ails didn't even know what his real name was, but he was often in Lizzie's on a Saturday night till the wee small hours. "That's probably why he can't get up," Lizzie would say, mad at him for keeping her up late, too, but, because of Altnamore's unwritten hospitality code, unable to go to bed herself till he left.

At last Ails's Catholic bell started. It was different. It went more like a waltz. That's why she took that rhyme. She was good at figuring out rhythms but Fiona couldn't yet keep waltz time with it. Ails kept time using the 'Cuckoo Waltz' as a guide:

"Ding, DONG,"	*rest*
"Ding, DONG,"	*rest*
"Your MASS time is drawing NEAR,"	*rest*
"Ding, DONG,"	*rest*
"Ding, DONG,"	*rest*
"We're HAPPY to see you HERE,"	*rest.*

It started off well this morning, but when the two bells were ringing simultaneously Ails and Fiona tried to out-shout each other while trying to hold onto their own rhythms. The result was that they woke the baby; their parents got mad and Lizzie got up miserable. Not that Lizzie didn't get up miserable nearly every Sunday whether they were rhyming or not. Every Saturday night Lizzie's kitchen would be packed with 'ones in on their ceilidhe', telling stories and yarns and playing cards and singing till all hours of the morning. Lizzie always got up for early Mass in spite of that, for she "wouldn't be caught dead at the lazy man's Mass" at noon. The real reason was that she had to have big pots of tea and soda bread and butter and jam for all the country people coming from 12 o'clock Mass. Lizzie, like Jinny's aunt and uncle, ran an 'eating house.' That way she made some money. The trouble was that she had to have a lot of things organized before she left for 9 a.m. Mass. Mary Biddy, her niece who came in from the country to sleep overnight and help her, could then continue with the preparations.

Ails and Fiona always went to nine o'clock Mass with Lizzie. That was the first thing Ails hated about Sundays: Lizzie trying to get dressed up. Lizzie always seemed to feel uncomfortable in good clothes. She was very confident in her working clothes in her own house, "Ach, sure you know what it's like when you're cookin' all the time, and makin' drops of tea, you never have a chance to keep yer clothes lookin' decent." Maybe because she had that excuse, she never seemed to have to get dressed up. Somehow, though, going to Mass, she went on and on worrying about what she looked like. She could never seem to find a pair of stockings without a rip, and was always shining up her shoes at the last minute, putting them up on the kitchen chair to tie them. Ever since her sister in America came home to visit, Lizzie invariably said "God, if me sister Rosie saw me doin' this, she'd trounce me. Terrible country that, can't even put your foot up on a chair." Even though Ails and Fiona were perfectly capable of going on to Mass without her, and avoiding this performance, Lizzie wouldn't hear of it.

"Come to think of it," Ails realized with surprise "Lizzie rarely goes out." It was true, she thought; everybody came to Lizzie's, so Sunday Mass was about the only time Lizzie ever went out of the door of her own house, and then she was usually in a bad mood from having to get everything ready for Mary Biddy, who helped out after Mass with the food. That was the first thing Ails hated about Sundays: Lizzie's bad mood when she was getting dressed for Mass. The next thing she hated was the fear of missing Mass or being late. The huge, forbidding priest roared that was a mortal sin to miss Mass. For a mortal sin, you could go straight to Hell with the devil — who was really a fallen angel who 'flew in the face of God and said 'I will not serve!' For a smaller offence, a venial sin, you went sort of halfway to Hell, Purgatory, but you could get out of there, but *never* out of Hell. At the yearly Altnamore mission, the monk missionaries bore out Father McStay's sermons, giving such graphic depictions of Hell that even the most cynical Altnamore person, Packie McMenamin, was petrified into going to Mass on time for a few weeks after the mission.

Ails hated the rotten taste in her mouth because she couldn't eat anything, or even have a drink of water before going to Mass, because, now that she had made her 'First Communion' she had to receive Communion at Mass for the rest of her life. It was a 'venial,' sin, less serious than mortal, but nevertheless, a sin, to eat or drink anything before Communion. One Sunday she had sneaked one of the peas that were soaking on the table for the dinner as she was on her way out the door. She was afraid to go to Communion. Jinny, Brigid and Maura said she must have been real bad. To have stayed away from Communion, she must not have been in a 'state of grace.' This meant she must have done something terrible, and not had time to go to Confession to have Father McStay say 'Ego te absolvo.' This meant you were forgiven and had to do a penance of saying some prayers, and could go on living normally, and continuing to go to Communion.

"You don't know how lucky you are," the Pigby said at Religion time in school. "People used to have go around in public in sackcloth and ashes for their penance!"

Ails also hated all the rushing around and nobody having time to sit around in the morning. She hated the way bicycles wheeled too fast up the hill on Sunday mornings, and how panic struck everyone when the five minute bell started to ring, warning everyone to hurry up. The big priest yelled at people who were late, going as far as walking down to the back to get the ones who stood outside smoking. Ails didn't like Mass. It was all in Latin anyway. The priest always mumbled. It was too long to sit still. She got squirmy. If she talked, someone would report to her mother. Also she didn't like the taste of that dry wafer of Communion host which stuck to her tongue. Jinny said it was a sin to let it touch your teeth. It took a lot of maneuvering around to keep it in the middle of your mouth. It stuck everywhere and took a lot of saliva before it would slide around loose.

Ails hated Sundays even after Mass was over. There was nothing to do. The Altnamore street was always deserted. It seemed to her that it usually rained. On Sundays Ails's thoughts always turned to 'eternity.' That was the worst part of all. In school they learnt that eternity went on and on and on and on and on and on and on and on and on and on... The idea of no finality was terrifying to Ails, but even worse was the idea that whatever state you reached after death, you would stay that way for eternity. You wouldn't get fatter or thinner or older or younger. Your nails and hair wouldn't grow and even if you ended up in Heaven ... the idea of eternity still terrified Ails. As she watched from her perch on the gable pillar today in particular, the steady drip, drip, drip from the roof into the rain barrel, and the long shadows, with the watery sunshine slanting out from behind the ever-threatening clouds all combined to make Ails hate this particular Sunday more than usual.

There was nothing to do in this place. It wasn't like other days. Even in school holidays, on a Monday, for example, you could go down the street and give some of the women a break at the churning. Ails and Maura, even though they were not tall enough, could stand on stools and share the pounding of the churn inside the glug-glugging wooden barrel, waiting excitedly for the milk sound to turn to the butter sound. There would be people talking and telling stories, and lots of activity in every house, or shop, or even on the street. But on Sundays in Altnamore — nothing — nothing for girls, anyway, after the Sunday noon dinner things were cleared away. Boys and men got to go to football matches in the afternoons, and the 'bullets' at night. This was where they formed teams to throw a heavy lead ball along a straight stretch of road — for that they had to go a long way out of the village, for every approach to Altnamore was uphill. When she was in the hospital, Ails thought wistfully, the townspeople talked of 'weekends' when people 'went to the pictures.' Altnamore Sundays were boring, boring, boring, Ails decided. Today Lizzie had scolded her:

"It's spoiled you are, just like the McColgan lassie that got burned. Think you can get anythin' you want; showin' off all the time: 'In the hospital we did this, in the hospital we did that....' " Lizzie minced around the kitchen, imitating Ails complaining. "There's nothin' wrong with you any more, Dilsie, and you just get them dishes 'redd up' right now, and don't be

94

expectin' servants!" Fiona stuck out her tongue at Ails behind Lizzie's back. Her rotten sister! Just because Ails wouldn't let her play with Ingrid. Her father said Ails was getting too big for her boots. When she tickled the baby's feet and made her squeal, her mother said "Ails, will you for Heavens sake go and find something to do! Why don't you go and read a book?"

Everybody hated her. Boy, if she died, would they be sorry, the whole lot of them! She got down off the gable pillar and walked down past the byres where the cows came home to be milked. The byres smelt cold and rank. She sneaked up the back way to the rocks. Stupid rocks, you could hardly find a flat piece of anything to sit on, and it was a stupid place to play house anyway. She ambled on down the deserted street, through the now mizzling rain, sat at the pump and surveyed the dismal scene for a while. Hughie McCann was delivering the Sunday papers, his off-tune whistling echoing all up and down the empty street.

"Wanna play after?" she asked him.

"Naw, goin' to the football match and on to the bullets after," said Hugh. "Wanna gimme a hand with these papers? The paper lorry was late an' everybody's waitin'."

"Awright, but only if you stop whistling," sighed Ails. Hughie looked hurt. He was learning to whistle. He seemed to be learning for a hundred years, thought Ails.

"Can you do Dobbs's, Turtle's and Monaghan's?"

"S'pose so." She dawdled on down the street with the papers under her arm.

Mrs. Dobbs opened the door a crack. She still had on her Sunday clothes from Mass, her hair in a bun and unaccustomed lipstick running into the lines around her mouth. She'd spend all week working hard in the shop wearing the same dreary overall. Ails could see she just wanted to sit down with the paper.

"Thanks, Ails. Hughie away to the match?"

"Yeh."

Then she went to Trevor Tunbridge's, who was the caretaker of the Protestant church. The step at his house was scrubbed, and a mat on it said "Welcome" but Ails didn't feel welcome. It was too clean. The tiles leading into the hall were shining. Turtle came to the door himself in his socks. He was the postman and was always early. All the Protestants were early, but Turtle was particularly so. Obviously the paper was late today, Ails thought from his actions.

"Thank yooo," said Turtle drily, looking pointedly at his pocket watch.

"Looks even more like a turtle without his postman's hat," thought Ails looking at his receding hair line, hooded eyes, big hooked nose and no chin. Every morning, though, he swaggered through the village with his postman's bag as if he didn't know he looked like a turtle. Maybe he didn't even know they called him that, Ails thought idly. She looked over the wall into the big Protestant church grounds, with their laurels, manicured flower beds, clear walkways and graves with plastic domes over the flowers. It was not at all like walking through the overgrown Catholic graveyard, where you sometimes had to kick the moss off the stone just to see who was buried there. The Catholic graveyard only got cleaned up once a year there, unless somebody died in between.

"Jinny's right," thought Ails, "definitely ghosts in there. You would just know to look at it."

She shivered in the misty rain as she started down the hill to her Auntie Cora's. She usually loved to go there, but this was Sunday, and her aunt would have hundreds of newspapers spread all over the floor and the table, and wouldn't want children around. Usually they didn't bother her, but Sunday was her day to herself.

Ails opened the back door and stepped in silently. It was awfully quiet. She thought she heard ...did she hear someone sobbing? ... crying? ... There it was again ... She peeped around the door. No newspapers, no radio on, just her beloved Auntie Cora with her head on her arms, sobbing "Oh, God help me, please help me!"

"Don't cry, Auntie Cora," said Ails from the doorway. Auntie Cora looked up. Her face was tear-stained, her eyes looked hollow and hopeless.

"I didn't hear you come in, love." She held her arms out and Ails ran to her, and they squeezed each other tightly, and Cora sobbed and Ails's tears fell on Cora's shoulder, just for the moment of the hug.

"God, you're soaked, child, where've you been? Does your father know you're here? Gimme that cardigan and I'll get you a dry one." She took off Ails's cardigan and blouse and hung them up on the pulley clothesline above the range and pulled over Ails's head a dry, grey pullover that smelled of Shamie.

"I'll make us a cup of tea, Ails. You get the cups and milk and sugar, and I'll cut the apple tart." Auntie Cora was trying to make Ails feel good, the way she tried to make everybody feel good with great food and a warm fire and lovely comfortable surroundings.

"But you're still crying inside yourself, Auntie Cora," thought Ails, although she didn't feel the need to say anything. Again, Auntie Cora hugged Ails, holding her long and close.

"Everybody has bad days. Don't you have bad days, Ails?" Ails spilled out the whole day's events, from waking the baby to eternity to the ghosts.

"It's just that I don't like Sundays, Auntie Cora," she said. "Do you like them?"

"Usually I love Sundays, Ails. After dinner everybody goes off to football matches and fishing and Irish dancing and I read all me papers and write letters." Then, seeming to sense Ails's feeling of encroaching on her time, she added quickly "Oh, no, I'm glad you're here, Ails!"

Ails started chattering to make the mood seem cheerier and more normal.

"My daddy doesn't like Irish dancing. Says it gives young girls notions about themselves. Says they'd be better off reading books and learning to write and do numbers. But I know all the steps anyway, from Jinny and Maura and Brigid."

The tart was delicious, and the tea meandered down and warmed their insides. The fear or panic or whatever it was that Ails sensed was still recurring in Auntie Cora's eyes. A few times she started to speak and stopped again.

"Ails, how would you … eh … how do you think … do you think you and Shamie would like a new baby?" Ails thought of newborn Neeve.

"But we have a baby…Another baby?" Ails was puzzled. "Whose is it?"

97

"Mine."

Ails stared at her incredulously.

"Your baby, Auntie Cora? But you had five babies already!" Auntie Cora's eyes welled up with tears again:

"I know, dear."

"Why was Auntie Cora so sad about having a baby?" thought Ails. Wasn't that what women were supposed to do? She had never heard of anyone reacting this way before to the idea of a new baby. Mind you, once or twice Ails had heard a dreadful, desperate sadness whispered in Lizzie's kitchen, when different women had lost a baby, especially the one young Slane girl who bled to death in the process. 'She shoulda never gone to that murdering woman,' Ails had heard from her chimney corner hiding place. "But then, he wouldn't marry her, and her father would've killed her," Lizzie had told Mary Margit in the hushed tones reserved for the unmentionable in Altnamore. Ails knew that married women were supposed to have as many babies as they could. Sure, didn't Father McStay even go round to houses where they only had two children, just like Protestants. He'd tell them they should have more little Catholic children. Maura and Brigid had told Ails and the rest that the big priest had come to their house asking why they only had two children, and girls at that? Her husband needed strong sons to take over the business, the big priest had said. But there was still only Maura and Brigid. Maybe that's why their parents fought a lot.

But Auntie Cora? She was so lucky to be having another baby. She had a husband and a house and everything. Maybe Auntie Cora was frightened of having the baby?

"Are you scared of the blood?" Ails said, suddenly, "because Neeve is nice now and my mammy is fine too."

Auntie Cora smiled

"No, no, it's not that, Ails. I just haven't been used to babies around for a while, but I'll get used to it again.

"I'll take it for walks for you."

"Thanks, Ails, you're my girl."

"Are you going to take it to France when you go to learn French cooking?" Auntie Cora had won a cooking contest and the prize was a week-long course at the "Blue Cord-on" cooking

98

school in Paris, Shamie had said. She had studied in Paris when she was young.

"Naw, I was just writing a letter to say I'll not be going," she said. "Just look at it, Ails. We ruined the letter, dripping all over it, the two of us!" She laughed a crying laugh. "Babies are tiny, and they need their mother. Isn't it funny, Ails, baby calves and colts walk within a few hours, and birds fly away and build their own nests in a short time, but our babies take a long time to grow up." Ails hadn't really ever thought about it that way before.

"Yeh, s'pose so," she answered. They sat in silence for a while sipping their tea, each one feeling the comforting vibes going in a circle through one and back through the other. Ails had never seen Auntie Cora so quiet.

The door knocked. It was Maura and Brigid:

"You're gonna get it when you go home, Ails! Your mother sent us to look for you ages ago. We looked everywhere."

Ails got a trouncing when she went home. Her father smacked her hard for going off without saying where, and for complaints about her behaviour all day long, from her mother, from Fiona, from Lizzie ...Ails hated Sundays.

She went to bed crying with her legs and her bottom stinging from the smacks. The last thing she remembered seeing, half awake, half asleep in the hostile darkness, was Auntie Cora's dear, sad face with its frightened eyes saying "Help me, God, please help me."

Ails sleepily wondered why her Auntie Cora needed help?

15

the finn mccool play

While visiting Ireland, Ails and Fiona, with their Canadian husbands and children, sat enthralled in Neeve's living room, as her children put on a concert. The three cousins had attended a Donegal summer camp, the 'Gaeltacht.', immersed in Gaelic language, culture and tradition. Coming back with a wealth of songs, stories, plays, myths, and legends, these children relayed stories with astounding agility and talent, moving from one role to another with the confidence and grace of seasoned performers in top theatre. The Canadians were totally captivated by this. Ails herself had forgotten this innate Irish talent. It had been evident in Lizzie's kitchen eons ago, but even then, she didn't think about it.

Ails's attention was focused back on the living room children's play about Finn McCool, that legendary Celtic warrior hero. There was a bloodcurdling yell from the makeshift stage. 'Finn McCool' had burnt his finger while cooking a salmon. He stuck the burnt finger in his mouth and seemed transformed. As

'Finn' moved into the pose of a man deep in thought, the narrator explained articulately that an ancient prophecy said Finn would taste the 'Salmon of Knowledge' and be forever wise.

The next scene showed Finn's wife 'Sava,' on stage, carrying a doll, her and Finn's brand new baby son, named Oisin. Sava vowed with Finn that their son Oisin would have "a real mother and father."

"Not like you, Finn," said Sava, his wife, looking up at him with great, sad eyes. "Your dead warrior father had so many enemies that your widowed mother couldn't risk keeping you with her, for fear of enemies killing you, her baby son, in revenge." 'Sava,' 'Finn's' wife, now swept across the stage, talking directly to their baby son in her arms.

"You know, Oisin, the women who reared your father did a wonderful job, teaching him how to run and leap and swim and hunt hare and deer." Sava then moved back beside Finn, her husband, addressing the end of her speech to him.

"Finn, our son, Oisin, will have all the love and the best upbringing and education a mother and father can give." They walked off the stage together, the doll between them.

"The End," announced the narrator, calling his brother and sister actors, along with the doll, over for a ceremonious bow.

Ails' and Fiona's four children — and their parents — were rapt in awe at the stunning performance, at the staging, directing and sheer raw talent of their cousins.

"Do you have any idea how good these kids are?" Fiona's husband asked their parents. "If they were in North America, they'd be child stars!"

"But this is not America," said their father. They can play, sing, act and dance all they want, but they have to study their medieval history and maths and the real things in our education system."

"Art and drama will get them no place in this country," added their mother Neeve firmly.

16

showtime!

After her Sunday episode where she learned about Auntie Cora going to have a new baby, Ails got up to a grey, drizzly Altnamore Monday morning. She was chastened, subdued. Even Fiona felt sorry for her because she had got whacked on Sunday night, punished for going off all day on her own, ending up in Auntie Cora's with nobody knowing where she was. Even Lizzie was halfways civil this morning. Ails walked slowly out to go to school and met Maura, Brigid and Jinny who were waiting for her at Callaghans'.

"Did you get whacked?"

"Does he use a stick?"

"Just his hand," muttered Ails, wishing they'd mind their own business. That Jinny was so nosey. She wanted to know everything. She never got smacked, just because she lived with her aunt and uncle who were real old, and had no children of their own. Jinny came in from the country to live with them, in the time-honoured Altnamore tradition. Years earlier Lizzie moved in from the country to live with her Aunt Nelly, who died, leaving Lizzie the house. These kind of children (like Lizzie and Jinny), said Ails's mother, were usually spoiled rotten, and this was certainly true in Jinny's case. Her aunt and uncle thought everything she did was funny or smart. They never shooed her out, even when people were in the eating house talking, so she heard the news of the whole townland.

"You're lucky, you know," continued Jinny, oblivious to Ails's annoyance. "Hughie McCann's father beats him with a coathanger, and Dingo Devine gets hit with a belt."

"Good," thought Ails remembering the crippling kick in her stomach, delivered by Dingo Devine, just because she said girls were as smart as boys.

"An' when my mammy and daddy get drunk, they throw dishes an' hit each other with them, an' smash them all over the floor. Sometimes they throw chairs, too," added Brigid. Ails was horrified. Brigid continued, oblivious. "One time my daddy had my mammy by the throat and he yelled that she was his wife, and he would do what he wanted, and he was just going to hit her with the big glass vase in the sitting room..." Brigid caught Maura's warning glance. She must have been told not to tell, thought Ails.

"Oh, they don't hit us," said Brigid, getting the message from Maura, "because we know how to hide under the bed till they forget about us. Then they get sober," she continued matter-of-factly. "Mind you, one night Aunt Rosie and Uncle Ned came and took us to their house, because they said it was bad for us to see all this fighting..." But again, Maura's silencing glance was on Brigid and she stopped. Stunned by this disclosure, Ails didn't feel too badly off, but looked at Maura and Brigid and tried to imagine plates and chairs flying through the air ... their skinny short father choking their roly-poly mother ... she just couldn't imagine it.

Whoa!! Ails was jolted out of her imagination by Jinny's exclamation about a bright red poster tacked on a telephone pole. "What's this?" exclaimed Jinny. Then she began to read:

COME ONE, COME ALL
TO THE GREATEST SHOW IN IRELAND
CLARENCE MCTAVISH
presents
"A TRAVELLING SPECTACULAR"
Family Entertainment
Featuring
MELINDA MCTAVISH

"MURDER IN THE RED BARN"

The excitement mounted as Jinny read out what the sign said. They all threw their schoolbags in the air and squealed and yelled "Yippppeeeeeeee!" They ran breathless up the hill to school, telling everybody on the way, and dying to tell the rest. Well, of course when they got there, Hughie McCann had already told all the Tuggan crowd that didn't come through the village, because he was the one who had put the signs up. They even had one in Hughie McCanns' own shop window, but the blinds weren't up yet.

Ails sat in Mrs. Digby's room mechanically doing her work, but her imagination was soaring, smelling the sawdust, seeing the striped tent, the brightly painted swing boats and wagons, the rifle range, the merry-go-round, and the man with the tall hat on the big stilts selling tickets, yelling:

"Roll up, roll up folks! Tickets here for the greatest peh-foh-mance in I-ah-land! Quiver in yor shoes, shake in yor boots, make yor hair curl with terror at 'Murder in the Red Barn!' " Ails couldn't wait for McTavish's show to arrive. They always came on a Thursday night, and were set up and 'ready to roll the show' as Clarence McTavish said, by Friday night.

And this was only Monday!

"Ails, you had better get to work, me girl, and stop thinking about that show. Write about it in your 'News' instead of daydreaming!"

"That's a great idea," thought Ails, for she certainly didn't want to write about Sunday, not the way it had gone yesterday.

"Y'know," she confided to Lizzie at lunch time, "ever since the school Inspector came, The Pigby hasn't been half as bad." It was true. Somehow Mrs. Digby seemed to belong to Altnamore as she never had before.

Every lunch time all week was spent speculating on this year's show, and getting ready for the Talent Contest. There were songs and fiddling, plays and spoons, sketches, riddles, jokes, lilting, dances and poems — anything that would get a person on that stage. The children's contest was always Saturday morning at ten o'clock. The Lilter McMenamin had won the Adult Contest three years in a row, and his nephew Whistler had won the Children's Talent Contest three times also.

"Ever since he was a wee nipper, that lad could sing and whistle like a blackbird. I declare t' God, he could sing before he could talk!" the Lilter always told everyone proudly. Anyway neither of them were allowed to win any more. Instead they both performed the opening number of both talent contests with the McTavish band. The band had a saxophone, a trumpet and a piano. The Lilter wore his funeral and wedding suit for that performance.

This year Ails's group was doing a play "Queen Maeve and the Brown Bull of Cooley" from a story Mrs. Digby told them in school. It was out of the Irish history book she hid from the school inspector. There was no point in asking her father some things, Ails had decided, so she had asked Auntie Cora why the book was hidden. Auntie Cora had said heatedly, "because we're not allowed to teach Irish history, the story of our own ancestors, our own story of our own people, in our own schools. It's a disgrace. We know about the glory of Britain all over the world, but Irish history doesn't exist — except as *they* see it."

"Oh," said Ails, not really understanding who 'they' were. Probably the English or the Protestants, who seemed responsible for most of the things Auntie Cora got angry about.

Jinny had 'buck-teeth' sticking prominently out over her lower jaw, but they weren't too buck to play Queen Maeve. Her best feature overruled the teeth. Jinny had huge eyes that she could do anything with. She could change her face to look any way she wanted: authoritative, scarey, heartbroken, guilty. No doubt about it, Jinny was a good Queen Maeve. Ails was the rival King because she had short hair. Ails swore to never cut her hair when she grew up. Her mother liked it short. It was easy to get ready for school in the mornings, with a big colored bow her mother made to match her skirts:

"Like cow horns," Ails complained bitterly, but it was easier to cut nits out of short hair when the head lice woman came around from the County Health Department each year when the gipsies were at school. Her mother was paranoid about nits. Fiona's hair was short for the same reason, so Fiona was a page boy. Brigid with the long ringlets was small, so she was the princess. There really wasn't a princess in the story, but they put one in anyway, because Brigid had a frilly dress her aunt had sent from America. Maura had to be the Brown Bull of Cooley who dashed his brains out on a rock. That way, Maura's squint would be covered up with the big brown blanket that Auntie Cora had lent them. The horns were two thick curvy sticks that Maura held out through the holes. They practised for hours, on the Rocks. Using for a stage curtain a big sheet, full of patches and pinned-together holes, they stretched the sheet with safety pins along a skipping rope, reaching across the deepest dips between the tallest rocks.

Well, Thursday did finally come. The town was humming. Lizzie had ordered special meat from Conor, the travelling butcher's van, in case the show people chose to eat there their first night:

"Even if it's Friday they come, I can still use it," she reasoned. "None of them's Catholics and heathens all eat meat on Fridays, anyway." Out of six evenings she'd get the McTavish players twice, because there were two other eating houses in the town, Jinny's house and McCallans' and the show people took great care to take turns "to spread business around" said Clarence McTavish. All the children who usually went in all directions home from school, today stampeded all in one direction, past the big stone Celtic cross, down the Monument road to the big field. Sure enough, there, right in front of their eyes, the big striped tent was rising like a giant magic balloon. The equipment was being unloaded. Clarence McTavish let them hang around, then handed out sweets and told them all to make sure and bring their families, friends, and neighbours and shooed them home.

"It's dangerous till we get set up, kiddies," he said. Of course, everyone just went across the road and watched from the Monument. Ails spotted her father going home from his country school. She ran home as fast as she could. She wanted to make sure he saw her coming home from school in time, so as not to ruin her chances of getting back tomorrow.

On Friday after school they were practising like mad for the Talent contest. The boys were their competition and kept trying to sneak up to spy on the girls' play. The boys were doing Cowboys and Indians as usual. They continually tried to sneak up to spy on the girls' play. One of Ails's group always had to stand watch, also keeping an eye out so they could alert the others to watch for the glamorous show people walking up into the village for their evening tea. Jinny was complaining bitterly that Maura, as the Brown Bull of Cooley, bumped into everything.

"I can't see through the holes in the blanket," whined Maura. She had a squint, so both of her eyes didn't focus in the same direction. "Anyway, Jinny, you're far too bossy," Maura went on. They all started fighting. Before they even noticed, Clarence McTavish, boss of the whole McTavish Travelling Show, was standing right at the Rocks in front of them. Jinny saw him first. Stopping in mid-sentence she nudged Ails. The rest looked up and all of them stood transfixed. Clarence spoke with calm authority, with everyone gaping at him in amazement.

"Now, I'd suggest you have the Queen sit over here with the Princess at her feet and the Page Boy back here and the King over there. That way all the characters can be seen and the bull has room to move. Good luck on Saturday, ladies!" And he was gone around the corner to Lizzie's. They all stood open-mouthed, staring after him. Clarence McTavish himself!

"Well, imagine that," whispered Jinny in disbelief, "we'll definitely win, with a famous actor telling us how to act. Now, what did he say?...You, over there, Fiona...," she ordered.

At six o'clock on Friday, the field gates opened. A big generator wheel in a special lorry roared to keep the lights flashing and the music playing. The entire countryside was alive with people. They came on buses and carts, on bicycles, crowded into old cars with people nearly coming out of the windows, arms and heads sticking out; on tractors, and 'Shanks's Mare' — what Lizzie called walking. Animated squeals came from the swing-boats, brightly decorated boat-shaped swings with steel 'ropes' that worked SO much better than rope swing seats. Lads took their girlfriends and swung them daringly high. The rifle range was crowded with people who won teddy bears. The bumping cars were accompanied by roars and yells and screams of people covering their eyes, waiting for bumps. It was just grand!

Jinny pulled Ails aside:

"Just look at the two of them ones over there!" Ails looked over and saw Jinny's cousin Briege Mullin, who looked like a golden haired angel. Her beautiful eyes were lowered shyly, as one of the men in the show group was obviously pressing her to go on the swing boats with him. He had hair as black as the crow and big liquid brown eyes. "Gravy-Eyes," hissed Jinny. Blonde Briege and the dark showman looked like a photograph and a negative side by side, Ails thought admiringly. After some persuasion, Briege finally went on the swingboats with the dark, handsome showman.

"Boy, just wait till Bouncer hears about this!" said Jinny. Bouncer was Briege's huge good-looking boyfriend. "He'll kill Gravy-Eyes for trying to steal his girl." Bouncer had been off in England for almost a year, working and saving so that he and Briege could get married.

The big show was ready to start. The lights flashed on and off faster and faster. A deafening drum roll sounded to warn all the children to go home, since the play was meant for adults. Of course Jinny got to stay. On the way out, Ails couldn't resist. She and Fiona, Maura and Brigid sneaked around the side and together they pulled and tugged, counting 1,2,3, PULL, until they managed to release from the ground the giant tent pegs from the back tent flap — just enough to let them lie down and watch the people filing in. The atmosphere was electric. Soon the tent was packed and steaming, with smells of people and drink and cigarette smoke and drying mud. The show ladies had on trousers and had sparkly eye-shadow, big black long curly eyelashes, bright rouge and lipstick.

"War paint caked out an inch from their faces. If you took it aff they'd be real hags underneath," they heard Mary Margit say to Lizzie, unobtrusively seated in the back row of chairs. Ails made a mental note. They'd have to be careful not to be seen. The show ladies wore gorgeous costumes. Their hair was like haystacks, all standing up high. The showmen were very debonair. They had skinny leg drainpipe trousers and wore colored satin shirts with chest hair curling up over the shirts, unbuttoned to show their chests.

The drum rolled again dramatically. There were always a few preliminary sketches before the big show. The band gave a fanfare and played "Jealous Heart" before Clarence McTavish came out as Clarrie. Clarrie was a man who wanted a three inch hem taken up on his new trousers that he had at home, before he could wear them to the dance that night. A woman with a headscarf and handbag came rushing by. She had to refuse when he asked her to hem his trousers, as she was in a hurry. Then another woman came by, and she also had to refuse to sew the trousers because she had to get home to feed the baby. A third woman said she couldn't do the hem before Thursday. Finally Clarrie gave up on trying to have his trousers shortened, and went into the pub for a drink.

The next scene showed the women all changing their minds, each one of them finding time to hem up the trousers. They went into Clarrie's house one by one, unknown to each other, each cutting off a large hem, making Clarrie's trousers shorter and shorter. The audience was giggling and nudging one another in anticipation.

In the next scene, Clarrie arrived home half-drunk, fitted on his trousers — by now neatly hemmed above his knees. Well, anything like the roaring and clapping and rollicking big hearty laughs, with toothless grins and false teeth rattling, was never heard in Altnamore. Pack McFelimy knocked a big fat woman right off the end of the bench with the whack he gave her, he was laughing so hard. Clarrie had the knobbliest knees anybody ever saw, with sinewy, spindly legs, big boney ankles and long funny shoes. Older women in black shawls grinned sheepishly and young girls teasingly asked boyfriends "Is that what your knees look like, Jimmy?"

So far, so good. Nobody had spotted the four girls under the flap. They were almost rolling on the ground, wiping away tears of laughter. Next came Amy McTavish singing "Nobody's Child" about a blind child in an orphanage whom nobody would take home. With the lines "No mother's kisses, and no daddy's smile" the audience earlier tears of laughter turned to tears of sadness. Then a troupe of dancers came on dressed as cowboys and cowgirls and everyone clapped in time to their dance. Then Clarence McTavish came on and said:

"The next dance is a snake dance. Will all those who snaked in, please snake out again, including those who snaked in under the tent!" In the excitement Ails and the other three had crawled inside, kneeling and craning their necks to see through the rows of chairs. They forgot themselves, stood up and forgot to hide! They crawled out, embarrassed, with grass stains all over their clothes, but it was just as well they were discovered, because they were sent home. Ails would otherwise have forgotten to go home and would have ruined her chances of returning the rest of the week. Her father said he didn't want them falling asleep in school the next day. It wouldn't have mattered, for everyone slept all that week anyway. Nobody listened in school at all, for they all lived in anticipation the entire week. Everyone who saw the big plays would act them out for the others in the school yard. Whistler McMenamin picked up the songs, and soon the whole village was singing them. As long as they had money, everyone went back all week.

Finally, too soon, it was Saturday, the day of the Big Contest. Alice the hairdresser, was run off her feet doing hair, and the children all took the rags out of their hair and came in ringlets. Brigid's were lovely; just like a real princess.

They hauled all the props down to the field in McMenamin's wheelbarrow. Despite their awful nervousness, the play went beautifully and Maura didn't bump into anybody. They watched all the other acts — the boys shooting each other wildly and falling down dead, the Indians with wild warpaint, the soloists, the fiddlers and Irish dancers. Eventually everyone waited with bated breath for the announcement of the winners:

"For their interpretation of an ancient Irish legend, 'Queen Maeve and the Brown Bull of Cooley,' the winners are....." But nobody heard their names. The four of them went screaming mad up onto the stage, and were presented with the ten shillings. Two shillings each! That was enough to keep them in luxury all week and they got to perform in the big tent before the Sunday night show! They flew home to tell everyone and savour this great honour. They didn't bother to go back for the adult contest, because Johnny McGee always won with "The

Tuggan White Hare." They knew that old country men with caps cocked over one ear and a hand cupped over the other ear, would be droning songs with forty-two verses — songs with no tune at all. Fiddlers would be complaining that Mrs. Aurora McTavish's piano accompaniment knocked them "off choon," particularly if they didn't win. This year a fiddler father and daughter did win. After the adult prizewinning highlight performance, Ails, Fiona, Maura, Brigid and Jinny did a repeat Children's performance of 'The Brown Bull of Cooley.' Afterwards they listened in their glow of stardom to the McTavish Band playing lively tunes, prancing and dancing and clapping at the back with their father and mother, Lizzie and Mary Margit, before going home exhausted to bed Sunday night, fully fledged actresses.

The images of McTavish's Travelling Show danced through Ails's head: the contests, the rides, the games, the songs, the music, Gravy Eyes and Briege, their 'Queen Maeve Brown Bull' winning performance...all of it was etching in her heart forever the magic that permeated Altnamore for that week. It would be a lifetime, it seemed to Ails, before next year's showtime. But for tonight, the magic, like stars from a wand, still sprinkled over Altnamore.

17

Queen Maeve

Fiona was visiting Ails in prairie Canada, from her home on the west coast. Calgary's bitter cold meant the four kids couldn't play outside, so they had turned couches and chairs upside down and sideways and they had all the sheets and blankets off the beds, building forts and tents with clothespins, playing house, kings and queens, warriors and soldiers, all at once, it seemed.

"Thank God they're occupied for a while," said Fiona at the kitchen table. "I don't know how you cope with this cold here. They must get nuts in the house all the time." Tripping over one of the blankets, Ails was reminded of a long-ago image of playing in Altnamore. She put the crocheted blanket over her head and stuck her fingers out through the holes like horns.
"Do you remember us and Queen Maeve and the brown bull of Cooley at McTavish's Travelling Show?" she asked Fiona in a loud bull voice.

"I remember it just like it was yesterday," answered Fiona. "Weren't we proud stars?" she went on, smiling at the memory. "All the same, I couldn't get over the story the way I heard it later in Celtic Studies at University," continued Fiona.

"What do you mean?" asked Ails.

"Well, ole Maeve was a female stud!" laughed Fiona.

"Go on!" said Ails in disbelief.

"Oh, yes, sort of like that species of insect that kills its mate after mating," Fiona went on. "She didn't put up with no fooling around from her man!" she continued on in a country and western accent. "Ole Maeve there, she jest hired a hit man and had her hubby killed when she found out he was doin' her wrong — and her sleeping with every Tom, Dick and Harry."

"Hey, I never heard that!" exclaimed Ails.

"Of course she was a kind of half goddess," Fiona went on, "so she could transform herself into a beautiful maiden instead of looking ordinary, like us, and those high-powered men just fell hook, line and sinker, into bed with her. The thing I found strange, though," continued Fiona, "was that fertility was a big deal in those days, but it seems to have been Maeve's nymphomaniac tendencies that were emphasized more than her bearing of children!"

"Jeez, Maeve sounds more like she lived in the 1960s in North America!" said Ails. Fiona didn't answer. She had a faraway look in her eyes.

"Remember our play, though?" she asked. Ails detected a note of nostalgia in her voice.

"Indeed I do," answered Ails, smiling at the memory. "Maura with that squint and the cow horns sticking out through the holes in the blanket!" Ails put her fingers up like horns and turned her eyes in.

"I don't remember us ever being told in school that bull worship was a big thing back in Maeve's day," said Fiona. "This husband of Maeve's, y'know, he had a fine big bull, and ole Maeve heard there was a bigger one in Ulster, the Brown Bull of Cooley, so she mobilized her army and went off and captured that bull."

"Bully for her!" said Ails. Fiona laughed.

"But you know the weirdest part about Maeve," said Fiona. "After all that glorious copulation and warrioring and winning the Brown Bull, Maeve got killed by a hard lump of cheese shot from a slingshot!"

"What a cheesy end!" grinned Ails. "Are you sure you're not just making that up?"

"No, it just sounds so preposterous that you'd think I made it up," Fiona continued. "Maeve's nephew killed Maeve with his slingshot to avenge her murder of his mother."

"Well, you can see that our research into Maeve wasn't what won us First Prize in Clarence McTavish's Travelling show!" said Ails, as she tried to talk above the growing din of the kids, now fighting. Lizzie was crying,

"They won't let me be the teenager," she said. They're the king and queen and the prince, and they won't let me be the teenager!"

"There is no teenager, stupid!" said Nuala, her sister.

"Don't you call your sister stupid," said Fiona.

"Well, I ..."

"That's enough out of all of you," said Ails, as she separated the two boys throwing cushions at each other and jumping off the back of the couch.

"These guys are stir-crazy," she said to Fiona. "Let's get them out of here. O.k., guys, cleanup time!" she said, gathering up blankets.

"Why do we have to clean up? We want to play in the castle later," whined Quinn. "What was that story Auntie Fiona was telling you?" he said, hoping to distract them from the cleanup. It always amazed Ails that kids seemed to be able to tell what you were talking about, even when they seemed engrossed in play.

"Oh, it's a story we learned a long time ago in school," said Ails. "Now, come on and get this mess cleaned up."

"Oh, go on and tell us," said Patrick, stopping in mid cleanup. "Please?"

Ails and Fiona looked at each other.

"I wouldn't touch it with a ten-foot pole," said Fiona. "Would you?"

"Ditto," answered Ails. They both laughed as she added "We'd want it to be too authentic!"

"Let's get on our snowsuits and go out to the Mall," said Ails.

"Oh, goody," said Patrick, echoed by Lizzie, then Quinn, then Nuala, all rhyming "Goody, goody, goody." Then they got louder and louder, following Patrick's rhyming nonsense words, 'Goody foody moody loody spoody!"

"Thank God for consumerism and heated malls," said Ails, going out into the biting wind to start the car. When she came back, they'd put away most of the bedclothes, replaced the furniture and were struggling into snowsuits and boots.

"To think that Maeve had husband, lovers, armies, and children and went off to capture mighty bulls," she said to Fiona. "And it's as much as we can do to get ourselves organized to go the mall."

"Look at it this way," said Fiona, "Maeve didn't have to beat this Calgary winter!"

18
Disappeared, Disillusioned

every night at Altnamore had been electric while Clarence McTavish's Travelling Show was on. The five girls had gone down every single night: Jinny, Maura, Brigid, Ails and Fiona. And each night Jinny and Ails had followed handsome, swarthy Gravy-Eyes and beautiful Briege Mullin and had watched Briege become more and more bewitched by this debonair showman. From behind swingboats, hedges, tent corners, they watched him look deep into her eyes, and walk with his arm around her waist down into the valley below, hidden by the hedge. They did a melodramatic re-enactment of this in the playground at school, with Jinny saying:

"Do you love me Briege, my angel?" and Ails answering:

"Yes, I love you Gravy-Eyes."

It was another of the many enchanting events that had happened under the spell of the McTavish's Travelling Show. All week long, work-worn faces had had a look of abandon about them. Lizzie, who never went anywhere, had watched from the dark shadowy areas, finally drawn into the whirl of magic and exhilaration of the swing-boats, flying high in the air with her cackling laugh echoing out through the din of music and people.

On Wednesday after school, the flattened grass in the field and the thousands of muddy footprints were all that were left of Clarence McTavish's Travelling Show. The showpeople seemed like characters in a dream, now gone.

Shockingly gone, also, was Briege Mullin!

Her clothes were gone from McAnallan's where she kept house during the week, looking after McAnallans' retarded boy,

117

Jimmy. Jimmy was crying for her: "Beege, I want Beege!" She wasn't at her home in Legnamarsh when Tommy McAnallan went to look there. Briege's boyfriend, Bouncer, had been working in England with his uncle, for months now, to make some extra money so he and Briege could get married. They sent for him immediately. He was home a day and a half later. He came straight to Jinny's, "an' the look of that lad would have broke your heart in smithereens," Jinny told Ails. "This'll be the finish of him." Briege's whole family, Bouncer, the McAnallans, the priest and the new policeman were all in Jinny's, trying to find a way to trace Briege. Tommy McAnallan had already gone with the new policeman to the next village where McTavish's Travelling Show was playing.

"I coulda told them all the time," Jinny said knowingly. "See, didn't I tell you?" But Jinny wouldn't admit that she was as shocked as anybody by the disappearance of Briege.

Clarence and Aurora McTavish were very upset, and drove back to Altnamore to Jinny's house to try and help. Clarence McTavish told them that Gravy Eyes had left the show without a word.

"Apart from the fact that we go to great lengths to protect our public image, we have very high moral standards," said Clarence McTavish. "I'm deeply sorry this happened. We value Altnamore patronage very highly, and I'm very angry with Bruno."

"Bruno — that was Gravy Eyes' real name," said Jinny when relaying all of the happenings to Ails and the rest. "Sounds like a name you'd call a dog," she added wryly.

Aurora McTavish continued, "Clarence and I will do everything in our power to trace them, Mrs. Mullin," she said, putting her arm around the shoulders of Briege's distraught mother. "Sergeant McNaughton here will be in constant contact. We have to get back for tonight's show. This is a dreadful state of affairs. Bruno was a very valuable part of our cast. He has no family, and has been with us since childhood."

"I knew his gravy eyes weren't normal!" exclaimed Jinny to Ails and Maura. "I bet you he's a changeling like in that book in school and the fairies left him in the McTavish's caravan."

118

"Don't be daft," said Maura suddenly, "he was born like other babies, from his mother's stomach that grew from a seed in his father's thingy."

Ails looked at Maura in amazement.

"WHAT?" said Ails in disbelief.

"What do you mean 'What' Ails? Everybody knows that.

"Aye, *ordinary* babies are made from a seed in the mother's stomach," said Jinny "but Gravy Eyes is not ordinary."

"What seed?" asked Ails, "How did a seed get there? Do they eat it?"

"God, don't you know nothin'?" said Maura, enjoying acting superior to the rest of them; for a change. Jinny joined in. Ails was mad at herself for being so ignorant. Now Jinny and Maura would get together. Maura didn't usually know much about most things:

"I know lots of things," said Ails, nettled.

"You know plenty of things out of books, that's all," challenged Maura.

"So?" defended Ails, "Where's the seed anyway?"

"The seed comes from the father, silly, and it comes out of their thingy that they pee with."

"You mean that it's *seeds* they pee into the toilet, not water like us?" asked Ails. Jinny and Maura were now laughing at her and giggling with each other as if they had some big fat secret.

"You mean you don't know that a man puts his thing into a woman's pee-pee hole, and that's how they make a baby?" Ails was utterly flabbergasted, and felt like she was going to be sick.

"That's how Auntie Cora got the baby," she thought to herself. "No wonder she was upset!"

"But that is *horrible!*" said Ails aloud. "My mother and father would never do that. It's disgusting," she said shuddering.

Everybody's mammy and daddy do it. Sometimes my mammy won't let my daddy do it," said Maura, getting carried away, "and they have a big fight, and he gets drunk, and she yells, 'Take that thing away, I don't want any more of your babies' and she locks him out of the bedroom. They do it in bed, you see," went on Maura, enjoying the look of complete shock on Ails's face.

"If your father never did it to your mother, you wouldn't be here," added Jinny, and went on talking to Maura. Ails didn't hear another word they said. Her world was shattered.

"How could Uncle Peter have done such a terrible thing to Auntie Cora?" she thought, "and this was the sixth time." He seemed like such a nice, clean, gentle man, and everybody said he idolized her. Poor Auntie Cora. No wonder she'd been so upset, thought Ails over and over.

As for Ails's own mother and father, now *that* was repulsive. Ails just refused to believe it.

Ails walked around in a daze for the next few days thinking. Everybody did this? Every baby in the world was born this way? Well, Jesus wasn't. Mary, Jesus's mother wouldn't allow any man to do that to her. There was no blood or mess either when Jesus was born. Ails couldn't even eat. There was no-one she could ask without looking stupid. She tried bringing up the subject with Auntie Cora. Auntie Cora had a way of talking around and around about everything and anything, while saying nothing, when she didn't want to talk about something in particular. Ails's father and mother, she knew, wouldn't let her play with Jinny if they knew what was being discussed, so Jinny and Maura were her only source.

That was why the boys had wanted them all to dance with no clothes on in the barn down the back lane — to see where to put that thingy! And she and Maura and Jinny had danced with only a necklace on, just because the boys had paid money: Jerry Gallagher, Dingo, Shamie, Pat Doran, Nailly McCarten and a few more. The boys had told them:

"This is what actresses do in big shows in England and America." Ails had felt just terrible at the time, and couldn't figure out why. She felt a whole lot worse now. Boys were rotten. She was alone these days a lot. Maura and Jinny had ganged up on her, leaving her out, and making her feel stupid.

Ails kept looking at the bulge in men's trousers. One day she even saw up the leg of Peter O'Neill's trousers when he was sitting on the ground against the wall of the school with his knees up. The 'Thingy' was a small fleshy pink pointed thing with sort of round shaped fleshy balls at the bottom near the split in his legs. It was very harmless looking. He had no pants under his short trousers. Ails couldn't see very well, and didn't want to stare.

"They must be wrong," thought Ails, "that pink thing couldn't have seeds in it."

Auntie Cora's new baby was a boy called Colum. She'd had to go to the hospital because she nearly died. She came back very white and pale and shaky, and had been told to have no more babies. So, luckily, thought Ails, Uncle Peter could never do that awful thing to her again.

Ails's mother went down to help every day, and Ails minded both babies, Neeve and the new baby boy, Colum. Ails's father didn't like them going down to Auntie Cora's every day, even it if was the summer holidays. He didn't like Auntie Cora very much, nor her rebel opinions, wanting an Irish Free State. But Ails's mother, usually quiet, was really stubborn.

"She's my sister, and our Ails might not be half the child she is today if Cora hadn't dropped everything to help me. Sure she practically raised Ails for two months till I got back on my feet." Ails and her mother wheeled Neeve down to the bottom of the village every morning of the summer holidays, where they washed clothes, cooked, and cleaned up after the other five children, while Auntie Cora got stronger daily.

Colum was lovely even if he was a boy. Ails often changed his nappy and looked at his wee pink thing and thought how crazy it was that that could be stuck in any girl's pee-pee.

"But they can't do that till they get hair on their face, and then they get hair all around their thingy, too," Maura and Jinny told her when she checked when men did this thing. "And anyway, you have to be married."

"No, you don't.....I mean you can.....Well, there's ones that's done it that's not married. Take Briege and Gravy Eyes . . . " Jinny baited all of them, but then clammed right up and would say no more. What did she mean, Briege and Gravy-Eyes? Did they do it? Ugh! Golden-haired Briege. She couldn't have! Jinny had probably heard it wrong. Sometimes Jinny didn't know any more, but she always left other people thinking she knew more, but just didn't want to tell them. Ails usually knew when Jinny was bluffing. Her eyes would sort of blink and quiver.

"No," continued Maura firmly, "you need to get permission from the priest to do it."

"Well, everybody knows that," said Jinny, uncertainly, "but if a man has a beard growing on his face, I'm telling you, he can just DO it."

Ails saw her chance to get back in again with Jinny and Maura. There was some doubt over this matter.

"Anyway, nobody's ever going to do it to me," said Ails, who didn't want to deal with this any more.

"Why don't we do act a play?" she asked the rest of them. "I saw curly wood shavings in the barn where somebody made shelves for the shop. We can use them for long curly hair" Ails got hair clips from Lizzie and some old sheets. They pinned the planed curly wood shavings to look like ringlets on the ends of their hair. They dressed up and performed a play from their school reading book. It was about three princesses whose father the King had sent them out to look for husbands. One of the husbands would rule the kingdom.

19

surprise artist on the rocks

On their way down to the Altnamore Rocks to play house, the seven and eight year old girls had old sheets and dolls and cutlery and a few other odds and ends. They had just arrived and were beginning to set up the downstairs part when they looked up at the upstairs part of the Rocks. There was a strange man up there. He was sitting on top of an upturned whisky barrel out of Heaney's pub. He was doing something on a piece of paper on the side of the telephone pole. They all moved quietly closer till they formed a semi-circle behind the man. He was sketching. He had piece of white paper pinned on to the pole and he was drawing shapes and shading them. They watched his big bony hands move the pencil deftly around, sometimes touching the paper, sometimes not. He had long legs and arms, was gangly, thin, and wore sandals with no socks. The only other person they ever saw in Altnamore wearing sandals and bare feet was a Franciscan monk with a long robe who came to the Mission and preached very angry sermons.

They all stood still on the Rocks for a full minute or so watching this strange sight. Fiona broke the silence, asking in awe:

"Are you a artist?" he gave a start and looked around at all of them, flustered, embarrassed, shy almost. His wispy, reddish hair was uncombed, and his greenish eyes looked like a surprised rabbit.

"Yes, I s'pose I am, sort of, a potter actually. I'm very sorry. I didn't realize I was in your way." He had a bit of an English accent. He left his picture, put his pencil in the pocket of his open-necked shirt and got up.

"Oh, that's alright, you don't have to leave," said Jinny. Maura added "We don't need the upstairs Rocks today anyway."

"Oh, no, please go ahead. I…I have to go…" and his voice trailed off vaguely. He backed away from the rocks apologetically, looking embarrassed that all of them had been watching him. Then he turned and walked down onto the road.

"Who was that?" asked Fiona.

"The Blind Widow Carragher's son, Brendan. He comes home to see her sometimes," Jinny said knowingly.

"How does she *always* know these things?" thought Ails, nettled. Nothing was ever new to Jinny, it seemed. The rest of them stood gawking after this stranger. Of course, Jinny went on arranging the sheet, as if she knew everything. Fiona was standing transfixed looking at the piece of paper on the telephone pole. She yelled after Brendan Carragher.

"Mister, can I keep your picture?" He didn't hear her. He just walked on with his hands in his pockets, his lanky frame stooped.

"He looks lost or something," thought Ails, strangely fascinated by him, "but how could anyone be lost in Altnamore?" She shook her head as if to make this thought clearer.

Since Brendan Carragher left, they decided to set up the upstairs part of the playhouse in the higher Rocks. Fiona took down the sketch, folded it up carefully and put it inside her vest. Today the ground was just damp enough so it was easy to sweep out the play houses without raising dust.

Later that evening Ails asked Lizzie about Brendan Carragher.

"Where'd you see him?" Ails told her about the Rocks. Fiona came in the middle of this conversation, proudly unfolding the sketch to showed Lizzie.

"Show me that again," said Lizzie. She shook her head. "Sure what kind of a picture is that, in the name of God. It's all shapes...doesn't look like fields or mountains or nothin'..." Lizzie put it down beside the butter. Fiona grabbed it.

"Don't get it dirty. It's mine. He gave it to me!" Yappy pest.

"He did not," said Ails. "You stole it."

"Did not."

"You did."

"Didn't."

"Did."

"Quet arguin'!" said Lizzie. "Youse have my head deeved. Run away out and play, the both of youse!"

"I'm gonna put this in my shoebox," Fiona said, leaving to go upstairs, folding the sketch carefully.

"With all her other junk," thought Ails drily, somewhat jealous of Fiona's 'art' collection of stones, old leaves, pieces of bright touchy fabric, leftover buttons, and now a real artist's sketch.

"I never saw Brendan Carragher before," said Ails with curiosity.

"Ach, he comes and goes like a ghost an' he's as about as much good to his poor blin' widowed mother as a ghost, too. Brains to burn, that lad had. Could have the best of jobs. All he does is make clay pots — mud pies, if y' ask me." Lizzie went on peeling potatoes.

"Where does he live?"

"Away in England someplace. Near yer Aunt Maisie. She knows where he lives, I heard. Like a hermit, they say he is. Thank god he has his sister Carmel to look after the poor widowed mother."

Ails didn't like the Widow Carragher, nor her sugary sweet daughter, Carmel, either.

"That Carmel's a saint," Lizzie said. "God, I must get these spuds on to boil. Away out from under me feet with youse. Run away out and play, for God's sake."

Carmel Carragher's voice was namby-pamby sweet. She smiled from the outside of her face not the inside of her eyes, and was always looking past you when she talked to you to see if anyone was watching her. Carmel wouldn't let them play ball against the gable of Carragher's house "in case it would disturb Mother." Ails had heard vaguely about a brother, but she'd never seen him before. The Widow Carragher was eerie. Her blind eyes were grey-white instead of coloured. Carmel took her everywhere, looking martyred. The people of the village called the widow "the blind banshee of Altnamore." That was because she wailed and keened and cried at funerals, sometimes even before the funeral, before the wake, even before the person was properly dead. Lizzie always said:

"Y'd hardly know y' were dead if the blind banshee didn't come to your wake. She's very fond of the drink at wakes, too." Right enough, the Blind Widow Carragher never missed a wake, with Carmel leading her in and out of the crowds in the wake houses.

"She's me eyes, God bless her," the Widow Carragher would say, and Carmel would bask in the appreciative looks of the people listening.

Ails saw Brendan Carragher briefly a few more times. He walked self-consciously around the village. "It's almost as if he'd lost something a long time ago, and he was searching for it — a piece of a jigsaw or something," thought Ails. Then she thought how silly that seemed. She met his eyes a few times, greenish, trusting eyes that had a wounded look. Brendan Carragher vanished from Altnamore just as suddenly as he had appeared.

20

But you do not see ...

But you do not see, nor do you hear, and it is well.
The veil that clouds your eyes shall be lifted
by the hands that wove it,
And the clay that fills your ears shall be pierced
by those fingers that kneaded it.
And you shall see
And you shall hear.
Yet you shall not deplore having known blindness,
nor regret having been deaf.
For in that day you shall know the hidden purposes in all things,
And you shall bless darkness as you would bless light."

from 'The Prophet' by Kahlil Gibran 1883—1931.

21

a celtic enigma

many years ago, on a sunny June day, Pat McCabe the butcher arrived in Altnamore. He arrived on the bus. The tar was bubbling up through Ails's toes, soft and squishy and delicious. The trick was to keep it that way without breaking the skin on the tar. When the sticky tar broke through the skin, it got on skin and clothes and mothers all over the village complained and smacked and washed and scrubbed. Lizzie would be rubbing butter on Ails and Fiona to try to remove the tar. Ails, Fiona, Maura, Brigid, Shamie and Pat Doran were concentrating on controlling the tar when a black shadow fell over three of them: Ails, Fiona and Shamie. They looked up to see what suddenly chilled out the sun. Out on the front of his face he had the winningest smile ever you saw, reddish-blonde hair, thinning at the front, and puzzlingly cold blue eyes that didn't seem to go with the smile. Fiona started whingeing and hiding behind Ails as soon as she saw him. She took funny notions about people sometimes.

"Well, now, aren't yiz the right bunch of weans," disarmingly using the 'wee-'uns' slang of Altnamore. "I suppose yiz wouldn't want to come up to the shop for some sweets?"

On their feet immediately, all of them — except Fiona, who was still whining, clutching Ails's dress while Ails apologetically tried to shut her up.

"He's gonna buy us sweets," she snapped at Fiona, exasperated.

"No wanna go with that man," wailed Fiona.

"Nuisance," thought Ails, "just because she hasn't seen him before." But Fiona would usually go with anyone who was going to buy sweets. "Of course," thought Ails drily "she'll take the sweets just the same, as soon as he's out of sight." Shamie and Pat had gone off to show the new man the shed down beside the Hall. In no time at all, McCabe had all the lads of the town carrying out junk, painting and helping him move pieces of glass in to set up his butcher's shop. He paid them — more generously than he thought. He'd tell them to take money out of the tin box that was the till. It was Pat Doran who discovered that McCabe was colour-blind, and couldn't distinguish the difference between the notes or the coins, especially when he was on the top of a ladder, or any distance away from the till. Money didn't seem to matter that much to Pat McCabe.

The women of the town were thrilled. Fresh meat daily: chops, tongue, steak, tripe, liver, brains, kidney, pigs' feet, leg of lamb for Sundays — heaven! And McCabe would cut it whatever way they wanted, and sell them as little as they wanted — without wanting them to buy more. The travelling butcher van used to try to sell them more meat than they needed — to make it worth his while to come out to such a remote place as Altnamore. "A godsend" Lizzie called Pat McCabe. All the young lassies were offering to buy meat for the older women. There was constant flow of them giggling and talking nervously. All the young lads hung around, imitating the giggling and the flirtatious looks the girls gave McCabe. He was always getting the lads to run messages, deliver meat and keep the change, and buying sweets for them. The men loved the fresh meat, the women loved the handiness of the meat, the young lassies loved McCabe's possible eligibility, quick wit, smile and charm and his seeming to play 'hard to get' with all of them. It was like a game. Pat McCabe had charmed the town. Above all, McCabe, it seemed to Ails, had almost bewitched Auntie Cora. She reacted to his smiles and flattery and animated discussion of current political topics. Ails was dismayed and confused. Her natural instinct was revulsion of some kind towards this man with the bull-neck, wispy red hair, steely hard cold blue eyes and charm he seemed to turn on and off like a water tap.

But her beloved Auntie Cora almost seemed besotted by McCabe. Mind you, Ails reminded herself, Auntie Cora loved to cook and had always had trouble getting good cuts of meat, complaining bitterly about 'cows and sheep and pigs all around us and we can't get a decent piece of meat because it's all controlled from outside us.' Nevertheless, every morning now, Auntie Cora wheeled Colum all the way up the village, all dressed up, with lipstick on, smiling, to buy her meat. She didn't used to come *every* day, Ails thought. Then Auntie Cora started asking McCabe down to her house for his dinner, because she had a new recipe for pork, or because McCabe had cut the meat (with his big butcher's sharp knife that scared Ails), into wafer-thin slices, or tiny squares, or long, thin flat sheets required for whatever she was simmering, or saute-ing, or stuffing, or braising. These were all words from the from the stained, dog eared 'Cordon Blue' Cookbook which Auntie Cora kept with her writing things on the cluttered shelf, beside the big friendly range in the kitchen.

Maybe Ails was seeing things all wrong? Maybe McCabe assuaged Auntie Cora's loneliness and heartbreak over her two oldest children who had emigrated to America? Maybe Ails was secretly jealous, feeling her space with Auntie Cora usurped by McCabe? Maybe, as her mother sometimes claimed, Ails's 'imagination was running away with her'? When she thought about all of this, it was disturbing, so she would shake herself to shake it out of her mind, and her being.

But Fiona still whinged and girned and wouldn't go near McCabe — not even when McCabe was buying sweets for them.

Nice as he seemed to be to everyone else, Ails was secretly revolted by his bull-neck, the way his head went straight down to his shoulders with no narrowing, and the eternal cold, hard blue eyes that didn't match the smile. But nobody else disliked McCabe. Ails shook herself, remembering that people couldn't help how they looked: people with crippled, crooked, or missing limbs; hair-lip people; and Lucia Grogan who was not right in the head. Lizzie said Lucia's mother was too old when she had her, that's why she had that wide-looking face that looked stretched back to her ears, and vacant eyes. If God made all those people, reasoned Ails, He also made Pat McCabe and

130

his bull neck that Ails hated to look at from a certain angle. His head stuck out from it and his eyeballs seemed to bulge cold and watery blue. Ails had to shake herself out of this every time she saw him. It made no sense for her to be feeling like that.

Sure, wasn't McCabe the talk of the town! He was that nice of himself, and great crack. He slept at the back of the shop. He was always ready to lend a hand to anybody that needed it. He helped out the blind widow Carragher. Her daughter, Carmel was sugary sweet to him, but McCabe had a handy way of brushing her off. None of the lassies of the village could get near him without a bevy of lads buzzing in and out through them and McCabe constantly directing operations. He was great at cutting meat just right, every day except 'damned fish day,' Friday, when only the Protestants shopped for meat. He starting bringing in fresh fish for Fridays and talking to the women about how good it tasted with champ. 'Just add a wee bit of butter and a few scallions on the pan, now, Missus. A couple of eggs, and yer old bread in crumbs and make a coat over the fish and fry it, and ye'll nivir miss the beef, I'm telling you, now!.'' Complaints about Fridays seemed to grow less and less. McCabe even charmed the seemingly impenetrable Lizzie, starting to sell Lizzie's eggs for her on Fridays, when no Catholics bought meat. Lizzie had Ails, Maura, Brigid, and even Jinny, who never did any work, washing the chicken dung off the eggs with baking soda, which McCabe kept telling her not to use.

"Weakens the shells, Lizzie," he'd say. But Lizzie did things Lizzie's way.

"Ivirybody knows you can't get eggs clean without soda, but don't let on to McCabe. Only rub it on the bad spots," she'd say. She'd even send down an extra one for McCabe himself.

"Him on his own, with neither chick nor chile," she'd say.

For a while, Shamie and Pat even shared the candied fruit and chocolate bars and sweets they bought with the money McCabe gave them. Not that Dingo Devine nor cross-eyed Jerry Gallagher nor Nailly McCarten nor any of the rest ever gave them any, though. But then they never knew Ails and the rest existed, except to tease and terrify them. Although McCabe didn't seem to have a girl of his own, he was nice to all of the young lassies when they went in. He got on great with all the men in the pubs, never drinking too much, but going to a different pub every night, ceilighing in some houses, always accompanied by Shamie, Pat, Dingo, and two or three other lads. He started to go to Auntie Cora's a lot, first for his dinner, and then it just became habit. Auntie Cora's face would light up when he talked about politics and how things were going to change. He assured her that she was perfectly right to be mad about the state of some things.

"Maybe she can't see his bull-neck," thought Ails to herself. She watched him look straight into Auntie Cora's eyes when Uncle Peter was gone at work, or was out shooting pheasants, or out at the pub. Ails thought of the snake in the book she was reading — how it could hypnotise people with its eyes. Again she had to shake herself out of thinking like that. Auntie Cora would talk of her University days. Her eyes would light up with a living, breathing, pulsating awareness of people and places and cultures and countries and all kinds of things. McCabe seemed to link into all of it, animated, supportive and encouraging. At times like this, it seemed to Ails that Auntie Cora was soaring high above Altnamore, seeing it as a part of a huge patchwork quilt. Ails loved to watch her like this: excited about ideas and the newspaper editorial, and books she lent McCabe, and the magazines he lent her. Ails even loved to watch the drama of the cold, hard angry look in her eyes when she talked about the way Altnamore was neglected by the county council.

"We might as well be living in the backwoods of Macnatassy," she'd say angrily. "As far as the government of this country's concerned we're not even on the map. Just look at that ridiculous estate down there below the village. That's no different from the summer castles of the French Kings, for Heaven's sake!" McCabe would ask questions and suggest solutions. He was genuinely interested in all these issues. Ails had heard Auntie Cora say these things to other people in the village who'd look at her quizzically, shrug their shoulders and say:

"Don't get yerself so upset, Cora! Sure we've a grand town," citing the big monthly Fair Day for all the people in the surrounding countryside to buy and sell their animals and wares, and the Bank coming out every Friday from Unragh, and now we have our own butcher. "We'll get them other extra things sometime," they'd say, with the weary resignation of a people out of the centre of things. "Sure, as long as we have our health."

"Why are they so accepting?" she'd ask McCabe. "Don't they know people can change things? People in other countries have done it ..."

No matter what McCabe said or did, Fiona still started whimpering as soon as he appeared, even when she watched him from Lizzie's window carrying boxes of meat, surrounded by lads helping him. Once, at Auntie Cora's, Fiona was getting downright obnoxious when McCabe was talking to Auntie Cora. She whined and wailed louder and louder, hiding behind Ails, and she wouldn't stop.

"What's wrong, lovey?" said Auntie Cora to Fiona. But McCabe turned and looked straight at Fiona, and at Ails who was blushing with embarrassment. That look almost silenced Fiona, and frightened Ails.

"Ach, she does this all the time. She's a nuisance," said Ails, feeling like nipping Fiona's knuckles clamped around her own behind her back. But those eyes, hard as flint, even though the face was smiling, and that bull neck . . . Ails had to shake herself and remind herself of how everybody loved McCabe.

As was the heartbreak of all Altnamore families, Auntie Cora had lost her older children to America. She looked sadder and sadder. Her oldest son Pat and her second daughter Mags had left recently. Ails would watch her sometimes looking into their beds. But Auntie Cora still had Shamie and Colum and her nieces, reasoned Ails. Auntie Cora kept frantically busy these days. Her baby, Colum, was growing, leaving her freer to cook and go out for her errands and messages and talk to people who dropped in and McCabe when he came to visit in the evenings. Sometimes Colum even trailed around with Ails, Fiona and the rest and he wasn't that hard to mind. They'd take turns carrying him around.

Things had changed as far as Shamie was concerned, though. He was never around the village the way he used to be. He always happened to be where McCabe happened to be.

It was October. Auntie Cora's older son and daughter wrote to their mother to say they were now settled in America. Her other two older ones were out working in other towns and boarding in those towns, but that was different. They did come home from time to time and she always knew she could see them any time. The weather was getting colder. McCabe stayed later at Auntie Cora's before going home to the back of his shop, away up the other end of the village. One particularly cold night Auntie Cora said

"Ach, away up to Pat's empty bed in Shamie's room. Sure you'll get your death of cold goin' out in the bucketing' rain and it freezin' out there." So she gave him a hot water bottle and sent him upstairs to sleep — so Ails heard her telling her mother on one of their Saturday talks that Ails loved to eavesdrop on.

"It's a terrible thing him goin' off to that barn of a place," she said, "an' him with no wife."

McCabe never really officially moved in to Auntie Cora's. He jut kept bringing one piece of belongings after another till finally all there was in the back of the butcher's shed was a mattress, a pillow and a blanket. Auntie Cora was lonely, lonely, lonely. Her heart seemed to visibly ache with longing for her two older children. When Ails was sitting cutting up scraps of sewing material in the corner of the kitchen, she often watched Auntie Cora's faraway eyes and occasional quiet weeping. Auntie Cora was sort of absent-minded when you asked her a question or talked to her. She would answer with a start, but go back into her wistful stare. She would rock Colum and say 'their eyes look over the ocean more and more till they go." She'd squeeze him, then go on with her work. She'd sing 'Noreen Bawn," or rather she would hum it, but Ails knew some of the words from the wireless, even if Auntie Cora didn't want to sing them. It was a song about a widow and her only daughter Noreen Bawn living happily in Tir Connell (Donegal, her father said it was, showing Ails on a map). But one fateful day arrived:

>*"Then one day there came a letter*
>*With her passage paid to go*
>*To the land where the Missouri*

134

And the Mississippi flow...

So Noreen Bawn went, like so many of the Irish, to America, to a better life, it seemed. In her case, however, she got deathly ill.

> *"But two scarlet spots appearing*
> *On her cheeks, the story told."*

Ails father said that meant she was sick with consumption. The song ended with Noreen Bawn dying, and coming home to be buried. *"There's a grave in old Tir Connell ...*
> *Where a broken-hearted widow*
> *Tends the grave of Noreen Bawn."*

Ails didn't know all the words, but last line she always remembered, because often when Auntie Cora had hummed a verse, she'd sing these words aloud:

> *"...'Twas the curse of emigration*
> *brought you here, my Noreen Bawn."*

"Why did they leave?" Ails found herself asking herself. When she'd asked Auntie Cora, the answer was "They have Westward-looking eyes, Ails, my love, Westward-looking eyes." But that didn't make sense to Ails. How could they have Westward-looking eyes when they'd never seen westwards? Everyone had loved them in Altnamore. They seemed to have such a good life here, thought Ails. They must have known it would break their mother's heart to see them go, and they loved her so much ... and the village was left with such a hole in it when they'd gone. How or why on earth could they possibly leave?

tradítional love songs - ?

There blooms a lily fair
The twilight gleam is in her eye
The night is on her hair
And like a lovesick lennin she,
She hath my heart in thrall
Not life I own, nor liberty
For love is lord of all.

From 'My Lagan Love' — traditional.

With gold and silver, I did support her
But I'll sing no more now till I get a drink
I'm drunk today and I'm seldom sober
A handsome rover from town to town
Ah, but, I'm sick now; my days are numbered
Come all ye young men and lay me down.

From 'Carrickfergus' — traditional.

23

BOUNCER

Bouncer was big, one of the biggest men eight-year-old Ails and her friends knew in Altnamore. He was called Bouncer because pubs and dance halls hired him to break up fights and get rid of unruly characters. Actually, though, Bouncer was as gentle as a lamb, and usually was able to persuade village drunks to leave peaceably. He didn't drink himself, and had never broken his 'Pioneer Pledge' he had taken as a boy, promising not to drink alcohol till the age of 21. Never, that is, until Briege disappeared. Bouncer used to leave the pubs sober as a judge at closing time, often walking a drunk man home. After Briege left, however, Bouncer 'took to the drink,' as was said around Altnamore, or alternately, 'The Drink got a hold of him.' It was uttered as if 'The Drink' was a living entity which put its hands around someone's throat, thought Ails when she heard it first. Like all local sayings, however, after a while they were commonly understood by even the smallest child, without explanation.

Bouncer was to be found behind the black-draped windows of the pubs, drinking with the all-night crowd after hours. These pubs often did more business from midnight till dawn than throughout daytime hours. Ever since Bouncer had come home from England, he had been working for Johnny the Miller. Lately, though, he kept coming to work later and later.

"Never seen a lad take it so hard about a girl," lamented Johnny the Miller. "Can't talk no sense into him. He swears she'll come back, that Briege. Ach, she was a lovely lassie, no doubt about it. Strange carryon that was, that showman turnin' her head, it was indeed." Johnny the Miller went and got Bouncer out of the pubs and tried to get him interested in other girls, but it was hopeless. Bouncer often wandered down by the Monument during the day and stood looking down over the field where the swingboats had been, as if he might find a clue about Briege.

"I shoulda never went away," mourned Bouncer to Brian McGribben, "an' I'm not much good at the writin' — not but I didn't think about her all the time. But she'll come back …She'll come back. Bouncer kept repeating, like a broken record, over and over again "She'll come back …" But as the weeks wore on and there was no sign of Briege, Bouncer was in the pubs more and more. He drank with the men who came in and spent all the money there was for food for the children. He drank with the ones that wanted to get away from crying babies and cows to be milked and the never-ending drudgery of work to do to make ends meet. He drank with the ones who were restless and didn't know why, or had a limp, or were too small, or too frightened or needed the camaraderie and warmth to feel able to face life. He drank with the ones that "went on the tear" every so often, — sober most of the time, but on a total binge every so often while neighbours kept things going and waited till they came out of the binge. He drank with those who left their women at home to deal with all of it, women who never seemed to break down, and who made them feel like wayward boys when they came home; these same women who produced one of their children yearly, each birth zapping another measure of strength from them, and then they'd drink to forget that. Bouncer drank with lads awed by the ability of a girl to render them powerless by rampant wild desire and bittersweet tenderness, while the priests at the Mission were preaching to them how wrong it all was anyway. He drank with lads like himself who desperately wanted their arms around the girl of their dreams, but it was only in their dreams. The girl wasn't there, or if she was, they watched from afar and didn't have the courage to approach her or ask her out, or touch her.

No doubt about it, Bouncer was a mess. One night in Heaney's pub, at three o'clock in the morning, the lookout man came running in at the very same time that there was a loud 'rat-a-tat-tat' on the big wooden door.

Lights out.

Everyone scattered up into the kitchen in the dark, stashing glasses and bottles of stout under couches and chairs and in suspicious-looking bulges inside jackets. Pat Heaney opened the big door in the semi-darkness. Constable Burbridge walked up the stairs into the empty pub, on up the house stairs into the kitchen, brightly lit with Mrs. Heaney appearing to be making tea for all the men; the baby still at his night feeding; the kitchen full of storytelling, ceilidghing men, looking like they'd been there all night.

"G'night, now, Constable. Why don't you draw up a chair to the fire? I'm sure it's drizzly and cold out there." There was an anxious hush, while all waited for the Constable to speak:

"Maybe a cup of tea, then, but aren't you all gettin' a bit late with the ceilidghing? It'd be a good idea to finish it up earlier." Constable Burbridge knew, and was playing along with all of them.

"Oh, indeed you're right. That's a fact. A person forgets the time sometimes." — Pat Heaney.

"Aye, indeed."

"We were goin' soon anyway."

"The Missus here was just makin' a last cuppa tea."

Bouncer felt terrible. He looked at the patient, worn face of Mrs. Heaney, bent down towards the fire with the baby to feed, and he looked at the face of Pat Heaney, scared that his pub, his livelihood, was going to be shut down, and his licence suspended. It was nearly dawn when Bouncer fumbled for the keys of the old car. He felt rotten, miserable, cold, and his head was spinning. If he could just sleep for a while ... He started down the street, shivering in the grey damp dawn, blearily watching the sun trying to rise through breaks in wispy rain clouds. He thought he saw a cat dart out like quicksilver out of nowhere with what looked like a small crooked figure of a child chasing the cat. Bouncer slammed on his brakes. Was he dreaming? ... drunk? ... hallucinating? ... a child and a cat ...at this hour?

There was a sickening thud, then a scream. Bouncer became instantly lucid and sober. Fear gripped him. He got unsteadily out of the car and saw the small body of Jimmy McAnallan, McAnallan's retarded boy, sobbing over a motionless cat. Bouncer was paralyzed with fear, but realized Jimmy was alright when the boy flailed his fists uncontrollably at Bouncer's legs.

"My cat . . . Beege . . . Where's Beege? . . . Beege gived Jimmy baby cat . . . Then little Jimmy turned his full sorrowful gaze, now turning to a scowl, on Bouncer. Bouncer stood there, ashen white and shaken. His first reaction was relief that it was the kitten he hit, not the boy. Then he realized that it was the kitten Briege had taken from the litter at her home to give to Jimmy.

"Oh, God, what have I done?" thought Bouncer. By this time Jimmy was screaming and howling like a banshee. Bouncer was becoming vaguely aware of lights going on in houses. Mrs. McAnallan came running out wildly:

"Jimmy! My God, how did he get out?" Briege always did tell Bouncer that Jimmy got up at the crack of dawn. She had often found him wandering through the house, but usually she just carried him back to her own bed, where he curled up in the crook of her arm and went back to sleep, safe and peaceful.

"Are you alright, Jimmy?" said Mrs. McAnallan, almost in hysterics. Grabbing her sobbing son she glared at Bouncer and screamed "You could have killed him! You almost killed my son!"

Bouncer stood in the middle of the street, his head hanging, the car still sputtering. Curtains were pulled back and eyes peered out at him.

"I'm sorry, Briege," choked Bouncer, "God, I'm so sorry, Briege. I'm a terrible mess altogether. Bouncer's sobs alternated with Little Jimmy McAnallan's, in a cacaphony of heartbreak, echoing up into the watery dawn sky. "Briege, why did you go? Why? Why? Why?"

When Bouncer went to bring Jimmy McAnallan one of Johnny the Miller's new kittens, Brian McGribben went with him. Bouncer was ashamed and afraid to go alone. Mrs. McAnallan didn't want to open the door more than a crack, but when she saw the kitten and Bouncer's clean-shaven face, new haircut, clean shirt and Brian with him, she called Jimmy. At first Jimmy wouldn't come near Bouncer. He stood crookedly watching the tiny ball of fur with the big grey liquid eyes peeping out of Bouncer's huge hands, holding and gently stroking the cat.

"He's called Blue," said Bouncer gently. "He's for you, Jimmy."

"Boo," echoed Jimmy. "He called Boo."

"I'm sorry, Mrs. McAnallan. I'm off the Drink now," said Bouncer.

"That's alright, Bouncer. We all have them kind of times. Thanks for bringin' the kitten," said Mrs. McAnallan, as she watched Jimmy falling in love with Blue, the new kitten.

Bouncer went often to see Jimmy and Boo, as the kitten came to be known. Bouncer carried Jimmy on his shoulders. Sometimes Jimmy put Boo on Bouncer's head and they'd walk up and down the street.

Bouncer in the Pub

24

gipsy song

my mother said I never should
Play with the gipsies in the wood.
If I did, she would say
"You naughty girl to disobey!
Your hair shan't curl
Your shoes shan't shine
You gipsy girl, you shan't be mine!"
And my father said that if I did
He'd rap my head with a teapot lid!

Anon.

gipsy poem

gay little Anna, the gipsy child
Has a husky voice, and a gaze, half-wild.
"Her dress is of scarlet and tattered blue,
And her shoes have holes where her toes peep
through."

From Ails's school reading book.

25

the gipsies

Callaghan's flour-bag store was the best place in Altnamore to play. It was like being in a muffled, padded world where everything was soft and plump and white and powdery. If they were lucky, the bags would be stacked so that there were steps along the edge to get their bare feet into, and each person could have a level to herself. Voices sounded different in there, and it could be a completely different world in its semi-darkness. They never got bored in the flour store, but then they never got time to get bored because they were always chased out by pompous Seamus Callaghan, the owner, who lived right beside the flour store above the shop. He had eyes in the back of his head and ears that could hear better than a dog. This time, as usual, Seamus rounded them up and chased them out.

They were now playing house on the rocks. Everybody was starting to fight:

"You copied me. I had curtains on the window first," complained Jinny.

"Well, I pretended to have twins first," whined Maura.

"Somebody stole my floor besom," whinged Brigid

"Well, I was the one who asked Lizzie for it," Fiona whimpered.

"I'm sick of playing here," frowned Ails, "Why don't we go back to the flour store?" It was worth it, for the short while they usually did get to play before Seamus emerged to clear them out.

"How do we get in?" asked Maura on the way over. Seamus always kept it locked, and they usually sneaked in and hid one by one while flour bags were being loaded and the men weren't looking.

"There's a hole behind the drainpipe that you can put your hand in, if you know how to pull back the bar," said Jinny.

"How do *you* know?" asked Ails

"I just *know*," answered Jinny in a maddeningly superior tone. And she did know. They sneaked around the back and through the hedge. Sure enough, Jinny got them in. As usual, they had to assign a lookout person:

"You're first." Jinny pointed at Fiona.

"Why do I always have to be first? I was first the last time."

"And you got us all chased out of here because you quit looking out for him and missed him coming in," said Ails. "You be first, or you're not playing," she added with finality. Fiona reluctantly climbed up to the top beside the square ventilation hole, and sat there pouting and looking out while the rest of them were having a great time.

They were only there a few minutes when Fiona called:

"C'mere everybody, quick!" Hearing the urgency in her voice, they all scrambled over beside her and tried to look through the square hole all at once. Fiona made them take turns to look.

"It's my lookout place," she insisted, "It was youse that put me here. Now youse have to take turns. You first, Jinny," said Fiona, trying to build up some points with Jinny. They could all see a little bit.

Across the street at Lizzie's and McCann's shop were two women in brightly coloured skirts and hob-nailed boots. They were wearing big hoop earrings, scarves tied around long, black hair, and big colored plaid shawls that contrasted wildly with the stark, black shawl of Mary Felimy hurrying over to McCann's shop to get away from them.

The gipsies had arrived!

Mary Felimy was standing watching them at McCann's shop window, but pretending to look in the window. One came over to Mary and held out the baby with the plaid shawl wrapped around it. Mary pulled her black shawl tighter round her and turned away. Like everyone else in Altnamore, Mary knew they only borrowed the babies in order to beg. It was now Ails's turn to look out. She saw Lizzie open the door, take one look, and slam it quickly. Ails could just hear her muttering behind the slammed door:

"Thievin' rascals. Tryin' to melt the heart out of you with a baby. You give them a sup of milk for the chile, an' the next thing they want sugar and tea and flour and soda bread. Y' can't let the buggers in on you at all, for they'd take all y' have about the house, and leave you with nothin'!" It worked both ways, thought Ails. The gipsies knew they were mistrusted, and were as sly and cunning as foxes. They were quick and agile, and picked their houses. There was always a softie somewhere. They were now heading down the back way to Heaney's pub.

"My turn," yelled Fiona, but by this time everyone was tumbling out through the back door — forgetting to pull it shut and to lock the inside bar from the outside. This would haunt them later that day. They were off to follow the gipsies. They all ran across the street and down by the byres, with Fiona yelling:

"Wait for meeeeeeee!"

"Nuisance," flounced Ails, "nuisance, pest, nuisance, pest," she chanted about her sister, as she ran to catch up with the agile gipsies.

When they got down by the byres one of the gipsy women was coming out of the henhouse with her apron full of eggs. Ails knew because she had straw sticking out of the bulge in her bunched-up apron. When the gipsies saw Ails and the whole crowd following them, they hurried down past Heaney's back door. Ails heard Rosie Heaney barring the door, which she never did. The word always spread like wildfire through the village about the gipsies. They moved like mountain goats down over the Rocks, hob-nailed boots, babies and all, with a smell of horses and dogs and stale sweat lingering in their wake. When Ails, Maura and Jinny reached the road, with Brigid and Fiona tagging behind, one gipsy woman had vanished. They were as quick as a flash. The one with the eggs was heading down by the big stone Celtic cross to the Monument field. Ails and the rest followed.

146

Sure enough, there they were, camped all around the Monument: myriads of them, colorful, dirty, exotic and fascinating. A dozen or so brightly painted wagons had washing strung up between them, and squads of dirty, tanned, big eyed children climbing up and down the Monument, and running around the brown and white piebald ponies and shaggy dogs. The men were weatherbeaten, shabby, quick to laugh, quick to fight, and sly. When Jinny and Ails got up closer, the smaller gipsy children sidled closer to their mothers, and hid behind their long skirts and boots. There was a feel of sunshine and rain, with the wind blowing the smell towards Ails of heather and whins and campfire smoke and trees and damp glory, all of it coming at her at once. Ails loved the gipsies being here.

But the village didn't. The doors were locked, and the doors that didn't have locks were barred with makeshift planks. Everyone's eyes rolled heavenward at even a mention of the gipsies.

This time it started the same way as always. The gipsies appeared overnight, then all of a sudden the village was flooded with them, women with babies begging, small children climbing into cars and pretending to drive them, young and old gipsy men in the pubs, "things" missing all over the place. This time it was Seamus Callaghan who went down to confront the gipsies and tell them to get off village property, and quit spreading their camp onto neighbouring farmers' fields:

"The dirty divils," Seamus was telling the people in the shop in disgust. "They have the ditches littered with everythin' — paper bags, horse dung, cans, jam jars, burnt out fires everywhere, lumps of fabric...."

"An' them with the best of good clothes giv' to them by decent people," ranted Lizzie later to Nora Andy while Ails was sitting in the chimney corner, her almost invisible spot, pretending to leaf through her school reading book, but listening intently, as usual.

"Not that I can stand the sight of Seamus meself," confided Nora Andy to Lizzie, "but they stole flour out of the storehouse — got the back door open some way, and it with the bar across it on the inside. Wily rascals, them ones is!"

Ails's face was bright red, her heart racing. The flour store door! She remembered in a flash that it was Jinny who had showed them all how to unlock the back door, and in their rush to follow the gipsies, nobody had remembered to relock it. Ails pretended to be concentrating on her book. She was panic-stricken. If Seamus Callaghan ever found out that they'd unlocked that door and left it unlocked, they'd all be killed! The gipsies stole every time they came — but never before had they ever dared to steal bags of flour! There was a lot of flour in each flour bag. Numbers reported stolen kept rising, depending upon who you talked to. Nora and Lizzie seemed to have forgotten Ails was there, half-hidden in the chimney corner.

"Near ten bags of flour I heard they got," said Nan Andy.

"You don't say," said Lizzie "Well, imagine that!" They didn't seem to notice Ails's guilty-looking face. She was going to have to make sure they were all sworn to secrecy...Fiona had such a big mouth...Brigid was kind of stupid like that, too...tomorrow first thing on the way to school... Ails furiously plotted a strategy to make sure they weren't caught for leaving the flour-bag store door open.

"...Y'know, His Reverence even went down to Heaney's pub to stop the fightin'" Nora went on in a hushed voice.

"Ach, no, go on!" said Lizzie in amazement "Who sent for him?"

"Seamus," said Nora. "He was ragin' about all the flour stolen, and wanted the police to get rid of 'them thieves', he said."

"Well?" Lizzie was hanging on every word.

Ails's stomach was tied in knots. If Seamus ever found out...her mother'd kill her...who told Jinny about the door anyway?...

"Well, *then*, His Reverence and the sergeant said that *if* they didn't spread their camp out into the other fields, and *if* they put their children in school, and *if* they came to Mass, and *if* they didn't drink, fight, or steal, they could stay awhile, and nobody'd bother them."

"Is that a fact? Lord bless us," said Lizzie, shaking her head.

"Mrs. P.J. says she knows for definite that in other big towns the council gives them houses to stop them camping in the farmers' fields," Nora went on.

"Ach, sure, it's no good," said Lizzie, "No matter what you do, they'd put years on you. Even if the poor children, God help them, get put into school, they can't learn. They'll never read. They're 'illigiterate.' They're just different." Lizzie shook her head again.

"I know," said Nora, "Mrs. P.J. says come the Spring they'll be off again, but His Reverence says they have to go to school for now."

"Oh, no," thought Ails, "the County Health nurse'll be back and I'll have to get my hair fine-tooth combed for nits and all that." Her mother would cut her hair again, just as it was growing long enough to seem like long hair.

That night in bed, Ails warned Fiona not to mention playing in the flour store. Fiona was delighted to have a secret.

Sure enough, the gipsy children were all in school the next morning. They were always polite and well-behaved in school, especially the older ones. Ails had waited for Jinny at the plantin stile and had already broken the news to her about the flour store door being open and the gipsies stealing maybe even ten bags of flour. Jinny looked maddeningly superior:

"I already know, and you're lucky that I do," said Jinny, triumphantly producing out of her pocket one of Fiona's socks. Young Brian McGribben, who carried in and stacked the flour bags, had found the sock and had given it to Jinny. Brian didn't like Seamus O'Callaghan either. Not many people did. This time Ails was genuinely grateful to Jinny. That Fiona was a menace, losing her sock in such an incriminating place. Just then Big Bunter McGuigan came out and clanged the handbell for everyone to go into school. He clanged and clanged it deafeningly till Mrs. Digby took the bell away and left him

149

crestfallen. Going in through the door, Mrs. Digby had the bell in her hand. One tall gipsy boy went up and opened the door, holding it from banging while she walked in:

"Now look at this boy living like a heathen, and he's got more manners than all you people from decent homes and families." The boy's name was Garrett. He was put in a desk beside Ails. He was all scrubbed and had his hair plastered back. His clothes were all too big or too small, ill-fitting all over him. He was bigger and older than Ails, or Pat Doran, or Shamie or Jinny or Nailly or Dingo, but he was put in their class anyway. He was big enough to be in the Master's Room. He had big calloused hands, scrubbed red, but still there were traces of dirt in the cracks. They stuck out of the end of his sleeves. The pencil looked all wrong in them. When he used a pen and ink he made a terrible mess — blots everywhere, but he turned the blots into dogs and foxes and clouds and every shape imaginable by spreading the ink blots with the point of the pen. Ails watched him in fascination, till the Pigby rapped Ails's knuckles with a ruler and told her to get on with her work, asking her drily

"Do you think you have all day to dawdle over your work, me girl?" Garrett just sat quietly, watching and listening. He never pulled girls' hair, didn't shoot erasers off the end of rulers or stick out his tongue and make ugly faces. He would try to do his work, biting his tongue and screwing up his mouth with concentration, but he always gave up. He was lucky. Mrs. Digby never corrected it anyway. Ails often watched his blue, blue eyes — he was the only blue-eyed gipsy she'd ever seen — while he stared out at the sky through the high windows, with a faraway look. Something stirred inside her:

"Y'know, he's really beautiful," she thought with surprise, "not like the other boys — a bit like the way Shamie used to be sometimes when they used to go with Bella for the cows. Then she shuddered and shook her head as she thought of what Shamie had now become. She couldn't bear the thought that Garrett might ever change, like Shamie had done, into one of those hateful boys. "No, no," she thought emphatically. "Garrett is different." Ails hated most of the boys, but Shamie was particularly miserable lately. When Garrett became conscious of her watching him he'd lower his eyes and become

150

embarrassed. All he ever said was "Yis," and "No," and "Tanks," with an accent like the Southern Irish people who came to visit Jerry Gallagher's grandmother every summer. Garrett always lowered his eyes when he spoke to anyone. Mrs. Digby was nervous and fidgety and somehow fearful around the gipsy children, even though they were so gentle. It seemed she knew she could never touch them. In one of those crystal clear flashes, Ails suddenly realized:

"None of us can touch the gipsies."

Day by day she was becoming increasingly aware of Garrett next to her. One day, late for school again, she knocked a pile of books onto the floor when she sat down in a hurry. Garrett scrambled down nimbly and quick as a wink he had picked them up and rearranged them on her desk almost before she knew what was happening. She felt all tender and sweet inside.

On Friday afternoons they did a "mat." Ails's mat was awful — a square of bilious green jute with cross-stitching in yellow wool, all soiled with sweat from her hands and knotted too tight so the jute was crumpled. She just wanted to burn it. The Pigby gave her a few heavy cuffs on the shoulder:

"You better get this sorted out before you go home this afternoon, me girl, or I'll be seeing your mother." Ails was in a panic. She'd been late three times this week from dawdling up the hill, and going to the secret place of her imagination — she thought a lot about Garrett. If the Pigby talked to her mother, she'd be murdered…The Pigby was out of the room. In despair, she went to pick up the horrible mat to do something with it.

It wasn't there. Ails was in a panic. She looked over at the malicious grin on Shamie's face, and Dingo sticking out his tongue at her. "They took it," thought Ails. "They hid it, and now they're just going to laugh at me searching for it, and watch the Pigby torment me…" She was seething.

But she was wrong.

"I have your mat, miss," said a gentle male voice. It was Garrett.

Without a word his big fingers were twinkling in and out of the crumpled sacking, untying knots, smoothing out the sacking. Ails watched him in astonishment. He couldn't do

151

sums. He wrote letters slowly and laboriously. His blue gipsy eyes showed enormous gratitude each time she had reached over surreptitiously to help him, or to correct answers for him. He got ink blots all over everything. Yet here he was like a magician, deftly and confidently pulling the big darning needle in and out as if it were quicksilver. Everybody was running around the room blowing bubble-gum or talking. Nobody even noticed. Ails looked at Garrett with undisguised adoration.

"Here, miss." He handed it to her — it even looked nice. When she said "Thanks" Garrett looked uncomfortable and lowered his eyes.

Scramble, scuffle, thunk, silence.

The Pigby was back.

Ails, Peggy, and Dingo, bring up your handwork!"

Where was the mat? Gone. Ails looked wildly around. Garrett pointed under the pile of books:

"Makes it smooth, miss," he whispered, his lilting brogue coming through, even in the whisper. That was the most he'd ever talked to Ails.

Dingo and Peggy got the cane.

"Ails, just shows what you can do when you put your mind to it." Garrett just smiled and bowed his head.

"What are gipsies?" Ails asked Lizzie.

"Don't talk to me about them divils!"

"What are gipsies, daddy?"

"They're a tribe of nomad people who originated in Europe, maybe even Asia — India, I think. The name of the tribe is 'Romany'."

"Why don't they live in houses?"

"Oh, they do in some places, but not for long. You see, there are nomad tribes all over the world. For different reasons, these tribes move from place to place. The reasons include food source, climactic conditions or religious beliefs. Now, take migration of birds, for example ..." But Ails had stopped listening.

"That's it," she thought. "Garrett is like a bird, inside himself, fragile, tough, and beautiful." God how she loved him, this blue-eyed gipsy!

"Of course, when I was young," — it was her mother talking, "there were real gipsies, selling flowers, and pots and pans they made themselves from tin. They sharpened scissors and knives too. There are no real gipsies any more. These are just tinkers." She went on bathing the baby.

"But we have commodities like that now, Eileen, commercially produced in factories," her father went on talking to her mother. "They can't compete with that market. It's happening all over the world. The war, of course, made a difference…"

But Ails started up from her chair, bolted out the door and down the street, completely ignoring Fiona yelling after her. She had a sudden gut feeling and knew in a flash that the gipsies were on the move again.

They always left just as suddenly and as magically as they came, taking everything:

"Ach, sure it's in them people's blood," Lizzie always said, "the call of the wild."

But this time Ails knew. She knew they were going. She could feel it.

She hurried out in the damp evening drizzle, running down past the stone Celtic cross to the Monument. Sure enough, the gipsies were going.

There they were, hitching up wagons and horses and shouting:

"Whoa back, there!" in their singsong brogue. They were laughing and bundling children up under the wagon covers, and tying on pots and pans and leading the extra piebald ponies from the fields.

Ails's heart jumped. There was Garrett. He didn't see her, hiding forlornly alone behind the hedge watching, with her cardigan pulled around her head to keep out the penetrating drizzle. Her shoes were soaked. Garrett was running with the dogs alongside the horses, noisy, alive, barefoot, bareheaded, free. Not like in school, not at all.

Eventually they were off, clattering, chattering, singing and squealing. Ails watched the procession long into the distance, till they disappeared, feeling the ache of the part of her heart that went with them.

She walked slowly, silently through the gathering mist, up past the stone Celtic cross, where she could almost feel the relief in the air.

"Goodbye, Garrett," she whispered softly, looking back with a lump in her throat, "Goodbye."

The Gipsies

26

the finn & oisin legacy

While working on her pottery, Ails often listened to Canadian radio. One morning, she slowed down her pottery wheel and turned up the radio when she heard the name 'Finn McCool.' Her mind flew back with a smile to her nephews and niece in their living room in Ireland, acting their play about Finn McCool, son of a king, raised in hiding after his father's death. Finn grew up to be a legendary warrior and ruler in Ireland. Once again, Ails saw mighty Finn, his wife Sava, and their baby son Oisin. She smiled as she remembered them promising Oisin the most loving and secure life they could give him.

The radio was talking about the huge influence of Finn and his son Oisin, extending to hundreds of years after his death. It was even reputed that Mendelssohn's wonderful musical piece from the 'Hebrides Overture,' 'Fingal's Cave,' was called after a Scottish cave with polygonal stones — thought to be a continuation of the Northern Ireland 'Giant's Causeway.' Legend had it that Finn McCool built this wonder of nature out into the wild Atlantic ocean, the radio documentary went on to say. Ails listened attentively to the account of 'Fingal and Ossian' (Finn and his son Oisin) centuries after their deaths. Research into the Celts just before 1800 led to those names becoming very popular, with fashionable ladies like Lady Wilde calling her son 'Oscar Fingal' after Oisin (which became 'Ossian') and Finn (which became 'Fingal').

As she continued to listen, Ails was mystified at these Celtic hero/warrior legends lasting right through the Christian era, into the Middle Ages, and in story and song, far beyond that. Not a word of Finn's mother, his wife, nor of the Druid women who raised him and developed his warrior skills by playing games in his youth. Not a word, either, of Oisin's shocking wife Naombh (Neeve).

So much for the childlike vision of Ails' niece and nephews in Ireland playing Finn McCool's wife, mother of baby Oisin, in their charming living-room play. She had promised the baby Oisin that he would have a mother and father, and the best and most loving upbringing possible.

"But there's no knowing how kids will turn out," thought Ails as she learned from the radio how the grown-up Oisin, out hunting as a young man, had fallen hopelessly in love with a beautiful woman who rode a white horse out of a misty lake. She was Naombh (Neeve) from the Otherworld. Naombh told Oisin he could live with her in *her* world, and he'd never age, as long as he never again set foot on Irish soil.

"Not a bad exchange!" thought Ails. So off went Oisin and lived for 300 years in a happy marriage with Naombh. However, Oisin got a yearning to see his land and his father again. He went back to earth with his boots on, so as not to stand on Irish soil, keeping the promise of Naombh intact.

Another echo of never again standing on Irish soil? Was this a threat — or a promise, or both? Ails thought of St. Columba, exiled from Ireland for secretly copying a book. When *he* was banished, he was told he could never again set foot on Irish soil.

The radio went on to report that an unchanged Oisin, living in eternal youth, arrived back in a *very* changed Ireland, finding only remnants and dregs of stories from very old people about his father Finn. Instead of Celtic warriors and heroes, all attention seemed to be drawn to a religious leader named St. Patrick. Oisin became discouraged, dejected, lonely — and careless — so careless, in fact, that he forgot the prophecy of his wife Naombh of the Otherworld. One night Oisin inadvertently took his boots off. As soon as he stepped on Irish soil, he withered into old age. Even then, though, Oisin went seeking the contemporary Irish phenomenon, St. Patrick. Until his own death at 300+years of age, Oisin went traipsing around the country with St. Patrick, telling him heroic stories of his father, Finn, and the Celtic days of glory.

Not exactly what Ails's niece, playing Oisin's mother in the child's play, had in mind for Oisin.
"But then," thought Ails, "does life explain myth, or does myth explain life?"

27

Bella, Shamie & McCabe

Whenever Ails and Fiona happened to be at Auntie Cora's, before they went home in the evening, they could almost feel Auntie Cora's anticipation that McCabe was coming for his tea. She would comb her hair, wash her face, put on lipstick, and start fussing around the kitchen. McCabe would come in whistling, with the newspaper or some books under his arm, and Shamie tagging along behind him, as usual.

"Well, Cora, what did you think of that 'Irish News' front-page article today, anyway?" he'd say, and they'd be off into another world of ideas, lifting Auntie Cora out of the housework and washing and ironing and cooking and cleaning and sewing. They would talk and argue animatedly. All the time Ails would be trying to maneuver Fiona out of the way before she started wailing when she saw McCabe.

Outside this happy kitchen talk picture, however, Cora's son, Shamie, was changing, thought Ails, right in front of her eyes. He and Pat Doran used to play with the girls sometimes, and were civil to them even when they were with Dingo and Jerry and Nailly and Ian and the rest of the lads. Pat Doran was still nice to everybody, same as he always was, but Shamie was starting to be downright mean and cruel, just like Dingo. He started to hurt Fiona. Even if she was a nuisance, he didn't need to pull her hair and nip her and pinch her, thought Ails. He used to play marbles and cars. He used to go with Bella for the cows on those golden evenings before Bella left for the Mental Hospital in Unragh.

Bella had returned again to Altnamore, as silently as she had left, shellshocked and vacant. As always, she just reappeared, with no talk that she had ever been away, and no big fuss or welcome; just a few whispers of acknowledgment here

159

and there, and the Dan would become more sociable again. This time, as always, it took Bella weeks to come out of her shellshocked state. "They put cords on your head and give you shocks in the Mental," she muttered to Ails this time, when she was beginning to speak again. " 'S awful. An' they tie your arms to your sides. I don' like it there, Ails." Ails couldn't imagine what it was like. All she knew was that Bella came back strangely broken each time.

Now Shamie wouldn't even look at Bella, much less go anywhere with her — or with Ails either, for that matter. When she first came home, Bella skulked past McCabe's, looking furtively at the tiny butcher's shop with curiosity. As time went on, she would walk past McCabe's with her head held high. Ever since she arrived back, Bella would set her lip in that funny way she had when she sorted people out as she saw them — no matter how anyone else saw them. Everybody liked McCabe. But not Bella. Bella never pretended.

Shamie was always, always with McCabe these days. And McCabe wasn't always nice to Shamie, Ails noticed. Sometimes he would be sitting while Shamie and Auntie Cora were talking, and McCabe would ask Shamie to get the sugar, or the butter "for yer mother and don't sit there bone lazy and her workin' all day." Strangely enough, Shamie would go and do as McCabe told him. Shamie would look sullen, and then scared. Auntie Cora didn't seem to notice, even when McCabe would say as an aside to Shamie "ye useless pup, ye." Instead, she brightened up when she realized that McCabe actually noticed that she *did* work hard. Usually nobody noticed.

28

cu culainn

fter her glaze lessons with Dora and Inder and Surinder in the pottery studio in Calgary, and after all the hullabaloo over the Celtic stories her children and their friends were acting, Ails's pottery took a quantum leap. She was the same person. The designs were of the same complexity. But inside her, Ails was more confident, more grounded. She had begun carving flat plaques separately, then, at an appropriate drying stage of pliability, attaching the plaques to the three-legged pots. This was working out so well that she decided to make plaques in their own right, not attaching them to anything. So she sat down at her pottery wheel with a ball of pure white porcelain clay. It felt like churned butter moving richly under hands. She flattened it out to cover the whole wheelhead, trimming off the edges like slippery pieces of wet silk. "Good," she thought, seeing in her mind's eye the glorious circular design, blue and purple, that would adorn this circular plaque.

Later, after she trimmed the plaque, and put hang-up holes through it with a fat milkshake straw, Ails was surprised, as always, at how the silky buttery feel had given way to a chalky texture. It was tricky to get porcelain to appropriate dryness to carve or paint. She got her paints and brush and carving tool ready. As she began to carve through the bluish purple haze, a gleaming white design began to emerge. Ails noticed what looked like a hound's head. As she followed the lines coming out from the neck, they continued on into what looked like a limb of a gigantic man. She was reminded of Cu Culainn, Cu pronounced 'koo' meaning hound, she remembered from her Gaelic (he had killed a hound, and he himself had become the guard 'dog') for Culainn of royal blood, of Irish myth and legend. She hadn't thought of Cu Culainn for years, at least not until her sons got the acting bug.

She remembered, in school, as a child, turning the map of Ireland sideways, where it looked like a furry little dog. That made it easier to draw the map. There was the neat rectangular shape of Lough Neagh. According to legend, this massive giant Cu Culainn left a sunken hole which filled up with water, now Lough Neagh, when he lifted a chunk of Irish earth and threw it into the Irish sea to become the Isle of Man.

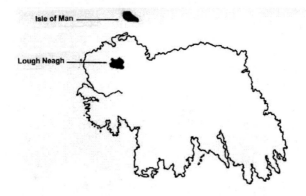

The shape of Lough Neagh didn't quite match the Isle of Man shape, thought Ails, smiling, but it made a good story.

"Larger-than-life giants who could protect and confront and create lakes by pulling up a chunk of square miles and casting it into the sea," went through Ails's head as she carved the circles that looked like jewels on Cu Culainn's sword, and wavy lines that looked like an ocean. Ails remembered looking at Cu Culainn's leather sandals, laced with straps up to his knees, and thinking how wet his feet must have got in such a rainy climate, and wondering what woman wove the wonderful yards of fabric pinned on his huge shoulders and flowing down his back. Was it his mother? Unlikely. She was royal and probably didn't weave her own clothes. Ails suddenly remembered, somewhat disturbingly, how she had read recently that Cu Culainn's parents were brother and sister. "We never learned that in school!" she thought to herself. Keeping the blood pure and unsullied, like gods in other countries. No common copulation could produce a man like Cu Culainn.

"Incest is what we'd call it these days," thought Ails of the sexual taboos of genetics and modern science. Still, Cu Culainn's mother must have been some kind of woman to give birth to such a giant son. Ails idly wondered about how much he must have weighed when he was born.

She thought of her growing boys play-acting Cu Culainn, and inventing other characters, a little more modern, jumping off the couch with capes from her sewing basket, or pieces of sheets pinned to their shoulders, and landing on spread-out mattresses with their swords of light, ready to take on the world.

29

nightmare

When Ails was growing up in Altnamore, babysitting was unheard of. There was always somebody — or everybody — to look after children. Altnamore was like the saying: "It takes a whole village to raise a child."

One rare night, when their parents were going to a teachers' dance in Unragh, Ails and Fiona got to sleep at Auntie Cora's. Lizzie would mind Neeve. Because they were sleeping there, McCabe stayed up at the butcher's — that way, Ails, Fiona and Shamie could all sleep in the room, Pat's old room, which Shamie had recently come to share with McCabe. In the middle of the night, Ails was awakened by the increasing volume of mutterings from Shamie in the next bed. He seemed to be sleeping...but not exactly dreaming...maybe in some kind of a dream-like state?

"No, no, NO, NO, my Master, NO!... mumble, mumble ...Don't hurt me tonight again...mutter, mumble...yes, I'll be your slave...but I'm too sore...mumble, mumble, sob...I couldn't play football and the Master'll tell me mammy and daddy on me...mumble, mutter, whimper...No, I won't shout and wake them up. Just leave me alone...o.k. My Master..." Then a desperate, muffled whisper, Shamie's head rocking wildly side-to-side on the pillow ... "Take yer hand off me mouth; I can't breathe. I'm gonna choke!" Then a stifled scream, and Shamie's face screwed up tight as a vice. " Oh Christ! don't hurt me bum like that. Oh, no, no, NO, NO! Take that thing outta me!... I'm bleedin'...alright, alright, alright, I'll say me nose was bleedin'..." Then quiet, pathetic whimpering, punctuated by desperate sobs.

Ails was sitting bolt upright, transfixed, even though she didn't remember sitting up. She looked across at Fiona, who was also transfixed. How long had Fiona been awake? "My Master? Somebody's slave?" Such a mixed-up nightmare, but Shamie was terrified. And so was Ails for some reason: white, shaking, frightened. Fiona was unusually silent for what seemed like a long time. Then Fiona started to scream blindly, wildly, flailing her arms around, waking Shamie in a panic.

"Shamie, you were talking in your sleep," said Ails.

Shamie's eyes filled with fear.

"What did I say?... Oh, my God he'll kill me... I'm not supposed to tell..."

Just at that moment, the door burst open and Auntie Cora came running in and wrapped her arms around Fiona.

"She had a nightmare," Ails lied instinctively. "We couldn't wake her up." She stole a furtive look at Shamie, and caught his eye, hard and hostile. Ails suddenly needed to vomit. Her stomach seemed to shoot right out of her and splatter all over the bedroom floor. All she could think of at that moment was the trouble they were causing Auntie Cora, with her comforting Fiona, then scrubbing the floor with a rag where Ails missed the chamber pot under the bed with the vomit. The stench was awful.

"You must have eaten something, love," was all Auntie Cora said. "You'll feel better now that you've got that off your stomach. Now you all need to go back to sleep."

But for weeks and weeks, and months and months, and for years and years later, it was not the stench of the vomit, or the screams of Fiona, or the comforting arms of Auntie Cora that would keep bubbling up in Ails's memory, even when she tried to push the memory down. It was the haunting fear in the eyes of Auntie Cora's son, Shamie, that Ails would remember, while his mother comforted his cousins. In dreams, in some dark place of scary secrets, Ails would involuntarily remember, then try to close out the sound of Shamie's sleep-talking, desperate voice "No, no, NO NO! Don't hurt me bum like that, my Master! ... ..."

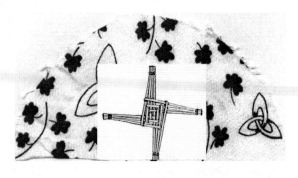

30

st. patrick & st. Brigid

(change agents)

t was St. Patrick's Day, in North America, in Ireland, and all over the world. It should have been named 'Emigrants' Day' as far as Ails was concerned, from the rush to post offices all over Ireland to mail St. Patrick's Day cards and boxes of authentic shamrocks to those who had left. At first, Ails had been puzzled to receive cards and shamrocks from people. Then she mused about a number of interpretations: Maybe it was to keep her from being homesick for Ireland? (which she wasn't) or perhaps, maybe they did miss her, and it was their way of encapsulating what they felt was a little piece of Ireland? Or maybe they needed to reassure themselves that Ireland was still the Ireland they thought it was? It was all speculation on Ails's part.

St. Patrick's Day had never played a great part in her life in Ireland. St. Patrick seemed to take all the fun out of dramatic, colourful, mythical characters who had come before him. But then, she had learned over the years, from her own studies, from her children, from stories of Jesus to Paradise Lost to Star Wars to Harry Potter, that being good never was a big, exciting deal; villains were much more interesting. St. Brigid and St. Patrick both seemed like pious, good, humble, anaemic people living their lives for God — at least, that's how it seemed to Ails

166

growing up, and even now, later in her life. Going to Mass as a child on the St. Patrick's Day holiday in Ireland, Ails could never find for her little safety pin an authentic bunch of shamrocks in the ditches by the plantin. She had often looked in vain for shamrocks, and settled for clover, with telltale white markings in the middle of each leaf — even though it looked in all other respects the same as a shamrock. Every year, ad nauseum, in school they did the story of St. Patrick teaching the concept of the Holy Trinity, three persons in one God, Father, Son and Holy Spirit. Just as there were three leaves on one stem, there were three persons in one God, blah, blah, blah. There were no St. Brigid's crosses to make with rushes to escape the boredom of the story. Nobody paid too much attention to the snake story, where St. Patrick was supposed to have banished all the snakes, although Ails had never in her whole life in Ireland seen a snake.

Even with all of these stereotypes, Ails had a sneaking admiration for St. Patrick, this dignified, tenacious man, who had come and lived among the Irish — an ethnocentric, complex, rugged, warlike, vibrant people who ate, drank, partied, celebrated, fornicated, and practised slavery and sacrifice. Mind you, thought Ails, St. Patrick wasn't there from choice the first time. He was kidnapped as an impressionable youth and worked as a slave, tending sheep on Mount Slemish. They heard the stories in school of how he prayed and prayed.

"I'm sure he did," thought Ails. "I can't think of a more boring job than watching a bunch of dumb sheep and making sure they don't wander off." She hoped St. Patrick had had a sheep dog to help him. Now that was an interesting animal.

St. Patrick's Day fell on a Saturday this year, so Ails's kids were happily playing off at their friends' house, all of them coming back in the afternoon. Ails took her cup of tea and went downstairs to throw some pots on her pottery wheel. As she was working, she turned on the radio, as usual. Today, of course, there were St. Patrick's Day celebrations everywhere. They had on some celebrities and musicians, and interviewed some Calgarians who put on phoney Irish accents, saying things like 'Faith & Begorra' that Irish people didn't say at all, as far as Ails knew. But she got into the spirit anyway, with the haunting music, and sometimes got up and jigged along around the basement, if the music was particularly infectious. She put a lump of clay on the wheel and started it with her foot pedal. Just as the drone of her wheel sounded, she heard on the radio 'Anya,' and missed the surname, 'an authority on hagiography is here to tell us about the authentic St. Patrick and St. Brigid, two Irish contemporary saints, who changed the face of Ireland forever.' Could this be the younger Anya, niece of Ails's friend Anya in Vancouver? Ails turned off her noisy wheel, straining to hear more information. All they said was that she was from Toronto, and was working in some University in Ireland. The girl had a Canadian accent, which would make sense, since she was raised in Canada. It must be the same Anya! Ails listened avidly.

The interviewer explained 'hagiography.' (Ails immediately thought of the study of hags!) It actually meant the study of saints' lives, and Anya was adamant that hagiography was *not* history. It was often written, she said, several hundred years after saints were supposed to have lived. In the case of St. Brigid and St. Patrick, who were contemporaries — Brigid was younger — that would have been the late 5th and early 6th Century. What really surprised Ails's journalistic way of thinking was Anya's statement to the radio interviewer that even given a list of historical facts, an author of saints' live might not even use them! She explained further that this was because there were many reasons for composing saints' lives. While celebrating the saints' sanctity might be one reason, propaganda for that saint's church was also very important. Ails smiled to herself while Anya described what could be construed as modern-day 'marketing techniques' or 'tourism development.'

"A good saint's life would have increased the number of pilgrims attending and journeying to the church or monastery," continued Anya. "Lots of pilgrims meant lots of money."

"And probably lots of accommodation, eating houses and transportation business, not to mention souvenirs and information books" thought Ails in the modern vein. She liked this professor's approach!

"In early Ireland, several groups of associated churches were also jockeying for power," continued Anya. "These power

168

plays are often inherent in accounts of the lives of the founding saints of these churches," she went on, citing later 7th Century concerns about the balance of power between Patrick's church in Armagh, and Brigid's church in Kildare.

"Well, whaddyaknow!" exclaimed Ails to herself, as haunting flute music punctuated the radio interview. "These hagiographers were a bit like marketing agents for the saints' real estate interests!" Ails remembered reading some stuff about how St. Brigid and St. Patrick really respected each other's territory, as far as miracles and 'showing off of power' (as Ails perceived it) was concerned. They seemed to have a mutual respect.

The radio interviewer was back on air, saying "Anya, I must ask you. What do we know in terms of cold, hard facts about St. Brigid?"

"Very little," replied Anya. "One theory is that she may originally have been a pagan goddess by that name, whose attributes were then transferred to a historical Christian woman of that name. Certainly the pagan goddess Brigid and Christian St. Brigid, have several things in common, such as their healing power, association with fertility, and association with fire."

"No wonder Mrs. Digby was so wishy-washy about St. Brigid," thought Ails. Anya was now saying:

"More interesting than historical truth, is how the figures of St. Brigid and St. Patrick represented certain aspects of Irish spirituality." Just at the end of the interview, the electricity went off in Ails's house. Mindful of Altnamore's unreliable electricity, Ails was left with a useless pottery wheel and a silent radio.

She sat for a long time, just looking out of the basement window at the angry, stormy March 17th Alberta sky, now turning into a blizzard. She thought of St. Patrick alone in the cold, camp silence of Mount Slemish, stolen away from his middle-class home, not much older than her own growing sons. Somehow, Anya on the radio had given Ails permission to sift through a whole lot of information she had heard all her life, and thought was real history.

"St. Patrick was brought by Niall of the Nine Hostages ('doesn't that sound like a pirate!' she thought) into obscure slavery, to being known and celebrated all over the world." That was quite a staggering thought to Ails.

"Myths, stories, fabrication, shamrocks or whatever," thought Ails, "St. Patrick must have been some kind of special person," she thought. Ails believed the stuff about his visions and dreams. Most major events of his life seemed to be preceded by a dream or vision, notably his rescue from slavery on a ship 200 miles away. Then his dream/vision message, handed to him in a letter from an Irish native, to "come and walk among us again," — a beautifully gentle invitation, Ails thought. In days long before liberation theology and before 20th Century missionaries were 'inculturated' to respect the local culture in such places as South America and Africa, St. Patrick seemed to have respected the Irish nature-based culture. In the 400 years of Christianity preceding Patrick, 'Christianize' had meant 'Romanize,' it seemed, but St. Patrick seemed to understand the people, language, culture and beliefs of Ireland. "Conversion without coercion," thought Ails. Ails saw this as an amazing feat. But mostly she admired his compassion for slaves — he himself had been a slave.

"What St. Patrick achieved was nothing to sneeze at," thought Ails, or St. Brigid either." St. Brigid seemed to Ails to be so connected to wholesome, nourishing food — probably from living on a dairy farm, she thought. St. Brigid stories were full of the healing powers of warm milk straight from the cow, butter, bread, bacon and beer. She was incredibly generous to the poor. It seemed to Ails that St. Brigid was more like a social worker than a bishop. Even though she seemed concerned about changes in the Catholic church from Rome, she seemed more like a front-line worker than a strategist or a power-player. But then, maybe the lives she'd been reading were written to get more of a certain 'target group' of pilgrims? All she knew was that Cu Culainn and Fin McCool and Oisin and Diarmid and Grainne and Queen Maeve coloured Irish history, but Brigid and Patrick changed it forever.

But St. Patrick bagged the shamrock and won the marketing game over St. Brigid.

"Ah, well, that's life," thought Ails, thinking of Frank McCourt and Maeve Binchy (Fiona called her Mauve Binky) and J.K. Rawlings, and remembering Paul McCartney of the Beatles, saying in a documentary: "The world was looking for something, and we happened to be it!"

St. Patrick was it.

Ails looked at her St. Patrick's Day cards and their messages of love hidden in clichéd sentimental greetings. They were great!

She looked at her now dried out St. Brigid's cross on the wall, winked, and said

"You done good, Brigid!"

hymn

Hail, glorious St. Patrick, dear saint of our isle,
On us, thy poor children, bestow a sweet smile!
And now, thou are high in thy mansions above,
On Erin's green valley, look down in thy love.
On Erin's green valley, on Erin's green valley
On Erin's green valley, look down in thy love.

31

english visitors

Aunt Maisie came home to Altnamore each year to see her mother. Ails's Aunt Maisie was married to a rich Englishman called Michael. She had a daughter Susan who was Ails's age, and a baby Michael, Neeve's age. Aunt Maisie had twinkly eyes. When the three sisters, Aunt Maisie, Auntie Cora and Ails's mother, Eileen, got together, they talked and laughed a lot, looking and acting like three young girls. Michael came to Altnamore with Aunt Maisie a few times. He didn't go into pubs much with Uncle Peter and the other men. He went for walks with Ails's father, both of them with walking sticks, and talked about gardening and governments:

"Th' Englishman and the Master, they look like landed gentry the two of them," said Lizzie.

"Why do they call your dad 'master'?" asked Susan, Aunt Maisie's daughter.

"Oh, all school teachers are called the Master or the Mistress here," said Ails.

"What does landed gentry mean?" asked Susan.

"What?"

"Landed gentry," repeated Susan.

"I dunno," said Ails. "I think they're people that live down in the estate at the foot of the town. They're very grand hoity-toity people," she said, adding "Oh, yes, and they're not Catholics."

"I see," said Susan thoughtfully, sounding as if she did not see at all.

Ails liked her cousin Susan. She was very quiet and thin and white-skinned with silvery blonde hair. Susan had a real fancy English accent, which Ails tried to learn. Susan liked Altnamore. She played with the others sometimes but Jinny didn't like her — said she was 'different,' English as well, and that she should go back where she came from like all the other English people who thought they owned Ireland. Jinny said it was terrible of Ails's Aunt Maisie to only have two children — just like an English Protestant. They'd definitely have to be spoiled and selfish, Jinny reasoned, with all that attention, money and their own beds in their own rooms. Ails didn't find Susan spoiled and selfish at all. She played a lot with Susan alone, because Jinny often persuaded the rest to stay away from them. Susan read a lot of books too. She and Ails acted some parts out of the books with Fiona hanging around them, as usual.

Everybody loved Aunt Maisie and said it was a terrible pity she ever left and married that Englishman "Michael Whats-his-name, an' all the great lads she could've had around Altnamore."

Aunt Maisie's husband had to go back to England "to attend to his business." Ails's father, Ails, Susan and Fiona drove him to catch the boat. On the way there Michael said:

"You've never come to visit us, Paddy. Why don't you come to England with the children? We'd love to have you."

"Well, maybe we will. Neeve's getting bigger. I'll talk to Eileen about it," answered Ails's father.

174

32

ꜰairꝺay

Ails awoke to accustomed mingled sounds: cows lowing, carts squeaking, horses neighing, dogs barking, and voices everywhere.

"How 'y' Jimmy?"

"Hello, gran' mornin'."

"Hope it stays fair."

"Where's the bull y' mentioned, Paddy?"

"Bring them cows on over this way, now!"

Ails jumped out of bed, flung on her clothes, tore downstairs, and straight out the front door, with the familiar "Wait for meeeeeee!"from Fiona echoing after her. The whole street was alive with activity. The horses were tethered to the big mossy stone gate post of Lizzie's yard, pawing the ground and clopping on the cobbles, with bags of hay hanging round their necks. The cows were steaming from their long walks into the village, their warm cow smell permeating the damp morning air. There were dogs barking around the cows' legs, keeping them in different herds belonging to different farmers. A group of big, ruddy-faced, raw-looking men wearing heavy coats, boots and tweed caps were blowing on their big rough hands, slapping each other on the back, guffawing and shouting. Suddenly there was silence, as they all turned towards the horses tied to the gate post.

There was Ails's baby sister, Neeve, picking her baby steps right underneath all the horses toddling in and out through the horses' legs, while they munched contentedly on the hay in their bags.

"Oh, my God!" thought Ails as she began to run to Neeve, "Fiona must have left the door open and Neeve toddled out!" Neeve was laughing and steadying herself, her small fat arms held out, walking under the horses' bellies. All eyes were riveted on her. One of the men grabbed Ails:

"No, chile, don't run, don't scare them horses!"

"But maybe a horse'll kick her!" Ails knew how, when she started losing her balance, Neeve would try to stay upright by breaking into a kind of run, then bash into the closest upright surface, and fall on her face or on her bum. What if she bumped into one of those big horse's legs? It might kick her, and she was so tiny, it would kill her! Ails felt sick with panic.

But Brian McGribben was there. Brian had seen the baby. He was walking quietly along, talking to the horses soothingly, "Awright, fellas, grand day it is. Easy, now, easy..." Brian got down on his hunkers. Ails's heart was beating wildly as she watched Brian coax Neeve closer. He took a sweet out of his pocket, and held it out to her to get her out from under the horses. As she reached, he grabbed her chubby arm, and like a flash, swung her up over his shoulder where she squealed with delight. There was an audible sigh of relief from the group of men. Then they all cheered. Brian smiled and swung Neeve down and placed her firmly in Ails's arms.

"Y' done a great job there, Brian!"

"Good on ye, Brian!"

"Thanks, Brian," said Ails carrying Neeve into the house. Lizzie called from the kitchen:

"Where were you, Neeve-kins?" Fiona, breathless:

"She got out the front door an' walked under the horses' legs, an' everybody was afraid she'd get kicked, an' nobody could get her in case the horses got scared an' Brian sat down an' got her to come out to him an'..." Lizzie's eyes were widening with the realization of what had happened. That Fiona was a pest, tattletale, nuisance, pest!

"Ails, you know you're not to leave that front door open especially on the Fair Day. Wait'll I tell yer father!"

"Fiona, you can't keep your big mouth shut. And anyway the horses didn't even know she was there. Isn't that right, Brian?" Brian was sitting on the window sill.

"Oh, they knew alright, Ails. Horses can sense a wean like Neeve, but they'd never kick unless somebody panicked them. Trouble was they mighta got scared if she bumped into one of their legs...Ah, well, she's safe now. Thank God it wasn't under the cows she went!"

"Phew!" thought Ails. She felt shaken from the incident. She didn't have the heart to make faces at the cows to try to make them blink, or to scratch their ears or ruffle their goldy brown fur like she usually did. She just looked over at the wreaths of mist that hung over the plantin and was glad Neeve was alright.

"Thanks, horses," she said on the way in for her breakfast. It was boiled eggs. Ever since she went to the hospital, Ails couldn't stand the sight of boiled eggs, but Lizzie gave her one every morning anyway. She left it in its shell as usual, going off out the door with "starvin' childer in India" ringing in her ears. She wended her way through the Fair, with Fiona, the pest, coming after her. She dawdled backwards up the hill to school, looking down at the moving mass of people and animals and dogs and vehicles on the street.

As usual it was clean-up day at school, the third Friday of every month, Altnamore Fair Day, when only a handful of children came to school — all the others were helping at the Fair. Country children led very different lives from city, town or even village children. They stayed home from school at potato-picking time, at haying time and harvest time, to mind babies while their parents both went out to work in the fields.

"Youse don't know how good yiz have it!" Lizzie drummed into Ails and Fiona, describing how she, as a country child, "worked harder than youse town childer ever knew how to!" The County school truant officer had given up trying to get working country children to come to school on this important trading day, so the teachers decided the best thing to do was to have the remaining children clean the school. Ails dusted and brushed and she and Maura cleaned behind the maps and washed the blackboards and banged out the blackboard dusters, making chalk patterns and matchstick people on the wall outside. The very few bigger ones in the Master's Room scrubbed the wooden floors, removing chewing gum with penknives. Everybody who could carried buckets of disinfectant and threw them down the wooden, outdoor toilets. The Master and Mrs. Digby sat at their desks correcting books, hardly looking up except to spot a place someone had missed in the cleaning. The incentive to clean was that everyone got out of school for lunchtime as soon as the cleaning was finished. Today, as usual, they worked feverishly, got out early, and ran like mad down the hill into the Fair.

It was easy to make money at the Fair, running messages for people. They all ran to the furniture van which was now unloaded. They sat in the big plush green velvety couches. When they were shooed away, they hid under the heavy wooden tables and chairs, running their hands over knobbly legs and rungs, rocked in the big padded rocking chairs and made faces at themselves in the big mirrors propped up against the Rocks. They bounced on the big brass beds. Then they ate at Lizzie's. It was always a lovely dinner on Fair Days because it was cooked for everyone and Ails could sneak extra potato pudding and apple tart. Potato pudding was her favourite. It was potatoes cooked and cooked for hours and hours with butter and milk, until, inexplicably, they turned into a sort of paste that tasted like butter made from nuts! It didn't make sense, but tasted delicious. Lizzie usually paid Ails to go down before and after she ate her lunch to count how many people were going into Jinny's eating house or into McCallans' — who only opened up on Fair Days. Then she had to count how many were in Lizzie's at the same time, since Lizzie herself was too busy to have time to count. Ails wrote down the time on Jinny's grandfather clock she could see through the window, and the numbers in three columns under it, and Lizzie would later look and look, cluck and ponder, asking Ails what they had been eating in Jinny's eating house, since she had been able to see through Jinny's window.

On the way back to school, Ails watched the men buying and selling cows. They took out big, thick wads of crumpled pound notes, shouted a rigmarole of figures, haggled, argued, and sometimes yelled, cursed and got mad. When the deal was finished and the animals sold, they'd give each other a great resounding slap on big horny work-worn hands, and let out a huge, bellowing laugh. Today Ails heard one dealer turn away immediately and mutter:

178

"Thievin' bastard, take the eye outa yer head, he would."
Ails and Fiona pushed their way through the nervous giggly
sheep moving this way and that, bleating and crying like babies.
They teased one of the goats, jumping in front of it, and making
faces. When the goat put down his head and ran at them, they
jumped nimbly out of the way. It was Packy Martin's goat, and
he shook his stick and yelled at them to get back to school.

"Some of youse childer wouldn't be alive t'day if it
wasn't for that goat's milk, and that's all the thanks youse have!"

Back to school. It was easy. On Fair Days they had art
class in the afternoons. Ails painted Neeve under the horses'
legs. They legs weren't very much like horses' legs, and Mrs.
Digby didn't like the red colour of danger all around the baby.
That's why it didn't get put up on the wall. The same art was
always on the wall because the same ones got art every Fair Day.
Barney Og Toner was different. His art was up all over the place
because he drew beautiful birds and animals with shading and
clouds and trees all round them. Barney Og was never even there
on most Fair Days when they did art in school. He spent a lot of
time drawing on pieces of paper. On the way out Ails noticed
Fiona's picture of Neeve under the horses' legs. It was up on
Miss McCartney's wall. She could draw really good pictures,
even if she was a pest.

As soon as the art stuff was cleaned up and the place
spotless, they could go home from school. That was the time
they could go down to the Fair stalls. Ails thought all the way
down where to spend her money she had got from Lizzie the last
Fair Day. There were thousands of things: second-hand clothes
and shoes, jewellery, combs, buttons, hair clips, toys, ornaments,
spools, tools, pots and pans and kettles, spoons, shoe polish,
black lead, irons, silver polish, camphor, chamois…It was hard
to decide. The people minding the stalls were always the same.
They wore big aprons with money jingling in the pockets. They
had flasks full of steaming strong tea and thick sandwiches. Ails
finally bought a plastic round ornament. When turned upside
down and back upright snow fell on trees, houses and mountains.
Altnamore rarely got snow. It was lovely. Every Fair Day Ails
looked wistfully at the silver music boxes where the ballet

dancer turned around when the music played. They cost a lot. She sighed, wishing she could buy one.

Now, for money for sweets. She went up to McCallan's to dry a few dishes. Mrs. McCallan paid her immediately, not like Lizzie who'd wait till the Fair was over and all the good stuff gone. Good, it was nearly time for the auction. It was hard to get a place where you could see the auctioneer, who stood on a box beside the big stone Celtic cross. Everywhere was crowded with men, women, bicycles, cows, sheep, goats, vans, lorries, carts and stalls. Today Ails, Fiona, Maura and Brigid crawled through people's legs, right to the front. Jinny was already right at the front. Even though she stayed home to help her aunt in the eating house all Fair Day, she never missed the auctioneer. Even with her buck teeth, Jinny was the best at playing auctioneer. They all watched mesmerized, while the auctioneer interspersed figures with "Whaddleyegimmenow?" or "Whaddimibid?" while people raised a hand or nodded a head or moved an eyeball. One item after another went: furniture, hammers, saws, cans of oil, tractor parts, plough fittings...When it was over, the Fair began to break up, with lads marshalling dogs and animals, stall owners packing up and men drifting into pubs. Ails and the rest wandered slowly down the street. They had to be home early, because often there were fights on the Fair evening. They were standing at Oiny's pub door when the new young policeman, replacing Constable Burbridge, walked stiffly past them. Policemen never stayed long in Altnamore. As soon as they got to know the people, they were transferred to another town. It was said this new man was a Catholic, but he didn't look it. He was young, fair-haired, tall and clean-cut.

"Ach, hello, Constable, so you're the new man? You came in place of Constable Burbridge? Terrible nice man, he was. Used to come in here all the time." It was Annie Oiny, her arms folded over her enormous bosom. She waited and they all watched.

"Yes, my name's McCullough." They could see Annie pondering his name and probably trying to figure out which side he was, Catholic or Protestant. It was hard to tell. Sometimes a Catholic man married a Protestant woman, or vice versa, and the name could be misleading. But not too many Catholics were policemen. Annie went ahead talking to the new policeman.

"Well, glad to meet you, Constable McCullough. Now any time you're around you're welcome to a cup of tea in your hand, or maybe a wee drop of the 'cratur'...?"

"Oh, I'd never drink while on duty, but thanks for the offer of the tea. I may take you up on it at another time." As he walked on up the street, Annie's smile changed quickly to a frown, as she called Packy, her man out to the door.

"Closin' time tonight, not a minute over. No drink in the kitchen, Packy. D'you hear me, now? That's a hard man, that one!"

The streets were almost cleared up and dusk beginning to gather as Ails and the rest walked up the street, jumping over the cow and horse dung and kicking around the hard balls of goat and sheep dung. They were standing around the pump, squirting water in jets with their fingers, nobody really wanting to go home, but knowing they had to. The last bus came up and stopped at McAleavey's. Miss Prim and Miss Prissy, secretaries in the town of Unragh got off and minced down the street. A few others straggled off the bus into McAleavey's shop.

Then a slim, blonde lady in a powder-blue fashionable suit got off the bus. She was carrying a beautiful baby boy with dark, curly hair, and big, round, dark-brown eyes.

The lady looked vaguely familiar. She walked towards Jinny's house.

"My God," said Jinny in disbelief. "It's Briege Mullin!"

Altnamore Fair Day

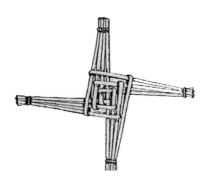

33

st. Brígíd's crosses

From a west-coast Canadian marsh, Ails and her sister Fiona were cutting rushes with a picnic knife. Ails was quite excited to find rushes growing there — they didn't grow on the prairies where she lived. Looking out the window of the car for a picnic site, here in the West European-type climate, sure enough, there were thousands of rushes growing in a boggy-looking expanse, that could have been in Ireland except for huge bulrushes and some unfamiliar-looking species of ducks. Ails had the idea of cutting rushes and making St. Brigid's crosses, thinking it would be great to show the kids. But the kids couldn't care less. Ails' and Fiona's four children were busy getting sodden wet and muddy, chasing wildly around among bewildered ducks.

"Ach, let them tear away," said Fiona. 'There's dry clothes in the car." Ails and Fiona brought the rushes over to the plastic tarp they had spread to sit on.

"I don't know if I remember how to make these," said Fiona.

"How could you forget?" retorted Ails. "We made them often enough!" Ails and Fiona had done this every year in school in Ireland, on the first of February, St. Brigid's feast day, all the years they were in school. As soon as they started bending the second rush around the first one, then another one around those two, adding the fourth to start weaving, it was like riding a bike. They automatically knew how to hold the ends and rotate them, keeping the tension to form the shape of a cross. An old, familiar, comforting, geometric square began forming in the centre, bearing an uncanny resemblance to the Celtic designs Ails used to decorate her pottery.

Ails and Fiona worked quietly, keeping half an eye on the squealing, splashing kids, until Fiona reminisced:

"Remember those stories about how subservient and martyred St. Brigid was? She went around with the priest to help the dying die?" asked Fiona.

"That's the way we heard it, alright " answered Ails, remembering how wimpy and saintly and utterly boring St. Brigid sounded, never complaining, standing beside some priest or other, giving the Last Rites, and holding the cross up before the dying person's eyes. She was a sort of handmaiden of the Lord, they were told, which sounded to Ails, even then, like a lowly servant hanging around to see what bits and pieces of tasks she could perform, and keeping out of everyone's way. Although Ails loved making the St. Brigid's crosses, she never was that impressed with the St. Brigid story, but at school they were usually making the crosses at the same time as Miss McCartney or the Pigby or the Master were droning on about St. Brigid, so she never really listened that closely. Fiona's and Ails' crosses were shaping into fine, thick, healthy-looking specimens, with gorgeous, woven middles, Finished weaving, however, they had nothing to tie the ends of the crosses with. Ails noticed a thread hanging out of the bottom of her blouse under her sweater. She pulled and pulled. Luckily, it was one of those that unravelled the whole hem. They broke off pieces of thread with their teeth,

184

winding them around and around the fat rushes, and then tied knots to secure the edges. When they had finished all four sides, they cut the rushes off so they had straight edges.

"Pity they'll dry out and lose their plumpness," said Ails.

"Just like us drying out," said Fiona, "except we don't lose our plumpness!" They both laughed.

"Oh, yeh, I forgot — I was gonna tell you what our course said about St. Brigid," said Fiona. "Y'know, in a University class, we watched a film about women in religion, and it said St. Brigid was actually a very powerful woman. In this film, she didn't sound at all like the wimp we learned about."

"Well, remember that story I told you about her plucking out her eye to avoid getting married and calling up a stream from the dry earth — that's not the way we thought about St. Brigid in school at all.".

"She was the daughter of a Druid priest and a Christian woman, I think," said Fiona. "Anyway, she sort of straddled the Druidism-Christianity thing and understood both sides, and I think she was even a Bishop, managing the transition from 'pagan' gods to the god of Christianity."

"She was around as a Bishop in St. Patrick's time, and worked her share of miracles, I've heard," said Ails.

"And that old bat, Mrs. Digby, telling us St. Brigid was just going around behind the priest, giving dying people sips of water and making sure they saw the cross before they died!" exclaimed Fiona. "St. Brigid sounded worse than that old Biddy McGinn. Remember Lizzie used to talk about her kneeling, muttering at the altar rails like a goat eatin' a hedge. She spent her time cleaning up after that big lump of a priest, Father McStay, we had in Altnamore!" Fiona got up and trailed around in that deadpan, lacklustre way Biddy used to, with her head bent in mock respect. Fiona was a good mimic.

"Is there anythin' else you'll be wantin' done, now, Father, before I go?"

"Wonder what St. Brigid would have thought of Father McStay, shaking his jowls and shouting at her, and her a Bishop?" said Ails.

"It sounded like she must have had to deal with plenty of guys like him, dragging a country kicking and screaming from Druidism and magic and herbs and cures and gods into something that was alien to them. Can you imagine the resistance? And a *woman* steering through all of that!"

"I'm amazed, all right," said Ails, "especially given what we were taught about her."

"So much for St. Brigid's hard work," said Fiona. "Scratch the surface and you find Druid. Sure, look at all the cures, folk and herbal and spells you can get down the country. That stuff has survived and been passed down through centuries."

"Well, plenty of other things sure changed since ole St. Brigid's time," said Ails. "Can you imagine a female bishop now — anywhere? But especially in Ireland? The land of saints of scholars, with no birth control, no abortion, no divorce, no escape from the glories of womanhood."

"I know," said Fiona cynically, "I don't know how many times I've heard 'Ach, Fiona, it's a pity you only have two children. Eh...Er... female problems, maybe?'"

"Wait for meeeee!" It was Fiona's younger daughter yelling. The other three kids had left her behind in the marshes, trying to plough through on her short legs. Ails and Fiona got up.

"Now, what are you doing, leaving her behind?" Ails scolded her two boys and Fiona's older girl, Nuala. "You know she's smaller and younger. You guys were small like that one time too, you know!"

"I don't see why we always have to look after her!" chimed Nuala. "She's too slow. We always have to bring her everywhere!"

"Jeez, it's hereditary," thought Ails, remembering herself complaining about Fiona in Altnamore. The kids started examining the St. Brigid's crosses, as Fiona went towards little Lizzie, calling:

"Come on, love, you can make it." She toddled up. Her wails stopped immediately when she saw the others turning over the St. Brigid's crosses in their hands. All four of them were totally enchanted, dripping wet, eyes shining.

"Wow, these are really neat!"

"Can I hang this up on my wall?"

"Mom, you should draw these on your pots!"

"Did you guys *really* make these from rushes?"

"Where'd you learn to make these?"

"Did you make stuff like this in the olden days?"

"Can you show us how to make these? Is it hard?"

"Couldn't you just tie the ends with grass?"

As all six of them gathered up armfuls of rushes to bring home, Ails and Fiona told them how all the schoolchildren in Altnamore learned to make St. Brigid's crosses every February 1st.

"Like a special art class every year?" asked Quinn, Ails's younger boy.

The four children changed into dry clothes. They ate on the rush-strewn tarp, munching sandwiches and cookies and drinking juice. Ails and Fiona told the two boys and two girls the story of St. Brigid, the powerful woman Bishop who lived in Ireland a long time ago, and helped guide the population from the old folk faith of Druidism, with its many gods, stone circles and magic practices, into the era of Christianity, with only one god. They told them she was as powerful as St. Patrick, and worked miracles and took care of the poor.

They also told them that Brigid was their granny's middle name, in honour of this powerful saint — not that Granny would believe their version of the story. Nor would Brigid, Maura's sister, with eight children and an alcoholic husband — Brigid, who'd always been so proud of her name, the name of a powerful woman, on February 1st. For too long on that side of the Atlantic they'd had their own version — closer to the holy Biddy McGinn one ...

"Cool story!" agreed all four kids.

Ails and Fiona sent Granny photos of the kids making St. Brigid's crosses at Fiona's kitchen table.

34

guess who's Back?

Long ago in Altnamore, the Fair evening that Briege Mullin got off the bus with a curly-haired baby boy, everyone still left on the street stood there in shock. Jinny walked down towards her house. Ails, Maura Brigid and Fiona followed as if the whole procession was in a trance. Briege home again? And a baby with gravy eyes! They all went up the hallway in Jinny's to the tea room where Briege sat, with the baby playing on the floor. Briege was very thin and very pale with dark circles under her eyes, but she still looked like an angel — more ethereal than ever, as if you could see through her skin.

"But Briege, you never even said you were alright or nothin'...over two years...yer poor mother, aw God the shame on yer family..." It was Jinny's Aunt Kate talking. Briege bristled.

"We got married right and proper, in England," she said, showing a wedding band. "Ricky has a father and mother, and I brought no shame on nobody. I brought him home because I didn't want to go to America. Bruno had to go there to get work. He was always in show business, and not used to construction and brick laying. I didn't want to bring Ricky up in America." Ails looked at Ricky. He was the loveliest child any of them had ever seen. He was half-crawling, half-walking, and playing with Jinny's cat.

"But what about Bouncer?" asked Jinny's Aunt Kate.

"What about Bouncer?" said Briege defiantly, but her eyes softened momentarily. She held her head up again:

188

"He was away a long time, and he never even wrote. I could marry who I wanted!"

"Ails and Fiona, youse have to go home!" This time it was Mary Margit on her way home from the Fair. "Kate, I'm here for a bottle of milk..." Her mouth fell open when she came in and saw Briege and Ricky. She ordered tea and soda bread just to hear what was going on, even though she'd already had her tea at Lizzie's. Ails and Fiona went off home, mad to be missing everything at Jinny's, but dying to tell everyone Briege was back. The first one they met was Brian McGribben:

"Well, Ails, yer wee sister findin' any more horses to walk under?"

"Briege Mullin is back."

"What?"

"Briege is back — she's in Jinny's."

"Are youse jokin'?"

"No, honest."

"My God, Bouncer.... must get Bouncer..." Brian went off into Devine's pub. They ran after him and stood peeping through the crack between the doors. They saw Bouncer's face drain of colour when Brian took him aside and spoke to him. They had to go home in case of fights on the Fair Evening, with all that money around, and men drinking, their father had said. But there was a new policeman, and Annie Oiny said he was a hard man, so it would be quiet, reasoned Ails. Maybe they could follow Bouncer to Jinny's?... Their father was standing on the cobbled street by Lizzie's looking out for them. They started to run. He lifted Fiona up and took Ails's hand.

"You're late, y'know!" he reproached them.

"But Briege Mullin is back," reported Ails.

"Oh?" remarked their father, with only mild curiosity.

Then Fiona started to go on like a gramophone record, as usual.

"We saw her comin' off the bus, an' she has a baby, Ricky an' he's lovely an' they're in Jinny's an' Jinny's Aunt Kate says her mother's heart was broke an' that Bouncer took to the Drink he was that wrecked an' what does she think she's gonna do now, with that chile on her own an' no husband an' everybody in the village'll be talkin' an'..."

"Whoa there, whoa! You don't need to be getting into all this gossip. Straight up to bed, now," said their father. He hated gossip. Fiona went reluctantly.

"I have to go round the back to go to pee. Fiona went already," said Ails, although she didn't have to go at all. She just *had* to be the first to tell Lizzie and watch Lizzie's expression. She went back in through Lizzie's scullery, where Lizzie and her niece Mary Biddy from the country were washing mountains of dishes from the Fair. Mary Biddy looked just like a horse, as usual.

"Briege Mullin's back." Lizzie dropped a plate, and her mouth fell open. Ails went on with glee. "She has a baby called Ricky and the Bruno fella from McTavish's show went away to America on his own." Lizzie's eyes widened with a hundred expressions, and she dropped the cloth, speechless. Ails was enjoying this. The horsey-looking niece, Mary Biddy, said:

"Where is she? When did she come? Did you see her? Does Bouncer know?" Meanwhile Lizzie regained her senses.

"God save us all. After what she done, that hussy has the nerve to come back to this part of the country. No shame, after her ruinin' that Bouncer's life, poor lad."

"Oh, she got married." Ails added more fuel.

"Married, me foot!" spat Lizzie, "in one of them registered offices, I'm sure. Them people's never married right." Lizzie shook her head. "What's she doin' back here anyway? He likely left her. An' a chile. What's the chile like?"

"He's gorgeous," answered Ails. Lizzie to her niece:

"Mary Biddy, away down to Jinny's with them milk bottles and see how things is goin'. Mary Biddy grabbed the soapy bottles and was gone like a shot, ostensibly to return the milk bottles to Jinny's uncle, the milkman.

"God bless us, this is terrible." Lizzie didn't seem to know what to think. "An' where's he again, that dark show fella?"

"America — goin' into show business."

"Ricky, did y' say? Such a name for a chile. Sounds like hay ricks to me. Not a name for a Christian at all, at all." Lizzie clicked her tongue.

190

"Ails come on. *Bed*, I said." Ails had been unaware that her father was at Lizzie's kitchen door, glaring at Ails. He had obviously been listening, and was not at all pleased that Ails was 'getting involved in gossip.'

Ails lay in bed listening to the bicycles creaking up the hill, the ting, ting in Fergie the Blacksmith's forge, and wondered about Briege — timid, quiet, angelic Briege who vanished so suddenly and dramatically from Altnamore, to return later with pride in her eyes.

Next morning Ails sat on the stairs with her ear to the wall of Lizzie's kitchen. Mary Biddy always stayed in Lizzie's the Fair night. Mary Biddy was telling Lizzie:

"An' Bouncer come in an' near fainted. Briege got red in the face. That lad's daft in the head about her, and that's a fact."

"An' after what she done to him, the slut!" Ails could just see Lizzie's eyes, hard as brown nuts.

"She's not a bit sorry, y'know. Very proud, she is, an' when her mother arrived — Tommy McAnallan went and got her mother — she wanted Briege to come home with the chile, and Briege said no, she'd work for her keep. She asked Mrs. McAnallan then and there if she'd take her back for less pay on account of the chile with her. Of course, Mrs. McAnallan said surely — y'know how good Briege was with wee Jimmy, the retarded lad — an' anyway Mrs. McAnallan said Briege was a great worker. Bouncer carried the chile down to McAnallans' for her. God I wish I had a man as daft about me!" said Mary Biddy, and Ails could just see her horsey face lengthening.

"Oops," thought Ails, as she heard Neeve's baby steps coming across the landing with her mother. Not wanting to be caught eavesdropping, Ails opened the door quickly and walked up the hallway.

"Ails!" called her mother, "Can you run over to Callaghan's for a white spool? I have to sew those buttons on your daddy's shirt first thing. Can you take Neeve?"

"Yeh," grumbled Ails, taking Neeve by the hand. "If it's not Fiona, it's Neeve." Callaghan's wasn't open so she walked on down to the Post Office. After the Fair there was always money to be found on the street. Today she was lucky. She found two threepenny pieces and a sixpence. While she was hoking around looking, she heard baby sounds and Bouncer's voice. She looked up and saw Bouncer walking towards her with Ricky toddling along holding one hand and Jimmy McAnallan, the retarded boy swinging off the other hand. Ricky was walking unsteadily. He shook free of Bouncer's hand and held out his arms to Neeve. They both fell. Ails and Bouncer laughed.

After that Bouncer was inseparable from Ricky and McAnallan's retarded boy, Jimmy. He played with them and always seemed to have one of them on his big shoulders, and another by the hand. But Briege wouldn't marry him, though everyone in the village said she should. She held her head high at Mass on Sundays, and apologized to no-one. People began to look at her almost with envy. Was this the same timid angel who left Altnamore with the travelling showman?

One Saturday when Ricky was two and a half, Briege and Bouncer got married by the big priest. Nobody knew except the McAnallans. Not even Jinny. Biddy McGinn had been praying "like a goat eating the altar rails" as usual, and rushed down the hill to tell the whole village. By that time, Briege and Bouncer had already left to go away for the weekend to Dublin.

Again, Briege had done things her own way, and surprised everyone.

35

gossip poem

Gaelic language	Pronunciation	Translation
Dubairt bean liom	Durch ban lum	A woman told me
Go dubairt bean leite	Go durch ban layhee	That a woman told her
Gur dubairt bean eile	Gur urch ban ella	That another woman told her
Gur innis bean di,	Gur innish ban jee	That a woman told her
Go bfaca si bean	Go wawka she ban	That she saw a woman
Ag bun na sceice	Egg bun na skay-he	At the bottom of a bush
Agus bean nar bean	awgus ban nar van	And it wasn't a woman at all
A's go sidhe bean i	iss go she-van ee.	But a Fairy Woman.

Ach, but I'm weary of mist and rain
And roads where there's never a house or bush
And tired I am of bog and road
And the crying wind and the lonesome hush
And I am praying to God on high
And I am praying Him night and day
For a little house, a house of my own
Out of the wind and the rain's way.

From *The Old Woman of the Roads*

193

36

sατurδαy sort-ουτ

a regular event of Ails's childhood was Auntie Cora coming up to talk to Ails's mother most Saturdays.

"No more bad dreams, Fiona?" asked Auntie Cora, referring to the awful night they slept at her house when Shamie had the bad nightmare, and Ails threw up.

"Shamie bad dreams," said Fiona, shaking her head.

"Yes, you had a bad nightmare," said Auntie Cora. "What did you dream about?"

"Shamie bad dream," repeated Fiona.

"You'd nearly think it was Shamie who had the nightmare," said their mother. Something stopped Ails saying "Yes, yes, it was Shamie, and he was terrified!" But she said nothing. Ails's stomach was still rumbling days after Shamie's nightmare. She couldn't eat for a few days. It wasn't that she was still sick. It was more that her stomach seemed to be paralyzed with strange, unfamiliar fear. She couldn't get Shamie's haunted face out of her mind. Yet he had threatened her the next morning.

"You say nothin' about me talkin' in me sleep, y'hear? If you do, I'll get Dingo to beat you up." Shamie was no longer the Shamie Ails used to know. He was cruel to her, and getting into fights at school. Once a great footballer — to the rest of the school lads, anyway — now he wouldn't play. After school he went straight to McCabe's shop every day. McCabe — bright, laughing McCabe whose cold hard blue eyes turned on Ails and

Fiona, and even Shamie, when no-one was watching. Ails shook herself out of her thoughts.

"Sorry they were so much trouble that night," said Ails's mother, seeming guilty about leaving Auntie Cora with nightmare and sickness problems, while she was off enjoying herself.

"No bother at all," said Auntie Cora. Then her voice lowered. "Eileen, I don't know what we're going to do with Shamie." Ails's mother immediately shooed them outside to play. Then she called "Ails, how's your stomach?" Aside to Auntie Cora, she said "Her stomach has been queasy for a while, and she's bedwetting again — she'd stopped for a few years." Back to Ails she called "You better not go out till you're completely better. Go upstairs and read a book." That usually meant 'don't be listening to what we're talking about' when Auntie Cora and her mother were talking in those hushed voices.

That was when Ails hid herself in her hiding place in the cubby hole under the stairs, with the hole in the wall nobody knew about. She had a trick of opening the stairs door, sounding her shoes on the lower stairs getting softer as if she was going up the stairs, then the door swinging carefully shut while she tiptoed around to the under-the-stairs cubby-hole, where she could hear everything that went on in the sitting room, and even look through the hole — unnoticed on the other side with the patterned wallpaper. She always sat in absolute silence, still as a mouse, hanging onto every word her mother and Auntie Cora said, even when she hadn't a clue what it was they were talking about. It was so much more dramatic when they talked like that, more so than when they talked with everyone around.

"Y'know, Eileen, he was never a bit of bother, not even when Colum was born, till the older ones left for America. We don't know what to do with him ever since. We're at our wits' end. Pat and Mags going — God knows, it's affected all of us ... we bear children for export," she said with an edge of bitterness in her voice. "I know there's nothing here for them, but it breaks your heart, all the same." Auntie Cora cried less and less when she talked of Pat and Mags who left for work in America, one shortly after the other. She might as well have cried, though. Her eyes showed her grief. "They might as well be dead," her eyes

195

said. Ails thought of the few that went to America who ever made it home for a visit. Not many, despite all the talk of millionaires and loads of money they all made. 'Unskilled labourers' was what Ails's father called those who went to America. "You work at your schooling, child, and you won't have to go," he said after each announcement of someone else leaving Altnamore for America. The women stayed with relatives and cleaned houses or worked in food places. The men worked in construction trades or in whatever business the relative could get them a job, usually in New York or Boston. Mostly the young men seemed to join the Army and Altnamore would hear of their exotic travel.

They all had some things in common. They were all successful, some outstandingly so. They all sent money home. Everybody knew in every village, that the postmistress opened these letters and counted up exactly how much people got. Then she would be the first to know who would be the next to be 'doin' up their house,' plastering up walls, making new curtains, getting new furniture made, and buying new clothes for all the other kids.

"Nosey old busybody," Lizzie always said about Altnamore postmistress, Mrs. McConnell. Money or no money, however, Auntie Cora's children were gone forever. No longer would Pat come in from work and say 'H'lo Ma,' in his slow, quiet drawl. No more would he tell her about the day's goings-on at the flour store while he washed the flour off himself in the scullery and changed his clothes for his evening meal. No more would he sit and sketch wonderful, lifelike drawings of dogs, of Cora, of Shamie and Colum and joke quietly with his beloved ma. Years later, they would find all the sketches in a book beside Auntie Cora's bed when she died. Her older daughter, Mags, was the light of Auntie Cora's life. She was as lively as Pat was quiet, always with a quip on her lip. Auntie Cora loved sewing dresses for her to go to dances. All the boys loved Mags, and one special one, John Slane, was left with a broken heart. He waited for her to come back for years, every so often calling into Auntie Cora's for news of her. He finally gave up on her, but not until after she married an Irish American in Boston.

Auntie Cora was now sobbing. "Honest to God, Eileen, Shamie's desperate. Peter gave him a hiding the other night, his work in school was so bad. God knows if Pat or Mags hadda been here, they could've talked to him maybe better than me or Peter. But he was never a problem when they were around. An' I must admit, I've been that heartsore meself about Pat and Mags goin' that I haven't had the heart for Shamie I maybe should have had... with Colum teething and up at night an' all. Mags used to put Colum to sleep ..." Ails leaned closer to the peephole in the wall. Auntie Cora's eyes showed her grief at missing Mags, and she looked weary and worn.

"Sometimes I sing to myself, Eileen, or say a poem to soothe my heart and stop me from going mad." She softly began rocking in the chair and saying,

> *"Ach, but I'm weary of mist and rain*
> *And roads where there's never a house or bush*
> *And tired I am of bog and road*
> *And the crying wind and the lonesome hush."*

"I'm sure I have the words wrong," she said. She was now weeping openly. Ails couldn't see her mother's face from her peep-hole, but she could feel her empathy emanating, even from a distance.

Ails knew all about Shamie in school. He used to be known as a kind of brain. The Pigby used to hold him up as an example at times, he was so good at sums. Not any more. He was in the corner with the stupid ones who got whacked every single Friday after 'Round the room for sums' session. Now Ails herself and Pat Doran did the best sums and the Pigby singled them out for praise. Shamie was rotten to both Ails and Pat all the time these days, but especially on Fridays.

From her hiding place, Ails could hear the women's voices becoming hushed again. She listened, spellbound, as Auntie Cora told her mother how Shamie had been beaten up the night before. "He was black and blue all over," said Auntie Cora.

"His balls were all kicked in," Ails was to hear later from Dingo Devine.

197

"My God, who did it?" Ails's mother involuntarily raised her voice in disbelief, then lowered it immediately when she realized she was not whispering.

"Oh, 'Durch bean liom, Go durch bann leahy' … You know how it is, Eileen. Everybody's talking about it, but nobody knows anything," said Auntie Cora. "None of the lads claim to know anything at all about it. Boys are so closed about talking about things, Eileen," she said. "Girls are just so much easier to talk to. At least they'll talk," she added in an exasperated voice, sounding as if she envied Ails's mother her three girls. "Imagine envying a mother of girls!" thought Ails, who knew her mother was kind of pitied by many in the village because they only had girls in their family.

"Ach, don't worry, Eileen, you'll have a boy the next time," Lizzie and the rest would say after each baby girl was born, just as if Neeve and Fiona and Ails didn't count.

Auntie Cora had four sons, and she seemed to think girls were easier, at least from the conversation Ails was now overhearing.

"When I grow up…" thought Ails…but then she remembered how babies were made…No, she wouldn't have any babies…Hushed tones between her mother and Auntie Cora drew her back into the conversation.

"But Shamie's been fighting with everybody in the whole townland of Altnamore, it seems like," said Cora, sounding tired. "It'd be hard to find anybody right now who wouldn't beat him up. And you know how boys are, anyway…" her voice trailed off. Ails hated boys. They just seemed to be able — even expected — to do what they liked.

Uncle Peter had taken the belt to Shamie, but it didn't do a bit of good. In fact he got worse. He was miserably cruel to Ails and Fiona. One day he whacked Neeve, just a baby, for nothing, and she cried and cried. Ails had yelled at him

"You're a good-for-nothin' skitter, Shamie. What'd you hit her for? She's a baby. She did nothin.' " Something strange almost happened. For a split second Ails thought she saw tears forming in Shamie's eyes before they hardened and he yelled back at her "Yiz are nothin' but a bunch of crybabies anyway, all of yiz. Sure isn't Fiona the Town Crier?" he taunted. "Waah, waah," he screeched, imitating Fiona's wailing.

Back in the warm kitchen, Auntie Cora continued in hushed tones talking to Ails's mother. "No, strangely he's not too bad with Colum, Eileen," Auntie Cora was saying. "I was actually watching him to make sure he didn't hurt Colum, he's been so awful lately. But he just ignores him. Another thing, Shamie won't go in the bath lately. God knows, he never did like water. The only way he'll wash himself is if we all leave him all by himself and he's the last one to use the water in the tin tub on Saturday nights before Peter empties it. I'm sure he doesn't half wash himself. I just get him clean clothes. I get so weary of fighting with him."

At the mention of the bath, Ails suddenly realized that these days, Shamie smelled. It was a strange, dank, sour, dark, somehow strangely male smell, puzzling to Ails. If he happened to catch Ails looking at him, Shamie would stick out his tongue and say "What are you lookin' at anyway?" At those times, thought Ails in confusion, Shamie's eyes seemed to take on that cold, hard look McCabe often gave the whining Fiona. Shamie even seemed to have McCabe's bull neck. At these times Ails had to shake herself and remember this was Shamie, her cousin, whom she'd known all her life. Then Shamie got in trouble for not playing football at school — Shamie who loved football, who was the most nimble player on the field, even if he was small.

Ails focused in again on the conversation between her mother and her aunt.

"Is he eating alright?" asked Ails's mother, always concerned about food.

"Oh, he eats alright. Takes more than his share when he can get away with it."

"So there's no point in bringing him to the doctor if he's not sick," said Ails's mother.

"Well, he's that skinny I give him worm powder, just in case. Sometimes he complains about his bum hurting. But you know boys, won't let you near them."

"Ach, they all go through these stages, Cora," comforted Ails's mother. "Look at our Fiona. She's impossible betimes."

199

"You're tellin' ME," Ails almost said aloud from her hiding place.

"Let me make you a cup of tea and you'll feel better, Cora," said Ails's mother, going out to the scullery adjoining the tiny living room, still talking while she made the tea.

Saturday was the day when they always sorted out the week's problems. There was always somebody at home to watch Colum. Ails watched for Auntie Cora arriving on Saturdays and always had some way to get rid of Fiona — collecting eggs with Lizzie, or playing with the Rafferty crybaby the same age. The two women were now drinking tea and Auntie Cora was smiling, once in a while, through her tears.

"Ach, well, thank God for Pat McCabe. He's great company with the loneliness," said Auntie Cora, dipping her oatcake into her tea. "Brightens up the house when he comes in the evenings. It's great to have somebody to talk to." Uncle Peter was quiet as the grave, thought Ails; always reading the paper with his glasses down on the end of his nose. Anyway Uncle Peter went out most evenings with the men to the pub, as most of the Altnamore men did. Ails's father went out maybe once or twice a week, but he'd rather smoke his pipe and fall asleep in the chair while Ails and Fiona braided red ribbons in his hair. Pat McCabe went out now and again with the men, but mostly he sat and talked with Auntie Cora after his evening tea.

"An' then there's always young lads comin' with messages for Pat McCabe. He eases the loneliness of the long evenings and nights. Y'know the bad sleeper I am, Eileen. An' you know, Eileen, Shamie doesn't give any bother when McCabe's around. Seems to be the only person Shamie'll listen to these days. Even makes him do things I can't get him to do," she added. "Maybe I'll ask McCabe to see if he can get to the bottom of this beating-up of Shamie. He gets along so well with all the lads," she added thoughtfully, drinking up the last of her tea and getting up to go home.

When Ails happened to be watching McCabe and her beloved Auntie Cora talking, him making her forget her lost children, and making her endless nights more bearable, Ails could almost forget McCabe's cold, hard, blue-eyed stare — almost. But the strange, frightening chill of McCabe never really

200

left her, despite her giving herself a 'talking-to' and trying to shake herself out of it. And Fiona continued to whine and wail at the sight of him — often starting to whinge and pout and cling to Ails and girn and whine, sometimes before he would inevitably actually appear. It was like Fiona could sense him coming. Ails hated Fiona's clinging, and resented how Lizzie excused everything Fiona did, by making excuses for her, saying "She's an old soul, a rare one, that Fiona Miona chile. She has the sight, I'm sure of it."

37

a view from the other side of the atlantic

ora was looking after the kids in Canada, while Ails was accompanying her Canadian husband, who was doing some work in the U.S.A. She had been so excited to have the opportunity to visit her cousin Mags in the Boston area. Their visit also happened to coincide with St. Patrick's Day weekend, and she'd heard about Eastern U.S.A. St. Patrick's Day celebrations for as long as she could remember. They were there for the Saturday night ceili, so off they went. Ails was amazed at the strong allegiance and loyalty to their Irish roots of these emigrants, with their strong Boston accents. All of their children did Irish dancing, played traditional Irish music and were immensely proud of their Irish heritage. At a break in the ceili dance sets, Ails was engrossed in reminiscing with Mags about Altnamore long ago. Close by, Ails's husband, always interested in intrinsic individuals, was talking to two women across from him. With half an ear, Ails assumed that her husband had asked them how they ended up in Boston. One lady, Mary Ann, described how her Aunt Annie had 'sent for one of the girls' — it didn't matter which one. This meant paying the young girl's fare to come out to America and 'get a start' in this new world. One of 11 children, Mary Ann's parents were grateful for the chance to give a child this opportunity, so they selected 'our Mary Ann' to go. This was a story so commonplace in Ireland that Ails could almost recite it herself. Some kindly uncle or aunt would help out the struggling large Catholic family in Ireland, who didn't have enough land, resources or jobs to stretch to provide for all the children. Mary Ann was describing matter-of-factly how her uncle got her a job in a fast-food restaurant, where she started at 6 a.m. and got home at 6 p.m., making minimum wage with a burger for her half-hour lunch. So far, Ails was familiar with the story. Everyone in Ireland knew that these emigrants worked very hard their first years in America and sent money home.

However, at this point in the conversation, Ails pricked up her ears. Mary Ann was describing how, on her way home from work, she got off the bus and picked up her aunt's children from the babysitter, took them home on the bus with her, changed out of her uniform, which she'd had to pay for herself and wash nightly, prepared supper for her aunt and uncle, just home from work, fed the children, cleaned up the house and dishes while the children did homework or talked to their parents, did the washing and ironed yesterday's wash, prepared everyone's lunch, bathed the kids and put them to bed, and got her own work stuff ready, before she fell into bed exhausted each night, only to repeat the same thing every week day. At the weekend, she did grocery-shopping, minded children, house-cleaned, vacuumed, cleaned windows or polished silver. On top of all of this, Mary Ann handed over every penny of her pay cheque to repay the fare which her Aunt Annie and Uncle Mick had 'advanced' for her to come to America.

Ails was stunned.

At this stage of the conversation, similar experiences were being recounted by all of the women at the table; then Mags echoed the rest. Ails was speechless. Her mind could not process this — she couldn't reconcile the stories she was hearing here, with the glorious ones she heard in Altnamore. Mags, even Mags, housed with an alcoholic uncle, who couldn't cope with anything; Mags, who had been the light of her mother's life; Mags, who had half the townland of Altnamore in love with her; Mags, who was reputed to have such a wonderful life in

America, Mags, envied by all the girls left behind, for her new, exciting life.

"Am I hearing this right?" she asked Mags.

"You are, indeed, Ails," answered Mags. "But, who could we tell?" Mags asked, to nobody in particular. "We were like prisoners in these relatives' houses," she said, to the nodding of the other women. The men, they said, hadn't fared much better, doing heavy physical work, overtime, working evenings and weekends, with no such thing as overtime pay; they handed over their wages also. This was no myth; it was real. These were middle-aged Irish-Americans, with grown families, who had no vested interest in fabricating their early life in Boston.

"The only way out was to get married," Mags said, and the women agreed. They'd been allowed out to a Saturday night ceili where all the Irish immigrants went. They married each other, and vowed to make a better life for their children than the one they'd had. And they did.

Ails had thought St. Patrick abolished slavery in Ireland, and it had been abolished in America.

But this was indentured labour, sort of.

And it was your relatives who were kind enough to bring you over in the first place. What was not to be grateful for?

38

pink candy

The dilapidated Dispensary was one of the places that Auntie Cora complained bitterly about. It was Altnamore's medical clinic, a damp part of a stone house near the Rocks, with a dank, cheerless waiting room — the actual 'examinin' room' was up a steep flight of stone steps. This was where Altnamore's only doctor, the Wee Doctor, held his 'clinic' hours — usually when somebody went and got him from the neighbouring pub. The Dispensary was 'like a pigsty,' Auntie Cora said, 'not fit for animals to go to be examined, never mind sick people.' The Dispensary was like a festering sore. It was cold, unwelcoming and filthy. But the local people often just went into the pub and the Wee Doctor would examine them there, or he'd go to the houses of the sick, since many of the older ones couldn't get into the village anyway. The Wee Doctor's area covered miles and miles of rural countryside. But there were Dispensary hours written on a curled-up, dirty notice nailed to the door, and so people came.

"The county council should be building a decent dispensary, and staffing it," Auntie Cora would say angrily to anyone who'd listen, usually McCabe, since nobody else wanted to think about the kinds of questions Auntie Cora brought up.

"We are citizens, too, you know!" she would often say in the Post Office, or getting her bread or milk or newspaper. Her remarks were usually met with puzzled stares.

The only time the Dispensary was ever cleaned was before somebody was coming out from Unragh to see the doctor from the hospital or Health Authority. This time, like wildfire, the rumour went around that there were official Dispensary visitors coming, and they all went trooping along to the dispensary to help clean it up. Nan Andy and Dolty Grimes, people who did odd jobs around Altnamore, were designated irregularly to clean up the dispensary. Nan cleaned up in eating houses after meals, and swept the floor in Altnamore shops; Dolty, Lizzie always said, 'nivir did a day's work in his life,' although he always seemed to be involved in some job or other, till he got enough money to go to the pub, and later to get in to a dance somewhere, where he was known as a great dancer who cut a dapper figure with girls and women of all ages. Dolty would start painting a wall, for example, and he'd come down off the ladder to talk to everybody who came along. By evening, he would still have hardly anything done. Where he had completed the job, it would be uneven and splotchy, with the paint having dried at different stages. But the Dispensary was not exactly a 'plum' job. Dolty and Nan were the two people who would pay those willing to help. Ails and all the rest of them would buzz around hoping for a few pennies for scrubbing the pee bucket stains off the linoleum, washing the stairs, scrubbing the oilcloth on the table, gathering up old needles and rubbish and trying in vain to make the hopeless Dispensary look clean, neat and hospitable.

Pat Doran's job had to be the rottenest one. He carried heavy, stinking buckets of pee samples down the steep stairs and through the draughty waiting room of the dispensary, emptying them down the road in the 'doughal,' a huge cess pool of manure accumulated from many Fair Days street cleanups. The buckets of pee were particularly full this time, and he even had to use a tin can to empty some into another large oil can, before he could even lift the heavy bucket. Pat valiantly struggled with the heavy, slimy load, with Ails holding onto one side of the big bucket handle with him. Between the two of them, the bucket became unbalanced, and teetered for a short moment before it spilled, cascading right down the stairs, the bucket coming clanking and battering down after the disgusting liquid. Right to the bottom of the stairs it cascaded and splashed all over the green-worn black shawl of Mary Felimy, who was in the waiting room on the scheduled day, but there was no doctor, since the Dispensary was being cleaned up. Pat called Ails and Maura and Brigid and they had to use all the Jeyes Fluid in the place to scrub away the stink of pee. Mary Felimy walked up the back way to Lizzie's. Lizzie washed the ancient shawl — which looked like it hadn't been washed for a century. Nobody had EVER seen Mary without her shawl, so she hid in Lizzie's scullery till the shawl dried over the fire. Then Mary smelled like smoke for weeks, but "it's better than the way she smelled before," Lizzie said, wrinkling her nose in disgust. Pat Doran felt bad about the mess, but nobody minded helping Pat out, because he helped everybody else out. Pat Doran was the only boy in the village Ails liked at all, since Shamie had turned so nasty. Pat was always doing errands and getting messages for people — even for Lizzie, whom the rest of the boys avoided like the plague. He was the first one to help Pat McCabe move in and was always running errands for him. Shamie used to be more like Pat Doran, before he got mean and cruel and nobody could stand him any more. But Pat was 'a good lad — even a bit of a softie' Lizzie always said, although she took advantage of his good nature, especially on Fair Days.

When the bucket of pee fell, it must have caught Pat sideways, because one side of his shirt and trousers and one shoe was soaked. The stink was awful, but Pat wouldn't take off any clothes with girls there. He seemed anxious to clean out his wet pocket in the corner beside where Ails was scrubbing the stairs. She stopped to watch the assortment of stuff coming out of Pat's pocket. "How on earth did he ever get all of it crammed in there?" she thought. There were bits of wire, marbles, string, hae'pennies, chestnuts on the end of strings to play conkers; butt ends of pencils and rubber erasers nobody could possibly use, wheels off toy cars, a few soggy cigarette butts, pieces of wood, a tiny penknife … and on and on.

"Dunno why he'd be so agitated about saving that junk," thought Ails, as he unloaded the stuff onto her clean stair. Then, as he turned his whole pocket inside out, Ails saw five or six bright pink things like round sweets, sticking to the lining of the pocket. They weren't the colored Valentine sweets, nor the candy packets they got at Rafferty's, nor the boiled sweets —

Ails knew her sweets. She knew every brand of sweets in Altnamore. No, these were big round bright pink ones, vaguely familiar. Somehow she'd seen them somewhere before. Oh, yes, that was it — Micky Faddy feeding them to the greyhounds. He used to crush them between two spoons and mix them in with the brown bread and the eggs he was getting ready for the dogs.

"Special vitamins from the Wee Doctor's office, said Micky, all hoity-toity and superior. Micky would never let Ails or Fiona touch or pet the greyhounds. "They're very high-strung," he'd say. "Youse weans stay away from them, now, or yiz'll put them off their form." These were the same pink tablets Ails was now looking at in Pat Doran's pocket.

"What're you doin' with the dogs' vitamin tablets?" asked Ails incredulously. Unaware that Ails had been watching from above him on the stair, Pat looked up at her like a startled rabbit. "Ssh, ssh," hissed Pat, "they're for Pat McCabe," he said sheepishly. "He needs them because of his skin rashes. If I hold the lining, can you pull these things off, Ails?" Ails climbed down into the corner behind the stairs. She pulled the stubborn, sticky, half-melted tablets off the lining. As she was doing this, she kept wondering idly why Pat Doran was bringing pink tablets to McCabe, mixed in as they were with all the filthy junk in his pocket. No bottle, no bag, just loose … She was putting them with the other junk on the freshly-washed stair when Lizzie came in with another bottle of Jeyes Fluid and another scrubbing brush. As soon as Pat saw her, he reached over and picked the pink tablets up quickly one by one and put them in his dry pocket, and of course that was the end of that, because Lizzie took over and started giving orders. Mary Felimy had told Lizzie what had happened and Lizzie arrived on the scene when most of the work was done. Of course, she pretended she'd done all the work herself — even told Nan Andy and Dolty she had organized all these 'weans' to get the work done. Ails and Maura and Brigid were just helping out a bit. She was such a poultice, that Lizzie, thought Ails. Nan gave Lizzie some money for the Jeyes fluid and all the work she did. Lizzie did give them all some money for sweets, but kept the most of it. It just wasn't fair, thought Ails. Fiona got more than the rest, as usual, "Fiona Miona workin' away with the bigger weans," and Fiona beamed.

"Sure, there's a great girl!" said Lizzie. All she'd done the whole time was sit on the window sill and swing her legs and look at all of them working. Ails got in trouble at home for getting her school frock and school shoes all stained.

"We were playing on the rocks when it happened," Ails lied. They weren't supposed to be hanging around the dispensary at any time, especially when there were patients going in and out.

"Well why didn't you come home and change your clothes before you went out to play?" asked her mother. "And how come Fiona didn't get filthy?"

Ails winced. That brat who got the money for sweets, did nothing, and now was so great because she didn't get her clothes dirty. There was no justice, thought Ails.

As she was falling asleep that night, and many, many times in the years to come, the thing puzzling Ails was Pat Doran quickly hiding the big pink tablets from Lizzie, the ones he was supposed to deliver to McCabe.

39

social activism.

Auntie Cora was really smart. Even though she took care of kids, house, and husband, washing and cleaning and cooking and sewing, like all the other women in Altnamore, she did all of it with a difference, with a flair. She cooked from 'Blue Cordon' cookbooks; she cooked pheasant and partridge that Uncle Peter hunted. McCabe was a godsend to her as a butcher, because she could get the cuts of meat required in recipes that nobody else would be using around Altnamore. She made clothes she saw in magazines, figuring how she needed to cut them, often without a pattern. Auntie Cora had gone to University, highly unusual for a person from Altnamore. Ails's father had told Ails, almost secretively, that, as a Catholic, Auntie Cora only 'got a place' in the University because her father, the local schoolmaster at that time, had lobbied the Unragh county councillors, all Protestants, to vote for her as a 'local candidate' for university. Ails was surprised at her father telling her this — even though it was in the context that she, Ails, and her sisters could also go to University. Ails was surprised because her father didn't like Auntie Cora. He didn't like Ails and Fiona spending too much time there. He didn't like how Auntie Cora got furious and rebellious over what she perceived as injustice in Altnamore village, as an outlying, remote part of the Unragh district. She complained incessantly about lack of basic facilities like roads, water, sewage, housing, banking, library and other services and consumer goods. Talking to McCabe, Auntie Cora would say:

"They can't use the war as excuse any longer, Pat."

210

"Yer right there, Cora," McCabe would answer.

Auntie Cora had piles of books of every kind. Recently, now that Colum was older, she had time to read while this contented little boy played happily alone, or Ails and Fiona took him off up the village.

Auntie Cora had always written letters, long, rambling letters. Ails was forever posting letters for her, weekly to her daughter Mags, and son Pat, in America, and to her University friends, and to catalogues and magazine and book companies everywhere. Of late, however, Ails was posting more and more letters to the County Council in Unragh. Ails knew from overhearing Auntie Cora and McCabe, that the most recent burning issue was one of housing.

"Sure look at my sister Eileen," she'd say to McCabe, "making good money with both of them working, and they can't get a decent house to live in with three children. There they are living in that onion box of that busybody Lizzie." Ails was shocked! She loved Lizzie's. Lizzie's was her home, the kitchen, cement hall, stairs, overgrown back yard, stack of turf, Fergie the blacksmith's forge, with its horses lined up down the back lane. There was always something going on at Lizzie's. It was Ails's home. What on earth was Auntie Cora talking about? She asked her.

"Well, I'm not saying there's anything wrong with where you live, child," she explained gently, "but we should have decent housing, Ails, with indoor plumbing, toilets and proper electricity not always breaking down," said Auntie Cora. But Ails didn't mind going poop in Lizzie's back yard, and using dalkin leaves to clean her bum and Fiona's. She didn't mind that at all. When Lizzie had to light the tilley lamp when the lights went out, it was a real treat, the way the lamp painted ghostly shadows on the walls, while the fire danced and the faces of the ceilighers were silhouetted on the walls.

But Auntie Cora showed Ails pictures in books of bath houses in Baghdad centuries ago, and hot water in heating pipes under floors of Moorish houses in Spain.

"These people had amenities centuries ago that we may never see in Altnamore," said Auntie Cora, dragging out another newer-looking book with pictures of modern post-war housing going up in England, and in other, more prosperous, more central parts of Northern Ireland. Ails found it interesting, but bewildering. She liked Altnamore the way it was. But she loved Auntie Cora. She kept on posting the letters to the County Council. Auntie Cora started to tell her what was in them.

"Things around here will never change, if the County Council thinks they can pull the wool over our eyes," she said vehemently. "Pat McCabe and myself have started a letter-writing campaign, demanding that our tax money we pay to the County Council be used to provide facilities to us in Altnamore. We have a *huge* housing problem here." Ails never saw McCabe's writing on any of the envelopes. He just talked to Auntie Cora, or rather it seemed she talked to him, and then wrote down what she reassured herself, through talking to him, that she should write.

Pretty soon, Ails noticed lots of letters coming back with typed addresses on them, all sitting on the cluttered desk, from the County Council, she supposed. A number of months later, a tract of land was cleared, big machinery brought in, and workmen started building new houses. Everybody in the village walked away down the road to see this happening. The country people went on Fair Days to watch these houses being built. People coming into the village on bicycles took a detour through Gortnabwee, to see the shiny bathtubs, sinks and toilets, and clean wood smell in the rooms that were shaping up inside the buildings. There were 14 houses. Nobody could ever remember houses being built more than one at a time, as needed. They didn't question things much. It was just happening.

But Ails knew how it was happening. It was the letters. She didn't tell anyone this. Nobody would have believed her anyway.

40

stretching wings

But I've nothing to DO," wailed Ails.
"Run away out and play and get out from under me feet,"
snapped Lizzie. Ails went to her mother.
"I've nothing to DO," she wailed.
"Run away out and play!"
"Naw, I don't wanna."
"Well, then, go read a book," said her mother in
exasperation. But Ails didn't feel like reading even though she
was getting really good at reading. A few weeks ago she had
begun to try to read pieces of her father's newspaper. Since they
had won the Clarence McTavish Travelling Show Youth
Contest, she really liked reading pieces about film stars and
actresses, especially when they had pictures as well, with their
hair all swept back, and shiny lips and arched eyebrows. When
she was asking her father some of the more difficult words she
could sense his disapproval of actresses and stage people, even
before he said: "With every single thing those famous people do,
they wonder what impression it's making on other people. It's as
if there's an audience watching them all the time, or an invisible
camera."

"Oh," said Ails, not quite understanding her father's
strong disapproval of these 'artificial people,' as he called them.
She started sweeping her hair up (it was too short, as usual), and
using her mother's old tubes of lipstick on her lips. She and
Maura stuffed rolled-up newspaper under their blouses inside
their vests to keep it in place to look like they had busts, and they

wore high heels. They had started practising being actresses. Since they started playing this, Ails didn't go much to her secret place in her imagination. Instead she was reading a lot of books. But books were not like her secret place. They were usually about places like England or somewhere which didn't fit with her secret place. Her secret place was sort of Altnamore, and sort of not. The 'not' part was how it was always dry, even though Ails knew that rain was needed for the rainbow that reflected different hues on different things at different times, depending on whether she was happy or sad or jealous or silly. Also the people in her secret place understood her, and they related to her, and she could talk to them, and they weren't the same as in the real world or even in the worlds of books.

But Ails liked acting because she didn't have to be herself; she could be somebody else. She went out to sit on the stone pillar by the gable, and go off in her imagination to her secret place, since there was nobody to play with and nothing to do. She settled back, sitting like a film star, with her hair swept up, just in case anybody came along. Somehow, though, her imagination would just not budge; it wouldn't move to her secret place as it had always done before.

Shamie, Pat, Jerry, Nailly and Dingo came along. They looked secretive and scheming and were whispering among themselves and pointing at her. Ails tossed her hair back.

"What's that stuff plastered on your mouth?" — asked Pat unceremoniously.

"None o' your business," Ails shot back at him.

"Looks like axle-grease." said Shamie, deliberately nasty.

"Or liver on a plate," said Jerry. Disgusting.

"Growin' tits, too." Dingo Devine was the most insulting person Ails had ever met.

"I'm an actress like in the pictures," she said with forced patience.

"Wanna come with us to the new houses? Jinny and Maura's comin'," said Pat nonchalantly. Ails was not allowed to go that far away below the village, but it was so boring today, nothing to do — and Jinny and Maura were going.

214

"The last time we went with youse we had to dance with no clothes on," said Ails suspiciously. Dingo Devine was not to be trusted. Ails climbed down and stood up unsteadily on her high heels.

"You better get out of them stilts or y'll not be able to walk," said Shamie, smirking. These boys were so crass, thought Ails. She did change her shoes but kept the hairstyle and the rolled-up newspaper breasts. Of course, Fiona saw them taking off and came running after them.

"Wait for meeeeee!"

"You're not comin' " said Ails.

"I'm tellin' on you. If you don't let me come I'm tellin'. You're goin' to the Septic Tank and the new houses and I'm tellin'!" Pest, nuisance, tattletale.

"Awright, then, c'mon, but if you open your mouth!" Pest. They called at Jinny's house to get her to come. Maura and Brigid were standing at the pump waiting.

"Do we have to take Fiona?" Groans all around. Same pest, same thing, always tagging along, she was. Maura and Jinny had their hair swept back with hairclips, too, and they had even brighter lipstick. Ails put some on and felt like a real actress. They went down the street past Auntie Cora's and the barracks. Well down out of the village they cut across the big barren field where the Septic Tank was. They rode around on the huge spokes that squirted water out on the circular gravel bed. It was great. Just like being on the merry-go-round at Clarence McTavish's Travelling Show. Somebody always spotted them, though. This time it was Brian and Bouncer.

"Get off that. It's dangerous!" Brian and Bouncer wouldn't tell on them, but they decided to leave anyway in case anyone else would see them. Somebody always spotted them on the Septic Tank pipes. Today's ride was too short. They walked on down to the new houses far below the village. There was a lovely smell of new wood, white shiny sinks and toilets, baths that water ran into; that you didn't have to fill and empty with buckets. Ails was pretending she lived there and was walking up and down the staircase when she stopped dead in her tracks. Pat Doran was smoking a cigarette, just leaning up against the

215

bannister smoking a cigarette trying to look just as if he was on a poster advertising a film.

"I didn't know you smoked," said Ails in astonishment.

"Do it all the time," said Pat. "Want one?" He flashed around a 20-pack of Players cigarettes. Ails's eyes nearly fell out.

"Where'd you get them? Off McCabe the butcher, I s'pose?" said Ails, who hated McCabe.

"None of your business," said Shamie curtly, appearing nonchalantly from around the corner, curling smoke out of his mouth. "Just take one and smoke it," he said in an American accent from the pictures. "And don't be such a yellow-bellied coward." When Ails hesitated, Dingo sneered:

"Thought you were supposed to be an actress? They smoke." Under the accusing glare of the hateful boys, Ails took a white cigarette and examined the tightly-packed tobacco inside it. She tapped it on the bannister. She took one, tossing back her swept-up hair. Jinny came out of one of the new-house rooms.

"Where'd you get that, Ails?" she said, looking at the unlit cigarette in Ails's mouth. Then she looked at Shamie, Nailly, Dingo, Pat and Jerry puffing away.

"Here, Jinny." Pat offered her a cigarette. Jinny took one, then Maura took one, wide-eyed. with wonder. Shamie lit a match and it burnt right down to his fingers because none of them could get the cigarettes lit.

"You're supposed to suck on it," said Shamie. "Breathe in!" and he lit another match. Maura's lit, but she coughed and coughed. Jinny said she'd smoked before and complained that Shamie wasn't holding the match in the right position to light her cigarette properly. She puffed in and sputtered just a little. Ails was nervous. She breathed in, nearly choked and blew out the match. She looked through her watering eyes at the glow on the end of her cigarette and tried again. It tasted awful. They looked at each other and giggled.

"See? Once you get used to it, it's easy." said Shamie, swaggering around puffing in and out clouds of smoke. Fiona and Brigid came running in and stopped, wide-eyed:

"I didn't know youse all smoked!" said Fiona in amazement.

"Wanna try?" asked Pat.

"Here's one," offered Jerry.

"Light up," said Shamie, with a lit match ready. Fiona looked at Ails.

"Maybe you shouldn't," warned Ails.

"I wanna. I won't tell," promised Fiona.

"Me too," insisted Brigid. They both coughed and choked terribly. After a while they experimented with different ways to hold the cigarettes. Finger and thumb like Pat, two fingers like Shamie, wee finger stuck like an actress, or...Maura and Brigid ran up the stairs retching. They both threw up at once in the white shiny porcelain sink and toilet. Fiona started to cry, and handed her cigarette to Ails. Pat and Shamie looked scared and said they should all go home and Dingo, Nailly and Jerry disappeared. On the way home Ails's head was a bit light, and Fiona seemed O.K. When they got home nobody said anything. They weren't even missed. Good.

They had pancakes for their tea. Fiona threw up green all over the floor.

"Why couldn't she have thrown up along with everybody else?" thought Ails. "Pest."

What on earth has that child been eating?" asked their mother, bewildered.

"Maybe it was the smoking. That's what kind of taste the vomit is..." Fiona clapped her hand over her mouth and looked guiltily at Ails, who was bright red. Silence.

"The what? What've you been doing?" Pest, nuisance, tattletale. No wonder Lizzie called Fiona the Town Crier. Mouth like a bucket. Now they were in for it. Ails told them. They weren't nearly as mad as Ails thought they might be. As usual, her father didn't like the idea of their going off without saying where. Of course Lizzie heard about it. She always heard about everything. She kept warning them that they'd never grow any bigger. For weeks Ails measured herself against the cigarette burn on the bannister door post . Lizzie said that's what had happened to the Wee Doctor. He smoked as a child and it stunted his growth. Then Ails was scared they'd grow up ugly to look just like the Wee Doctor, with strawberry noses and they'd have to wear big thick glasses. Of course Lizzie told Fergie the blacksmith, and that was like telling the whole village. Fergie teased her mercilessly:

"Let me see, Ails. Yes, it's definitely getting smaller, you are. Y'll have to quit the smokin'!" Her face burned.

It wasn't much fun being an actress, and smoking and acting sophisticated all the time, Ails decided. Her father didn't like her newspaper breasts. The high heels hurt, especially on the cobblestones. Her hair was too straight and too short, and her teeth too crooked. She started to go back into her secret place, where she was alright without having to change who she was, or worry what she looked like. Ingrid, now a character in her imagination, had missed her and was glad to see Ails back. All the flowers ran to meet her. The rainbow glowed beautifully and the button boots were much nicer than high heels. She wasn't bored as often now that she had somewhere in her imagination to go, and she didn't feel as lonesome when the long shadows stretched across the wet black roofs and the shiny black street on long summer evenings.

Smoking

emigrant songs

(Mountains of Mourne are in Co. Down, N. Ireland. This song is about
London, England. 'Force' means police force.)

You remember young Peter O'Loughlin, of course?
Well, you know he is here at the head of the force.
I met him today, I was crossing the Strand
And he stopped the whole street
With one wave of his hand;
And there we stood talking of days that were gone
While the whole population of London looked on.
And all of the time we were wishing to be
Where the mountains of Mourne sweep down to the
sea.

From *"The Mountains of Mourne Sweep Down to the Sea"*

Goodbye, Johnny Dear
When you're far away
Don't forget your dear old mother
Far across the sea
Write a letter now and then
And send her all you can
And don't forget, where'er you roam
That you're an Irish man.

42

across the irish sea

Summer holidays came, with whoops and yells and books flying high into the trees. The tyres on the master's car were flat. The bigger lads did this every year, and somebody always broke into the school over the holidays and stole the Master's cane and long ruler. Nobody ever knew who did any of this. By September everyone had almost forgotten these pre-holiday incidents. Mrs. Digby's cane went flying into the playground. Everyone ran down the hill. Ails felt the wind in her hair and savoured the smell of summer in her nostrils. September seemed far, far away. That night her father said they were leaving in a few days for a week in England. They were going by boat. They borrowed suitcases and packed clothes and toys. It seemed a long, long way to go from Altnamore.

The boat was huge. The sea smelled and Ails couldn't believe that the boat wouldn't sink, it was so big and heavy. It had beds and sinks in the tiny rooms and chug, chug, chugged all night long. In the morning they all walked sleepily in the damp dawn onto a train. They were in England. The train had mirrors, and long seats and sliding doors and Ails kept saying to the click of the wheels a poem they had learnt in school:

> *"Faster than fairies, faster than witches,*
> *bridges and houses and hedges and ditches*
> *trav'lling along in the wink of an eye*
> *As painted stations whistle by..."*

Uncle Michael met them at the station with Susan, who, of course, knew all of the poem by Robert Louis Stevenson, and told Ails how he wrote it as a little boy, sick in bed. Susan was very excited to see them. They had a lovely house and garden out in the country with lots of luscious lawns, flowers and magnificent roses, all tended by a gardener. The four adults talked a lot, while Susan, Ails and Fiona played well together — for two days or so. Then something seemed missing. Nobody walked up and down past the gates wheeling bicycles or shouting greetings. There was no plantin with trees silhouetted against the sky, no Rocks with dips in between to set up houses, nobody coming in and out to catch up on the village news for the day — it was strange, new, different. It was beautiful where they were, but different. Aunt Maisie sang and whistled and talked and laughed, but Ails saw from time to time a frightened, lonely look in her eyes, as if she, too, missed the plantin and Lizzie's kitchen and the warm feeling that everybody knew who you were. That feeling formed a sort of blanket all around you. That was good, thought Ails, as long as you didn't have to go outside that blanket's glow to get cold and feel buffeted by the world.

"Auntie Cora went outside the blanket a long time ago, and she doesn't seem to be able to be warmed by it any more," thought Ails. "And Aunt Maisie's eyes look just like Auntie Cora's, when they both look out the window and think nobody is watching," thought Ails sadly. At that moment Auntie Maisie came back to earth again, and was her usual cheerful, funny self. She went on cooking something good, poking the fire in the range to make a nice cheery glow, even though it wasn't a cold day. "Just like Auntie Cora does," thought Ails. "They both try all the time to make everybody feel good." Ails's secret place worked well in England for short periods of time, but as the week went on she felt lonelier and lonelier. She got on her mother's nerves fighting with Fiona and hanging around with nothing to do. Susan would just go to her room, and read and play alone at these times. The people from up the road came to eat one day. Aunt Maisie polished the forks and set the table with a white linen tablecloth, ironed really nicely, not like at Lizzie's or Jinny's eating house with the scrubbed wooden tables.

One day they all went in Uncle Michael's huge car to see Brendan Carragher, the artist son of the Blind Widow Carragher that they had come across unexpectedly on the Rocks in Altnamore. As Lizzie had foretold, Aunt Maisie knew where Brendan lived. His blind widowed mother and sister Carmel had sent him a fruit cake in a tin box. They went up a really winding narrow road, nearly getting stuck in the mud before they came to a tumbledown stone shack with smoke coming from the crooked chimney. Around the steps was an array of broken pots with plants in them that had beautiful exotic-looking flowers growing in them. There were pieces of pots everywhere, coloured chunks, plain pieces; chipped, broken shapes, and lids of all kinds strewn everywhere. The adults all looked at one another, shaking their heads. It was Fiona who went forward boldly and knocked loudly the scarred wooden door with a broken piece of a pot. Out came the man they had seen on the rocks, Brendan Carragher. His eyes looked even more like a surprised rabbit, and he seemed overwhelmed by the crowd of them arriving at his house unannounced.

"But you can't contact him," Aunt Maisie had said, "He has no phone." Unlike Altnamore where there were hardly any phones, people in England phoned or wrote letters to say what they were going to be doing — 'their plans,' Aunt Maisie had explained, even if it was only to visit somebody for a cup of tea. Brendan Carragher had on a big apron covered with mud. His face and arms were spattered with mud; his wispy reddish hair was flying all over the place.

"Hello, Brendan," she smiled, "there's an awful crowd of us. Your mother sent a cake with Eileen here, and we brought some barm brack and soda bread."

"Oh, come on in," said Brendan, wiping his muddy hands on a dirty towel. Aunt Maisie had been to Brendans house before and she led the way inside. They all filed in through the narrow door. There was an earthen floor and Ails got a warm feeling when she saw the fire on the hearth smoking up through the chimney and the crook with the big black kettle just like Lizzie's. Brendan's eyes lit up when Ails's father asked him about his plants and flowers in broken pots all over the place. He talked animatedly about how he planted slips from different

223

plants and species of plants, about pruning and growing seasons and watering needs. Ails looked around, fascinated by the room itself. There was a wooden settle bed in the corner beside the fire, and a wooden table just like Lizzie's. Brendan had hundreds of cups. Ails's mother was distinctly uncomfortable with the babies on the earthen floor, and looked at the hole in the roof with the bucket under it to catch the drips. Brendan saw her looking and apologized for not having it fixed. Ails's mother said quickly:

"Those are lovely cups. Where did you get them?"

"Oh, I made them," said Brendan shyly.

"You made them?" echoed Fiona in amazement. "You made them all by yourself? But how?"

"Oh, just over here." He pulled aside a curtain into another compartment of the stone house where there was a strange-looking contraption made from pieces of wood and iron bars and wire.

What's that?" asked Fiona.

"Oh, that's my wheel. Would you like to see it work?" There were pots everywhere, drying, wet, damp, dry and bone-dry. The place smelled of damp clay. Brendan was pulling lumps of clay out of a big thing that looked like a cement mixer and slapping them together in his hands. Ails remembered his big bony fingers drawing. He handled the clay the same way. When he had a ball of this stuff slapped together, he slapped it on a flat round steel thing and climbed on a stool. He gave the stone wheel under the contraption a mighty kick, put his hands on the ball of clay on the round steel, which started to move, wobbly at first. Then the wheel turned more and more smoothly, and the clay began to grow into a shape and look like silk, with Brendan's big bony hands caressing it in and out into different shapes, dipping his hands in and out of water, till it became a tall stately shape "Like a chinese vase," thought Ails. Ails, Fiona and Susan stood speechless, watching.

"That's beautiful!" said Fiona in awe. "It looks just like magic."

"No, it's just moving the clay with your hands on a wheel," said Brendan simply, his face flushing with pleasure at their interest, his eyes lighting up with excitement as he showed them how he mixed up clay out of the ground in what looked like a cement mixer, until it became smooth. He showed them the big brick oven for cooking the pots; also how he had dug a hole in the ground outside, lit a fire in it with straw and put the pots in. The fire then transformed the dull-looking paint on them into wonderful colours. He showed Ails's father how he tried to get some pots to turn pale pink just like the flowers, by throwing powdery stuff in the fire. Brendan Carragher was like a different person from the man they had talked to on the rocks in Altnamore. Gone was the lost, scared rabbit look. He was fascinating, excited and enthusiastic — not at all lost or awkward or searching like he seemed in Altnamore. This was the first place since Altnamore that Ails felt kindled and warm — there was a good feeling in this funny house as this warm, gentle man led them all back into the kitchen where Aunt Maisie was wetting tea in a big blackened teapot, and buttering bread. Brendan brought in a big jug of milk from the creamery can out the back. His farmer neighbour, he explained, brought milk, cream, butter and cheese every week or so. Brendan produced some wheaten bread from the rough wooden cupboard.

"That was very nice of you to bring the bread. Thank you, Maisie. I didn't have much left," said Brendan, adding thick slices to the other bread on the big pottery plate. They all took a big pottery mug of strong, sweet tea.

"This is good wheaten bread. Where do you get it?" asked Ails's mother.

"Oh, I made it on the griddle there," said Brendan. Ails's mother looked in surprise at the griddle, then at the wooden table, then at Brendan's hands, with clay in the cracks. Brendan was oblivious. He talked and laughed and obviously just loved their being there. Fiona told him she still had his picture in a shoebox. He drew more and gave them to her. He told them of the birds and the flowers and the trees and his pots and the colours and he gave each of them a pot.

"I'll bring some home to Altnamore for your mother and Carmel, if you like," said Ails's mother. Brendan's face changed dramatically and looked haunted and lost again.

"They...eh... They don't...I don't think they like my pots much," he sort of stammered, "but if you want...eh...if you

225

think they..." for a moment he looked hopeful, then hopeless again, and his voice trailed off. The subject was dropped. Ails was totally bewildered. Here she was in England, missing Altnamore, feeling so vulnerable and lonesome. In Brendan Carragher's place she felt at home and warm and good. Yet every time anyone mentioned Altnamore Brendan changed completely, becoming lost and lonesome. It didn't make any sense. They asked to play with some clay, and Brendan looked crestfallen when Ails's mother said the babies had to be brought home. They were getting very whiney because they couldn't move around much. Brendan was sad to see them go. He liked Fiona best of all of them, and she him. She hugged him, and he almost looked like he was going to cry. On the way back to Aunt Maisie's the adults talked about how Brendan lived like a hermit in squalor. They spelled out a lot of words, but Ails was pretty good at spelling. Ails's father said he thought Brendan was a kind of scientist. Fiona said no, he was an artist, and Ails thought he was just a person, or different persons, depending on where he found himself.

"I think I'm like that, too," thought Ails, so glad to be going home to Altnamore the next day. They went off on the boat train early next morning. As the train chugged away from the station, Ails watched Aunt Maisie's face, fun-loving, alive and mischievous in Altnamore, now somehow looking lost underneath the smile, and trying to be happy. It didn't make any sense to Ails. She looked out at the railway lines that seemed to go on forever. She felt the wind blowing her hair forward, blowing her back to the big boat to sail home, home to Altnamore.

Brendan Carragher, the potter's cottage.

43

the more things change

ever since they came back to Canada from seeing their cousins in Ireland acting plays of Celtic myths, Ails's kids were smitten with the acting bug. They wanted stories, Irish stories, stories of heroes and warriors like Cu Culainn and Finn McCool, who carried spears and wore armour, stories of people turning into animals and birds, stories of battles and kingdoms. They spent ages with their friends making swords and pinning on costumes. When they heard that Cu Culainn had an eye which popped out before battle, they used a ping-pong ball from an old Cookie Monster costume, stuck it on the end of a stick and hid it under a cloak until the moment of battle, then shot the eye out and charged over the back of the couch.

"So much for the Island of saints and scholars," said Ails to herself, looking around at the devastation of almost every square inch of the house. They went to the local library to get books — ones with pictures — these TV era kids weren't really interested in anything they had to read to get information. The trouble was, Ails didn't know a whole lot about all of this stuff. It was all a jumble of bits and pieces from her youth. She phoned Fiona, who had taken Celtic studies, to look for more Celtic superhero stories.

"Your kids too?" exclaimed Fiona. "Mine are driving me crazy. Princesses riding out of mystic lakes on white (broom) horses; a wicked stepmother turning four kids into swans. I haven't a broom or a piece of cloth about the place that's not strewn everywhere!"

"Same here," said Ails. "Although, to tell you the truth, Fiona, I can't believe how much I'm learning myself." It was true. Carving and painting celtic designs on pottery, which had caused Ails so much frustration, was falling into place in a totally illogical, intuitive way she couldn't explain.

At the pottery studio, while working, she and Dora and Inder and Surinder now took turns telling a story from their country each week. The stories had remarkable similarities about human nature. After recounting Finn McCool's marvellous feats and heroic status, Ails came one week with a further instalment of Finn as a grumpy, autocratic old man who wanted to marry a young beautiful girl, Grainne. (As they all often did for each other when telling stories, Ails had to carefully pronounce the name Grawn-ya for the others.) However, at Finn's wedding party, Grainne saw a handsome young wedding guest called Diarmid. A goddess had dubbed on Diarmid's forehead a love potion to make him irresistible. Diarmid and Grainne ran off together and for 16 years, Finn let his responsibilities and ruling go to rack and ruin while he pursued them so thoroughly that they could never stay two nights in the same place.

"Your basic mid-life crisis," agreed the women. "The more things change, the more they stay the same."

44

changes

auntie Cora had to go to see the wee Doctor. She was getting stronger all the time and Column was growing like a weed. Usually she didn't have to bring Colum, but this time he wanted to see both mother and son, so Ails went with them both to the Dispensary upstairs in the ancient, dank, stone house in the middle of the town. Colum was smiling now, chubby, cherubic and happy, aware and alert.

"He's not walking yet, so he's a lot easier to mind than Neeve is right now," Ails told Auntie Cora. "Neeve is walking and keeps falling and bashing into things and eating clay and cigarette butts."

"Oh, I know," said Auntie Cora wearily, but she smiled at Colum. Ails carried Colum and they went into the Dispensary. There was a fire in the grate, trying in vain to heat the damp, grey cement room. People were sitting around the walls on upturned boxes talking about all the health things wrong with them. Every so often one of them would get up and run into the pub for a quick nip, and run back so's not to miss a turn. But something was different today. Ails couldn't quite figure out what it was. On, yes, it was the smell. It smelled of disinfectant or wood varnish or something unfamiliar to the dispensary. Then there was a completely new sound — water gurgling down pipes. There was something else as well, something about the waiting people. Ails started noticing that instead of taking turns as usual, the next one in turn was hesitating:

"Ach, you go on up first, Maggie, you haven't much time," or

"You've farther to go home than me, Minnie, you go first." Ails was vaguely puzzled. She had been idly playing with the baby, but now started listening:

"He's alright for a prescription or two, but the Wee Doctor's the one to go to if you're sick."

That Rosaleen McGarvey one — there's nothin' wrong with her y'know. Up to see him with the lipstick and high heels — on them stairs, even." It dawned on Ails that they were discussing the new doctor. Just at that moment the lithe figure of a young man with blond hair came down the rickety crooked stairs. He had on a white coat and a stethoscope hung around his neck, just like a real doctor in the hospital Ails had been in.

"Can I help anyone here?" Many of the people just shuffled and muttered "I'm in no hurry, Doc," or "I have to get some papers from the wee doctor." It was embarrassing. Finally Auntie Cora spoke up:

"Yes, doctor, you can help me. Ails can you mind the baby for a minute?" After what seemed like ages, but was probably about ten minutes, Auntie Cora called Ails to come upstairs. She carried the baby up the stairs with her, and the young, blonde doctor greeted both of them.

"Now, then, who have we got here. Ails? I'm Doctor McKenna," and he even shook her hand. "And this is Colum. Gave your mother quite a time, mister, didn't you?" While the doctor examined Colum, Ails looked around in open amazement. The dispensary was cleaned up — not just the way it was cleaned up for the health inspector, but really clean and uncluttered looking. This time it was almost unrecognizable. The old washed-out curtain was gone. In its place was a new wooden partition with a smell of varnish. There was brand new thick oilcloth on the bench. All the old needle packages were thrown away with no sign of the old overflowing cardboard box that used to hold them. The biggest surprise was a shiny white sink and a real toilet with a door. The old bucket where the urine samples used to be emptied was now gone. There were no splashes on the walls. They were all newly whitewashed. Ails gawked around in open astonishment. It almost looked like a real hospital office. Ails had noticed Dolty Grimes and Nan Andy working around the dispensary, as they usually did before the

231

health inspections, but she didn't think anything of it. She had not expected this kind of transformation.

"Like I was saying, Mrs. Monaghan, I just said to the County Council, 'Just because Altnamore is remote is no reason not to have sanitary conditions. Money must be provided for some basic improvements. The Altnamore practice is a huge area of the country." Ails could hear the Wee Doctor behind the partition whistling away. So there were two doctors now?
The Wee Doctor was asking about the family and telling somebody:

"Jay-sus, woman, there's no more wrong with yer mother than there is with me. Just needs time and a bit of spoilin' to get over yer da's death. Hard on them, y'know. But she's not sick, not a bit of it. Don't let her play on your sympathy. You've enough work to do, let alone her thinkin' she's sick."

"Quite a character, isn't he?" smiled Dr. McKenna as they both listened to the Wee Doctor. "Really knows his stuff. You can dress Colum now, Ails." Auntie Cora said:

"I'm so glad you fought for this, doctor. I get so angry sometimes about the complacency in this place. The council doesn't even supply the basic needs of this village. Just look at our sewage, our medical facilities — up till now, anyway; our electricity, our education system. Sure it's shocking. We're second-class citizens in our own country!"

"It's a question of representation, though, Mrs. Monaghan. Those who shout the loudest, you know, and all that......Ready, Ails? Watch yourself on those stairs — they'll be replaced soon. I enjoyed talking to you, Mrs. Monaghan."

The faces in the cheerless waiting room were turned expectantly towards the stairs.

"Well, Cora, what's he like?"

"Just great."

"Well, mebbe I'll go then. Mind you, just this once, just to try him out."

Ails woke up early. It was Saturday morning and something was strange. Voices, that was it. Somebody was up. But the voices were outside. She hopped up to the window and pulled back the lace curtain.

"Fiona, look! There she is!" Fiona crawled over sleepily: "Who?"

"The nurse I told you about in the hospital — Nurse Mary Ellen." Fiona woke up quickly. There was Nurse Mary Ellen in unfamiliar dress — a grey coat tucked in at the waist, flared out full at the bottom, a little hat with net around it. Even wearing low-heeled shoes she was taller than the Wee Doctor. She was flushed and pretty. The wee doctor was beside her with a new suit and tie and his shoes polished. They were getting into the back of a car with Ails's parents driving. Where were they going? Ails and Fiona tore down the stairs and burst through the front door in their nighties, just in time to see the car turning the corner.

"Come in, you'll get yer death of cold out there!" It was Lizzie from her familiar stance at the window. "Well, there they go. Imagine that!"

"Where are they goin'?" asked Ails and Fiona excitedly, jumping up and down.

"The wee doctor's getting married."

"Where?"

"When?"

"Can we go?"

"No, it's a secret. Only me and your father and mother know it," said Lizzie importantly. "They're getting married in the town, and they'll be away for a while." Ails and Fiona got dressed and went tearing out to tell Maura, Brigid and Jinny and anybody else who'd listen. Nobody had any idea that this was happening. There were suspicions he had a girlfriend — Jinny knew that, but she was mad she wasn't the first to know about the wedding. Everyone they talked to was amazed and delighted.

"Well, now, isn't he the quare one, goin' off and doin' it like that!"

"So that's why that new Doctor McKenna fella is here!"

"Where'll they live?"

"Ah, more than likely the new houses."

"Well, isn't that great, now!"

The new young Doctor McKenna was very brusque and efficient — so much so that Lizzie said,

"You'd nearly think he was a Protestant, only Sarah-Ann, his housekeeper, says he doesn't eat meat on Fridays. 'Spose he goes to Mass in the town when he goes home Sundays."

True to his word, Dr. McKenna did have the dispensary stairs replaced, the waiting room walls whitewashed. As well as the fire at the front, Dolty protectively carried in a big box, warning all curious onlookers "jist keep yer hands aff that new electrificated heater!" On Dr. McKenna's instructions, Donleavy's Electric shop lads down the street put in a new plug for the heater, on the opposite side of the room, where nobody ever wanted to sit, it was so cold. When John Donleavy mentioned the price of running a heater, Dr. McKenna simply said, "I'll submit it to the County Council. Don't worry, they'll pay the bill." Over a few weeks new curtains were added, a sofa and some magazines. The dispensary began to look positively inviting. The nicer it got, the more healthy women went in there for shelter while waiting for their men to come out of the pubs to go home. The County Council paid Mickey James and Nan Andy to do the work on the dispensary. Doctor McKenna, "bein' from the town where they have them meetings, he knows who to ask," explained Dolty importantly to those raising questions about how on earth this transformation was taking place.

"Right enough, it's better," said an old woman with a shawl and nearly a beard, drying herself out in front of Nan Andy's cheerful waiting room fire. "But it'll be nice to have the Wee Doctor back, just the same."

Dr. McKenna worked diligently all week in Altnamore, making calls in the evenings after office hours. He went back into town Sundays only, and had to be phoned for emergencies. Many of the young girls in the village fancied the good-looking Doctor McKenna. However, they abruptly gave up going to see him for imaginary ailments after his girlfriend, Violet Carrow, visited one Sunday. Violet was tiny and fashionable, and wore the highest heeled, daintiest shoes anyone in Altnamore had ever seen. "Sunday Mass time is over, so I wonder does she go at all?

234

...She definitely looks like a Protestant," said Lizzie when Dr. McKenna brought Violet in for tea and to meet some of the country people in Lizzie's eating-house after the late Mass. "Carrow sounds awful like a Protestant name to me. Surely he's not a Catholic going into a mixed marriage? Tch, tch, tch," complained Lizzie.

Young Doctor McKenna left Altnamore shortly after the Wee Doctor came back from his honeymoon. According to later reports, he did marry Violet, the Protestant girl, and moved to Belfast.

The Wee Doctor came back with his new bride, to the refurbished dispensary waiting room loaded with sheets, blankets, pots, pans, potatoes, bags of turf, a creel and the promise of a chicken here, a duck there, a turkey there:

"Whenever the missus wants it, we'll kill it and bring it in, Doc!" Even before The Wee Doctor arrived home, Doctor McKenna had had to get Nan Andy to keep inventory of all the stuff when it started arriving in overwhelming amounts.

Nurse Mary Ellen became known as 'The Wee Doctor's Missus.'

"Isn't she the quiet one. Never says a word about anybody," remarked Lizzie, "an' got him off the drink, too!"

But not for long. It was hard not to meet with the old crowd for a drink, and miss all the crack in the pubs. He started to take one drink, then another, and another, and everybody was thoroughly enjoying him again.

But when the Wee Doctor's wife lost one baby, then another, he started to drink really heavily again. (Ails could never figure how a nurse and a doctor could lose a baby, anyway.) When he was drinking he'd run into fence posts and gates with his jeep. He knocked down a few cement posts with the wires running through them at the new houses — but the posts were really ugly anyway, not like the blackthorn sticks and barbed wire used everywhere else. Often Mary Ellen had red eyes and looked tired and worried but she never talked much to anyone. Ails, Fiona, Maura and Brigid took to visiting her after she lost her first baby. They brought bunches of snowdrops and primroses and she let them play and cut up magazines and play school with cushions on the stairs. She didn't mind the house being untidy. The hired girl always helped clean it up. But the Wee Doctor's wife didn't like Jinny. So Jinny didn't come, though she'd ask a lot of questions about the Wee Doctor's house. The Wee Doctor himself looked awful, not the same awful way he used to look when he was drunk before he was married; now he looked kind of desperate, like an unhappy, trapped animal.

One day he disappeared mysteriously and another young doctor came out from the town to stand in for him:

"Ach, they can do the doctoring alright, I s'pose," was the word that went around the village, "but the Wee Doctor's better drunk than two of them new lads is sober. Though, mind you, I have to say that McKenna fella done a lot for the dispensary . . . "

The Wee Doctor was gone for what seemed like a long, long time. Nurse Mary Ellen looked after many a patient that came to the door, not wanting to go to the new doctor. They were mostly the ones that were in the IRA, involved in shootings, wounded, or on the run from the police. They had always come to the Wee Doctor through the back doors of pubs, leaving a lookout man at the door. They couldn't go anywhere publicly in case of being recognized by the few in the town that would inform on them. Nurse Mary Ellen treated and bandaged as best she could. Every Saturday she went into Unragh on the early newspaper bus to get the bus to the Belfast.. Everyone supposed she was going to see the Wee Doctor in the city, although she never said.

After what seemed like an eternity to the Altnamore people, the Wee Doctor came back looking like a new man.

"Dryin' out, he was," nodded everyone, "thank God it wasn't his health, and only the Drink that was wrong with him." The people of the country said:

"Thank God he went off the Drink. It must have been the prayers of the people he cured, and he got himself a great missus, even if she doesn't talk enough." Then they'd tell a story of heroism from his bad old days, the stories growing with each new telling to mythical, heroic proportions.

"But he's never as good a crack any more."

They they'd sigh.

45

a Bucket of water

When Ails left Ireland forever at 24 years old, she imagined people questioning, the way she herself had questioned, how or why she could possibly leave. Didn't she have a good life there? Wasn't she surrounded by people who loved her? She was not one of a huge family with not enough land to go around. She was equipped to stay. Her father had made sure of that. Was it perhaps the very education she had received to enable her to stay, that had led to her leaving? Or was Auntie Cora perhaps right about 'westward looking eyes'?

Today in her Canadian studio, Ails was carving on a large flat surface a design consisting of what looked like a ship's prow in the midst of what seemed like waves — a welcome change from the angular designs she had just been working on. As she carved into the malleable clay, she thought of the thousands who had left Ireland before her. Sure wasn't St. Brendan himself reputed to have sailed away to North American shores, on a boat with a curving prow like the one in this design? She remembered that he was even supposed to have said Mass on the back of a whale. "Of course, he was a priest," Ails reminded herself. Ireland, 'land of saints and scholars' had sent missionaries and teachers worldwide. "But they belonged to God," reasoned Ails, knowing that St. Brendan and thousands like him would never have made it back to Ireland again. It was too far and too expensive, and maybe it was just as well.

About the rare few emigrants from Ireland who did get a chance to return for a visit, there were stories and poems written, none of them flattering. They were usually along the lines of '*I mind him, a young cub, leavin'* — a parent reminiscing about how hard it was to part with a child. Then when he came back, how he had changed, and now wanted special food, and had a wife with strange ways. When these people came home, they were a sort of curiosity, bearing no relation to the people they were before they left, it seemed.

Is that how she, Ails, appeared when she went back to visit? Many, many times she would ask herself this while she was adapting to the strange cultural rules of her adopted country, where quiet, conservative people on the street courteously passed her by, but never stopped to talk; where she didn't know anyone on the bus; where her behaviour often seemed out of place; where there was no crack — fun, banter, humour. In this land, it was not better. It was just different. This was what she had chosen, but she didn't realize that by choosing this, she'd given up so much. How could she think things would remain the same, and that she could hold on to both worlds?

After a number of years in Canada, on a visit to Ireland, Ails was walking down the street one day when she recognized an old face — Dolty Grimes, who had been so much a part of the landscape of her youth that it seemed he'd always been there.

"Hello, Ails! How're ye doin'? Haven't seen you for ages."

"Hi, Dolty!" Oops, she'd forgotten and spontaneously said 'Hi.' Nobody used that greeting there.

"I live in Canada now, Dolty," Ails went on.

"That's right, somebody *told* me you married a Yank!"

"Actually, he's Canadian," Ails.

"That's right, I *knew* he was a Yank alright," replied Dolty. Oops, Yank and American and Canadian were interchangeable here.

"I sound so technical," thought Ails hopelessly. This was Dolty, ageless, timeless Dolty of her childhood. Talking to Dolty used to be as easy as sitting in an old armchair. He had been part of everything that had seemed so dear to her. Now she felt awkward, a stranger, talking to him. What on earth had happened?

She'd noticed it the very first Christmas she was away. She'd happily sent Christmas cards to all of those people she had loved and left, thrilled with her new life — only to receive very few cards back. When she returned for her first visit, she heard such things as "Ach, sure, I lost yer address"; "I meant to send a card, but I didn't send any this year"; "I never did see yer mother to get your address." "Yer address was sittin' on the mantelpiece, and one day a gust of wind came through the door and blew the piece of paper into the fire."

Ails remembered the going-away-to-America parties, the bittersweet celebration of a community coming together to give its children a good sendoff. A little bit like a wake.

Too many had left, she thought.

As she filled a cup from her bucket of painting water, Ails sat quietly and watched the surface of the water gradually settle down again, smooth as glass, as if no water had been removed, except the water surface was a little lower.

To that collective body of Irish people, was she now dead? Involuntarily, she shivered.

The mantle of belonging to the tribe was gone.

And it was cold out there without it.

46

the going-away party

Brian McGribben was going to America. His uncle had sent over the fare and had a job waiting for Brian.

"Sure what would I be doin' movin' around flourbags for the rest of me days for Seamus Callaghan?" he said when Lizzie asked if he was glad about going. Brian was Bouncer's cousin, and they were originally both supposed to go together a year or more before, but Bouncer had never given up hope that Briege would come back. The bank down beside Peter Coyle's opened every Friday. Bouncer was there waiting every week when the banker came on the bus from the town of Unragh. No matter how much he had been drinking, Bouncer had faithfully put saving money in the bank when he got paid. It was to marry Briege, but Brian and the other lads kept trying to persuade Bouncer to take the money out and buy a ticket to America. Now, however, the way things had turned out, with Bouncer married, Brian was going alone to America.

So there would be a going-away-to-America party in Lizzie's that coming Saturday. Ails could hardly believe her ears when she realized her father and mother were going to a teachers' meeting and dance that Saturday in the city. It was almost too good to be true. That meant that she and Fiona could sneak down to the party and nobody'd even notice — although she knew Fiona would fall asleep and would kick up a ruckus if anyone tried to put her back in her bed, because she'd be afraid to go to bed after the ghost stories. Ails would have to go up to bed with her, but Fiona usually fell asleep fast, planned Ails, at

241

which time she could slip back down by herself to the party. Ails savoured the delicious feeling of anticipation all week. Jinny was coming, of course — she went to everything. So was half the country. Everybody liked Brian. Lizzie had to clean up the whole shop area above the kitchen and the tea rooms at the back for the fiddlers. There'd be a ceilidge dancing session in Heaney's hall, just outside the door beside the byres, and they could all wander around from one place to the other. It'd be great.

The whole day Saturday Ails was running up and down to the shop for buttermilk, butter and flour. Lizzie was always running out of things at the best of times. Now she was all up in a heap about everybody coming, nervously shouting out orders to move chairs, and paying a few pennies to Pat and Nailly and the other boys to carry up cases of stout. Ails's mother and father were getting all organized to go out. Every time she passed a door, either they or Lizzie had a job for her to do. If she tried to watch what was going on, they'd tell her to run away out and play. Ails took the baby down to Auntie Cora's.

"Do you want to sleep here, too, love?" Auntie Cora asked, and then smiled when she saw Ails's ambivalence.

"Oh, I forgot you wouldn't want to miss Brian's party." And she winked, "Ye'll not be goin' to bed too early, I doubt!" Auntie Cora made Ails some tea and soda scones, all hot with butter. Her house always smelled good.

"Can I go and see Ingrid?" Ails said when she finished.

"Go ahead." Ails went into the lovely sitting room with its marble fireplace and white plump fat cushions. This room reminded her of the 'nursery' she read about in the library books at school. It came to life on special occasions such as Christmas and birthdays. Looking up at Ingrid on the wall, she could imagine her shaking her flaxen braids and yawning and flexing her stuffed arms and taking off her bonnet and coming down to walk around in her button boots and speak. Of course Ingrid did this all the time in Ails's imagination in her secret place, ever since the hospital. She played with Ails and talked a lot in her funny accent. She came from Switzerland. Ails heard all the big boys coming into the kitchen, and she slipped out the front door that nobody used and out the side gate, up onto the road outside the barracks. Auntie Cora's big son Moss and his friends didn't

242

like Ails much. They teased her. Shamie had recently become nearly as bad as they were. Colum was lovely but still a baby. Ails didn't like boys much.

She knew that if she went straight home she'd be running messages all over the place, so she dandered up by the barracks. She climbed up the stone wall onto the grassy top, and took off her shoes. She walked along the grass on top of the wall beside the chain link fence, running a stick through the holes. At different speeds it made different sounds, clinking or rasping.

"Hello." It was Phyllis, the Sergeant's daughter. She was minding her sisters. "Would you like to play?" Ails hesitated. She had never been inside the shiny black barrack gate, and often wondered about the big, white forbidding building with bars on the windows where they put drunk people in jail sometimes.

"Just for a wee while, maybe." Ails went in and Phyllis said awkwardly,

"Would you like to see my dolls?"

"O.K." said Ails. Phyllis was nice. She seemed lonely. They went past the jail place.

"Is that a jail?"

"Yes, and my daddy's office is in there, too. We're not allowed in there." That settled that. She wouldn't see the jail. They went to the door of Phyllis's part of the house. Phyllis said "Wait here." There was a bright polished red-tile floor with a sunken place that fitted the floor mat to clean your shoes. Ails could see into the house, with its tiled fireplace and pieces of carpet on the tiled floor and a bowl of fruit on the polished wooden table. Phyllis came back with three dolls. One doll's eyes opened and closed. They carried them to the green smooth lawn and sat on a blanket. Phyllis's sisters came over shyly. The dolls were lovely. They were just starting to play when Phyllis's mother came to the upstairs window.

"You have to go to your piano lesson now, Phyllis," she called. "You'll have to go now, dear," the mother called to Ails. "But *do* ask your mother if you can come back and play another day!"

"Will you come back tomorrow...N...no, that's Sunday...I can't play...I mean...next Saturday...I go to Miss Pauline McKenna's at 2 for piano...could you come earlier?"

"Yeh, maybe," answered Ails evasively, knowing somehow she wouldn't. She dandered on up past the Protestant church and crossed the road.

"Ails! can you do a message?" Groan. It was Miss Trudy McKenna, Miss Pauline's sister. Their mother Mrs. McKenna, made extra money from bleaching and selling flour bags. She sent her girls away to be secretaries. They came home on the 5 o'clock bus on Friday evenings and had nice clothes, and went out with young men, and taught piano at weekends. Jinny, Ails and Maura called them Miss Prim and Miss Prissy. Their mother talked like she used to be English. Their father was a farmer who lived in the village but worked some land out the Tonnegan Road.

"Mother needs these flour bags delivered to Lizzie before tonight. Perhaps you're going that way?" Miss Prim smiled with her neatly lipsticked mouth. "Thank you, dear," and she pirouetted off in her high heels. Ails had thought she was far enough away not to have to run messages! She took the bundle of bleached flour bags and buried her nose in them. They smelled clean and felt soft and gauzy.

"Just imagine, I maybe jumped on these when they were full of flour," she thought idly, imagining the soapy water floating away the gucked up flour.

It was just impossible to get away from Lizzie's. Everywhere she stopped people were talking about the going-away ceilidghe and who'd be there. Instead of turning at the stone Celtic cross, and going home to be ordered around some more, Ails decided to wander on down the Monument Road and go up the back road by the forge. She liked to watch the horses standing waiting for shoes, all queued up, and she didn't want to go back too early, for the fuss would be terrible, with Lizzie shouting at everybody.

"As well, horses can't send you for messages," thought Ails with relief. She ambled on up the laneway poking sticks in the cuckoo spit on the flower stems. The horses were in a line chewing grass and turning around their blinkers to look at her. They looked at her differently from Bella's cows. Bella's cows were sort of thick. Horses were not. Maybe it was their long faces and the way they sometimes held up their necks very regally, or maybe it was the fact that in 'Gulliver's Travels' they were smarter than people. Whatever it was, they were nice. They stood patiently, lifting their hooves every now and then and clopping them down again. Ails climbed over the stone ditch so that she could cut in past the forge. She didn't want Fergie the blacksmith to see her. He was a terrible tease. He always teased her about boys. No, she wouldn't go through the forge, but there was a hole in the stone forge wall and she could look into the forge if she stood on top of the ditch. She could hear the men's voices as she approached, picking her way along the top of the stone ditch.

"Now, there's one with tits, that one." They were talking about cows. "You'd get the quare sup of milk from them, Jimmy!" She looked through the hole. Fergie was hammering away and taking the horseshoe in and out of the fire. Jimmy was working the bellows, and a bunch of other men she knew from the chapel were sitting around waiting, some smoking pipes, all with caps on. She was able to sit comfortably on top of the grassy knoll to look in through the hole, but it felt damp on her bottom, so she sat on the flour bags.

"Tell y' what, Jimmy, why don't you take her out for a roll in the hay out the back there tonight. Lord, them tits!"

"The cow for a roll in the hay?" thought Ails, puzzled.

"She fancies you, y'know, Jimmy." Ails looked over at Jimmy's face at the bellows. He was all red in the face. They were all teasing him. "Milkin' Mamie fancies you, she does indeed, Jimmy!"

They were talking about Mamie McGuigan! And Ails thought they were talking about a cow. They were talking as if Jimmy was going to milk Mamie.

"Must be like Annie Oiny," thought Ails. She had big full tits, just like Bella's cows before milking, and Packy, her man, was always grabbing them and pulling on them when he thought nobody was looking.

Jimmy came out with Fergie to fit on the horseshoes, and Ails had to climb down really carefully, because Jimmy's horse was standing right at the corner of the forge beside her, and they'd see her. She got down but forgot the flour bags. She hid, hoping they wouldn't see them. They didn't. Jimmy left.

245

"Don't forget, now, Jimmy. Tonight's the night!" Ails got up from her hiding place and climbed back up the side of the forge to get the flourbags.

"Wouldn't mind a roll with that Mamie and a feel of them tits meself!" Ails looked at the speaker with a shock. It was Miss Prim and Prissy's father!

Oops, somebody was coming out again. Ails climbed down and ran up the yard with the flourbags. Fergie spotted her out of the open forge doors.

"Who you been kissin' lately, Ails? Dingo Devine?" Ails's face was flaming red. She was furious. Of all the boys...She ran on, mortified, hearing the men laugh at her embarrassment.

"Where WERE you, Ails? I needed you to go for me flourbags and you never came back!" Ails handed the flourbags to Lizzie. "What under God did you do with these?" Ails looked at them. They were all green grass stains. Ails had to wash and hang them out on the bushes. She juked around to the front door, avoiding everyone, with the house in an uproar. She sneaked quietly upstairs with her book and fell asleep, hearing the 'ting, ting, ting,' and feeling her face burn with embarrassment.

When Ails woke up, it was quiet. She was cold. She had fallen asleep on top of the blankets. It must be about 6 o'clock. Funny, Ails always knew roughly what time it was when she woke up. She could hear Fiona calling her. She went downstairs.

"We couldn't find you, love," said her mother. Ails stared. Her mother looked beautiful. She had on a turquoise lacey dress and pearls and high heels and stockings, and a shiny bag with a diamondy clasp. Her father was all dressed up in a suit and a white shirt with gold studs in the sleeves. Fiona came in:

"Where were you, Ails? I ..." She stopped and stared also. They were not used to seeing their mother and father dressed up grand like this.

"Youse are lovely, like a king and queen," exclaimed Fiona.

"Yeh, you look like fancy, grand people," said Ails as she and Fiona followed them out to the car, while Lizzie hid behind the curtain looking after them.

"Be good!" they said as they drove off in the car.

Good, thought Ails. Nobody said not to go to the party, so they could go. Ails and Fiona sat up in the windowsill waiting for people to arrive. They started arriving on bicycles, cars, tractors, and some by horse and cart. They tethered the horses down by the forge. Fergie was working till really late into the evening shoeing horses, because it was hard for working farmers to take a day to make a special trip into the village to bring the horses. It was a nice evening, so everyone hung about outside, went to the forge, went in and out of the pubs, stood about in groups talking, finally drifting in and settling in groups here and there. Ails liked the kitchen best, but she didn't go there yet, for Lizzie was still warming up, and would be shooing them out till she had a drink or two, when she'd forget all about them being there. Ails and Fiona sidled up the hallway and sat in the back tea room where all the fiddlers were settling. Ails liked the 'tuning up' bit best. Every time a new fiddler came in, they'd stop and say "Choon hm up, boys!" and they'd screw up their faces and cock their ears over sideways to listen. A lot of fiddlers had no teeth. Then they'd start with feet tapping and bows and fingers dancing up and down. After a while it seemed they went

248

on and on and on and the tune always sounded the same. Mamie McGuigan was bringing up bottles of stout.

"Come on and give us a reel, Mamie!" they coaxed. Mamie was great at the Irish dancing.

"That lassie could dance on the edge of a plate," Lizzie said.

"Ach, alright then, just a short one," said Mamie, laughing good-naturedly, as they rasped back the chairs and cleared the cement floor for her to dance. As she watched Mamie dance, all Ails could think about was the conversation of the men in the forge today. Instead of watching Mamie dance, she began to watch the men's eyes watching Mamie's breasts jiggling. She was enjoying herself dancing, and liked the attention. But Ails could see something furtive and strange in the men's eyes, especially when they looked up her clothes when Mamie kicked her skirt high in the seven steps. Ails felt uncomfortable. Young Jimmy was there. Ails remembered the men teasing him in the forge. Shyly, he watched Mamie dance. They all clapped when she finished. She walked straight over to Jimmy, flushed and self-conscious. Later Ails saw them disappear out the back door together. She followed them, with Fiona tagging along, but they soon disappeared through the groups of people into the deepening dusk.

When they finally lost Jimmy and Mamie in the gathering dusk, Ails and Fiona sneaked in again through the back door to Lizzie's kitchen. Sure enough, Lizzie no longer even noticed them. Everything was in full swing. Rosaleen McVerry was singing 'Noreen Bawn,' the song that Ails had heard haunting Auntie Cora. Rosaleen had a really sad voice that broke as if she was crying at the parts where Noreen Bawn died and where her widowed mother sat lonesome by Noreen's grave. Brian McGribben's mother and sister were crying. Bouncer looked sad. He never left Briege's side these days, except to go to work. Briege had tears in her eyes, and even little Ricky and little Jimmy McAnallen stopped playing with the cat till Rosaleen was finished singing. Everyone always cried at a going-away-to-America ceilidghe, even though they were having a good time.

"It's kind of like a wake," thought Ails, looking around at the faces, "but here, instead of dying, the person goes to America." Though it was hard to tell the difference, because you never saw the person again anyway. They'd send home money and Christmas cards and photos and exotic presents — like beautifully colored paper tablecloths — but they never came home again.

"Maybe it's just as well," though Ails. She was thinking of Minnie Campbell with the funny now-married name that nobody could say — Sockolovski or something like that. She married a Yank in America. They both came home for a visit. They were just awful. Everybody said how changed Minnie was. She had pencilled eyebrows, wore rouge, and didn't want to be called 'Minnie' any more.

"Everyone in the States calls me Maria," she said haughtily.

"An' her called after her grandmother, God rest her soul," said Lizzie, "an' that Minnie Haughey was the finest woman in this townland. Sure, she must be turning in her grave!" The Yank himself was a real pain, according to Lizzie.

"Him in his sunglasses, an' it teemin' rain," said Lizzie. "Such a big poultice." The lad Minnie (Maria) left pining away in Ireland 'got cured real quick,' said Lizzie, when he saw how changed she was when she came back.

"Wonder why they'd change?" thought Ails. Maybe it was different there, in 'the States,' as the returned Yanks referred to it. She looked at Brian now, whom everybody loved. Would he change? She couldn't imagine it, with the lamplight shining on his face in Lizzie's kitchen. Brian, who gave them pennies, Brian who brought all his money home to help raise the other eight children on the tiny farm; Brian who always had a joke, walking in and out with the poke bag covering his head and neck like a hood to carry the flourbags; Brian who rescued Neeve from under the horses' legs on the Fair Day. No, Brian wouldn't change, decided Ails. She just couldn't imagine Brian different from the Brian now in Lizzie's kitchen, laughing and joking, so at home with everyone. Rosaleen's brother Paddy was now singing, with everybody joining in:

"Goodbye, Johnny dear, when you're far away,
Don't forget your dear old mother far across the sea
Write a letter now and then, and send her all you can,
And don't forget where'er you roam
That you're an Irishman."

The last line drew a cheer for Brian. His mother and oldest sister were weeping inconsolably.

"Give us a bit of a story there, Lizzie!" Brian proposed. Lizzie was delighted. Ghost stories were her specialty. Lizzie lit the tilley lamp, and turned off the light bulb in the kitchen. "This is the way Aunt Nelly, God rest her, liked stories told," she said. Lizzie's aunt had lived there long before Ails's family began to rent rooms there, but it almost seemed she was still alive in the house from the many times Lizzie, and other people coming in, referred to her as if she was still alive. "Indeed I remember, Lizzie, Nelly used to darn socks by that lamp when you were a wean sitting beside her." Lizzie's house was still referred to as 'Nelly's Shop.' Lizzie now used the shop part to serve teas on Sundays and Fair Days. Like Jinny, Lizzie had been totally spoilt by this ageing aunt and uncle who took her in from the country, since they had no children of their own.

The tilly lamp cast ghostly shadows on the walls and flowered curtains. The flames licking around the turf flickered sprinklings of light out on the faces around the fire, and up onto the ceiling. Every so often Lizzie would poke the turf, a shower of sparks would flash, and she would poke the extra red glowing red ashes down through the grating in the floor in front of the hearth. Ails looked at Lizzie. It was as if Lizzie was a different Lizzie that she didn't know. The scene was set. All was silent except for the crickets chirping in the chimney. Lizzie wrapped her sinister-looking hands around the tongs. Her hands were like witches' hands, boney and claw-like and could almost talk by themselves. Lizzie put on her ghostly voice:

"It was one night with a watery moon goin' in and out behin' the clouds. Mickey Dan was goin' up the road beyond the graveyard when he thought he heard — wheesht! There it was again — that noise behind him... "Lizzie paused.

251

All those listening glanced over their shoulders. Ails felt prickles on her spine.

"It was like footsteps, only different footsteps. Mickey listened again..." Pause...Fiona's fingers were digging into Ails's arm.

"There it was again — one footstep was human, and the other one was like a..." Pause..."CLOP." Lizzie clicked her tongue and curved her hands to make them go like someone walking slowly.

'But every time Mickey Dan would stop, the footsteps would stop, too. He done this three times. Then the sweat started to break on him." Lizzie wiped her brow, for effect. "He commenced to run, but them footsteps just kept comin' slow and steady." Her curved claw-like hands were moving menacingly. "But always the footsteps were right behind him, right on his heels." Ails had heard this story before, listening through the wall from her hiding place on the stairs, but she was still spellbound. She looked at the eerie glow the lamp threw on the faces around the kitchen, bewitched by Lizzie's storytelling.

"Mickey Dan, with the sweat runnin' down his face and neck, ran right up to the door, and battered on it in terror." Lizzie moved her wide, terrified, expressive, brown eyes menacingly around the listeners, "an' he turned around, an' there it was, leerin' at Mickey Dan." There was a hushed, scary pause.

'The man with the cloven hoof." A knowing hush.

"When Mrs. Paddy Flynn opened the door, there lay Mickey Dan, passed out with the shock of it. And from that day to this, y'll not get Mickey Dan to go up that road on his lone." Hush. "An' that's as true as I'm sittin' here in Nelly's kitchen." The tension broke.

"Lord, you're a powerful storyteller indeed, Lizzie!"

"Ach, not at all. Sure I'll never be as good as Nelly." Suddenly, Lizzie was the familiar Lizzie again.

"We'll have some tea." Lizzie wet the huge pot of tea and lifted the soda farls off the huge griddle on the chimney ledge. Women passed it around, all warm and buttery, smelling delicious, with the big mugs of hot tea. Some of the older country men took saucers from the cupboard and 'saucered' the tea to cool it, then drank it from the saucer.

'Strong enough to dance on, that tea is, Lizzie. I'll guarantee you, Brian, y'll not get tea like this in Americay," said someone, "or yarns like Lizzie's, either," added Brian's cousin. Everybody had got up and was stretching out the pins and needles from sitting on the hard chairs. Fiona was dropping off to sleep. Ails could hardly get her to move. Brian McGribben saw them and came over. He gathered Fiona up in his arms, walked down Lizzie's hall with her and up the stairs. Ails showed Brian where they slept. He put her gently under the blankets. He looked at her fondly.

"I'll not see her again, Ails, or you either, till maybe you're a grown-up woman," he said thoughtfully. "Will you remember me at all?" Suddenly Ails felt his sadness at leaving all that was familiar to him. The feeling of her and Bella and Shamie a long time ago, bringing home the cows, belonging in Altnamore — this picture flashed across her mind.

"I will remember, Brian," Ails answered softly. "An' thanks for getting Neeve out from under the horses." Brian laughed.

"Just mind you keep her out from under the horses!" he said. Those were the last words Ails ever spoke to Brian. Her heart was strangely heavy on the way downstairs. Everything was in confusion, as the fiddlers were leaving to set up down at Heaney's Hall for the dance. In the kitchen The Lilter McMenamin was singing 'O'Donnel Abu,' with Whistler whistling notes up and down behind it to accompany him. Then they sang 'Roddy McCorley' together to the sinister accompaniment of a boran drum. Their last song was 'Danny Boy.' It was beautiful. When they came to the part:

"And when you come and all the flowers are dying
And I am dead, as dead I well may be.
You'll come and find the place where I am lying,
And kneel and say an 'Ave' there for me."

Brian's father blew his nose for a long time in a big striped handkerchief. Was he crying? Ails couldn't tell. The Lilter went on:

"And I shall hear, though soft you tread above me

253

And o'er my grave will warmer, sweeter be.
And you shall bend and tell me that you love me,
And I will sleep in peace until you come to me."

Again Brian's father blew his nose for a long time. All the men shifted uneasily from foot to foot, or got fidgety in the chairs while the women all had tears in their eyes, some sobbing openly. The Lilter finished with those heavenly high notes at the end of the song. The sorrow was probably because the song was true, thought Ails. Brian would probably not see his father again. And then he could bend and tell his father that he loved him, for the only time you could say a thing like that was when a person was dead. If the person wasn't dead, you'd be too embarrassed to say a thing like that around Altnamore, even if you were leaving. The only person Ails ever heard expressing love was Bruno to Briege, and just look what happened there, she thought. In America, she knew people said 'I love you,' from the films on Friday nights in the Hall. But nobody in Altnamore would ever say things like that. They'd more likely give you a clip on the ear to hide that they might indeed love you. From her cramped chimney-corner seat, Ails looked around at the bittersweet expressions on the work-worn faces of the people gathered in Lizzie's kitchen in the lamplight's glow. She knew she would keep this always in her secret place inside her, and would recall it years from now. After this emotion-laden pause at the end of the song, everyone started clapping and cheering and calling for another song, but the McMenamins had to leave to practise with the fiddlers before everybody came down later for the dance.

"Aw, come on, Lizzie, another yarn!" they were all calling. This time it was about the fairy bushes and Pete Barney Ann. Pete's father Barney had inherited the farm from Ann, Pete's grandmother.

"Right in the middle of the field it was, this clump of fairy bushes," — curved hands showing the clump. "An' ever since the farm was there, Pete's father Barney had ploughed carefully, steering the horse and plough around them bushes. Pete's grandmother, Ann, she seen to it that the clump of bushes were kept peaceful and undisturbed. But that Pete, he girned and

254

yapped about them bushes an' how he couldn't get the plough aroun' them an' how he couldn't steer the horses around them. Awwww, awwww, awww." Lizzie shook her head ominously. "Awww, he was a headstrong one, that Pete. He wouldn't listen to ould Barney tellin' him the luck them wee people's bushes bring if you leave them alone." With her one finger up in the air, Lizzie's eyes held everyone in suspense: "But if ever you lay a finger;" down came the finger hard on her other palm "on them wee people, awww, well…"

Ails had heard this one before too, but was just as transfixed with it this time around, as were all the other listeners. One day when Barney was in the village getting his pension, Pete cut down the bushes against his father's wishes,. Barney took a 'turn' when he saw that the bushes were gone, and never really recovered from it. After Barney died, everything Pete touched went wrong: his best calf died; the hens quit laying; the potatoes got the blight. Eventually Pete went off to America. Everyone sighed knowingly. After a brief pause, Lizzie went on from there to tell great stories about cures: sprained ankles cured by charms; sties on people's eyes cured by gooseberry bush thorns; warts cured by rubbing them with a raw potato and then burying the potato; whooping cough cure held by two marriage partners of the same name; cures held by the seventh son of the seventh son, and on and on. Lizzie was wound up, making stories come alive. Lizzie's eyes were magical — coy, confidential, guarded, mirthful, sly, sinister, secretive, vicious — she could change them like pulling a switch.

Eventually the stories petered out, as different key people slipped down to get the hall ready for the dance. By now everybody was weaving down to the hall. Ails passed Pat McCabe's butcher's shop, which was full of the village lads, and a lot of men too. It looked like Pat was telling stories, just like Lizzie was, but Brian, the guest of honour, walked right past and didn't go in there at all. The music was like a magnet, drawing people in waves down to Heaney's Hall. Ails found Maura, Brigid, Jinny and many others from school when she got there. They had been ceilidhing here and there in the village and came together for the dance. They all danced the feet off themselves. Ails's feet had wings. Every time Fergie the blacksmith saw her

255

dancing opposite Pat Doran or Dingo Devine or Jerry Gallagher he'd shout over, referring to her missing teeth that he used to tease her about when she was younger:

"Was it him that kissed the teeth out of you, Ails?" pointing to his own teeth. Ails couldn't help laughing. There was a feeling of buoyancy and fun and kindness all around. There were there to send Brian McGribben off well. Surely Brian would etch this night in his memory, as Ails would, and remember it inside himself forever? Brian danced in every set dance and swung all the girls around, the littler ones right off their feet.

"He kicks his feet that high in the Haymakers' Jig that he near knocks out your teeth," complained Jinny, delighted that he had picked her to dance with in 'The Seige of Ennis.'

It was a wonderful night. Nobody wanted it to end. The streaks of dawn were showing in the sky over the plantin as Ails wended her way back up to Lizzie's. She went dreamily up the stairs not feeling the least bit tired, fell into bed fully clothed beside the sleeping Fiona. She drifted into sleep in a warm glow — more aware of the vague ache somewhere deep inside her than she was of her tired feet. She knew that tomorrow Brian, like all the others who went to America, would be gone...gone from Altnamore...gone forever.

Making Sense out of Life

glossary of terms used.

A leanbh	—term of endearment - 'baby'; also 'a-stor', 'a-roon' - 'love'
Banshee	— a woman who traditionally weeps (keens) loudly at funerals
BBC	— British Broadcasting Corporation
Besom	— handmade broom
Black & Tans	— a brutal special British force, brought in to stop rebellion
Black Pudding	— blood sausage, in round slices, fried for breakfast or grill
Bog	— marshy land where peat grows
Byre	— 'stable' where cows are kept
Caning	— common school punishment
Cardigan	— a button-up-the-front sweater
Ceilidhe	— socialize, talk, sing, have 'good crack'; name for a dance
Champ	— mashed potatoes
Chemist	— pharmacy
Chilblain	— an itchy lump on fingers, toes and heels, from damp cold
Conkers	— a chestnut game
Crack	— fun, entertaining humour, recently spelled 'craic'
Creel	— a woven basket
Cuff	— a blow usually inflicted on the shoulder or back
Daft	— crazy
Deeved	— mixed-up
Dispensary	— medical clinic
Drops of tea	— cups of tea
Fair Day	— market day for rural towns; also good weather
Farl	— triangular cake of bread
Fenian	— one of the names for Irish rebel nationalists
Frock	— a dress
Gable	— side of a house
Gaelic	— an alternative for things 'Celtic,' including the language
Girn	— whining with a pouty face
Gutters	— runnels dug to catch liquid from byre
I.R.A.	— Irish Republican Army
Jodphurs	— English-style riding pants
Jotter	— paper exercise book or scribbler for school work
Lair	— name given to a fox's hole, or home
Lilting	— Using 'la-la' to sing rhythmic melodies for dancing
Lorry	— truck
Malevogue	— mal = bad - threatening term, not serious
Mass	— Catholic Church celebration
Master, The	— name given to male schoolteacher
Messages	— errands
Midge	— tiny insects which travel in swarms

258

Mistress	— name given to female schoolteacher
Mizzling	— very light, but soaking, rain
Mortal sin	— Catholic bad deed
Nits	— head lice
Plantin	— 'plantation' - an area of land not used for agriculture
Poke bag	— cone-shaped bag
Poultice	— warm compress to draw out poison
Pram	— baby carriage
Privet	— a golden-green type of hedge
Quare	— queer - in Irish context, it means 'good' or 'great'
Redd up	— cleanup, usually housekeeping-related
Scallions	— green onions
Scullery	— Wash-house off a kitchen
Scythe	— a long-blade, long handled tool for cutting grass
Settle bed	— bed that doubles as a seat in daytime
Shilling	— a coin worth 12 pennies
Skitter	— brat
Slate	— a small square of slate, modern blackboard, for school work
Squint	— cross-eyed
Stile	— a raised wooden gateway, usually on top of stone steps
Stout	— dark beer — like 'Guinness'
Sweets	— candies
Swing-boats	— swings shaped like boats
Tara	— a specific design of brooch (also High King's residence)
Tart	— pie
Tea	— used to describe 'supper'
Tilley lamp	— oil lamp with a wick
Traipsed	— moved around
Turf	— peat fuel, carved out from bogs and left to dry
Up in a heap	— upset, upheaved
Vicks	— camphorated ointment, rubbed on chest for a cold
Waistcoat	— vest
Wake	— celebrating the life, and sending the dead off for burial
Wean	— derivative of 'wee one,' or 'wee'un'
Wellingtons	— rubber boots
Whinge	— onomatopoeic word for whining
Yarn	— tale or story

ISBN 155212967-5

9 781552 129678